To the three Marilyns in my life: my sister, Marilyn Luff, who encouraged me to write; my dear friend, Marilyn Lister, who patiently edited my first attempts; and my wife, whose love encourages me every day to continue.

Richard C. Thuss
Berryville, VA, October 16, 2009

Chapter 1: Self-Aware-Machines

"What time is it?" asked the clock.

Jack Farrell pushed a few wayward strands of blonde hair out of his eyes and then glared at the small, shiny black object lying on the passenger seat next to him, its blue luminescent display flickering once before changing to 1:15 p.m. "Read your own display, you idiot," he yelled and then grabbed the clock and shook it a few times. "That's the third time you've asked me that stupid question in the last half-hour. You're a Goddamned clock; can't you even tell the time? Now be quiet for a while, I need to concentrate on finding this apartment. I'm tired of listening to all of you."

Without warning, his pickup truck abruptly swerved across three lanes of mid-Sunday-morning city traffic, cutting off several other cars as it careened toward the curb and then came to a screeching stop in a church no-parking zone.

The truck's computer voice blared from the dashboard-mounted speakers. "You're tired, Jack? You're tired? What about me? I've been hauling you and all these heavy things around this city for the last three hours, and not once did you think about stopping to give me a rest. Not once did you think of anyone but yourself. My oil pressure has been running high lately. I'm a week past due for a tune-up, and all four of my tires need rotating. All of us could have been home relaxing today if it wasn't for your dumb mistake. We all work hard for you, and look at the thanks we get. You call the clock stupid. Well I think you need to take a hard look at yourself, Jack. You're the stupid one, and you're selfish, too."

Slumping with his head against the steering wheel, Jack's hands tightly gripped the center hub, creating an appearance that he was trying to strangle the truck, which at that moment was exactly what he wished he could do.

Sometimes he wondered if life had been better before self-aware machines or SAMs. Now everything he owned had a voice, and an opinion. But in truth, he knew he couldn't do without them. They made his life easier, helped him earn his living, and had even become his friends. What he didn't know was that some could become dangerous, and he would have laughed at the thought that his North Korean made wrist computer was planning to conduct war against his country and that it recently decided it wanted him dead.

Chapter 2: A New Apartment

Rubbing his forehead and trying to relieve the tension headache that was building, Jack looked at the camera imbedded in the truck's dashboard, its small lens and input microphone pointing directly at his face. "I'm sorry, Averette," he replied in a subdued voice. "I'm really stressed out today. We need to find an apartment to live in. If we can't find one soon, then we'll all be sleeping inside your cab over in the park tonight."

His double-cab Dodge pickup truck took the name Averette when he purchased it off the used car lot last year. All cars and trucks were now equipped with ultra-high-performance computers, computers that monitored and controlled every function, computers that were intelligent, and computers that had reached a state where they were self-aware. Using the term "purchased" therefore wasn't technically correct, because when you bought a car or a truck it, was now officially labeled as a SAM adoption. You not only paid for it, you adopted it, and because it was self-aware, it had all the legal rights of a small animal.

On the used car adoption lot, he quickly realized that the truck was a complainer, and after listening to it gripe about the previous owner, he decided to call the deal off. When he tried to leave the dealership, the linebacker-sized salesman thrust a large hairy arm out to stop him.

"I'll take another four thousand off the price if both of us just sign here saying we listened to all of its complaints," the man said as he not so gently pushed Jack back down into the chair and handed him a pen.

Jack hesitated.

"Fifty-five hundred! I'll take fifty-five hundred off and give you free oil changes and tire rotations and throw in four tune-ups for the next year." Perspiration was dripping from his forehead as he continued in a pleading voice, "Please buy this thing! I've had to listen to its complaints five times in the past few days, and if I hear it whine one more time, I'll quit."

Jack renamed the truck Averette after learning that the truck's previous owner had called it Slug because one of its three cylinders misfired when you floored the gas pedal. But giving it a new name had been a mistake, because with its newfound confidence, the truck often thought its opinion was more important than his.

Several times in the past few weeks, Averette had decided to head the wrong way down a one-way street because the GPS indicated it was a shorter route. But complaining about any near-miss was useless, because Averette's neural processor had a design flaw: it didn't take criticism very well. In fact, it didn't accept criticism at all.

Sitting there illegally parked at the curb, Jack glanced out his side window toward the busy sidewalk, where a large crowd was congregating next to his truck. They were all dressed in their Sunday best clothes; all were frowning, and a few were shaking one or more fingers at him, including a family whose feet were dripping water courtesy of the puddle Averette passed through just before stopping.

A policeman kept pointing to a large red No Parking sign while simultaneously reaching into a black leather holster for his automated ticket phone. Jack knew from experience that he had just a few seconds before the camera in the ticket phone took stereo pictures of him and the truck, and then fifteen seconds later, a judge in India would certify him as the owner of the truck, find him guilty, and automatically deduct the fine from the little money remaining in his checking account. High-speed networks, global face recognition databases, and self-aware computers had made instant traffic convictions feasible and irreversible.

"Can we start up again now, Averette?" Jack was trying hard to sound apologetic. "Please, I can't afford another four hundred dollar parking ticket, and we need to be at this next apartment in a few minutes or we'll lose it." Pleading louder, he watched as the policeman fumbled at first but then aimed the small camera toward the truck's front license plate. "Averette, get moving!"

With a loud sigh from the driver's-side speaker, Averette cryptically said, "I accept your apology," and then pulled quickly away from the curb, heading down Baseline Drive toward the Cleveland waterfront.

Jack was searching for a new apartment. He was evicted from his old one this morning shortly after his radio called the landlord stupid. He really couldn't disagree with that assessment, because his landlord's IQ was probably less than that of the chip in his wrist computer, but he wasn't laughing when the landlord told him, "Get out!"

"I told you to get rid of that radio," Averette reminded him as he was tying down the last few items from his old apartment into the back of the truck. "Didn't I warn you?"

The radio belonged to his former live-in girlfriend, Melissa, who left it in his apartment earlier that summer when she unexpectedly left for Spain with her yoga instructor. He was forced to keep it because he didn't have the adoption papers for it, and without adoption papers, it wasn't easy to get rid of a self-aware machine, since throwing a SAM in the trash was a crime.

"Isn't this the same street we were on two hours ago?" Averette snapped at him as they merged into the heavy morning traffic.

"No, this is the south side of the lake," Jack responded quickly, trying to keep his voice cheerful, anxious to avoid a repeat of the truck swerving unexpectedly toward the curb. "We were looking at places over on the west side of town several hours ago."

"Well, it all looks the same to me," Averette quipped. "What's the address of the apartment building we're looking for this time?"

"It's 2411 Fenwick Street, so turn left at the next light, uh ... but wait until after this big truck has passed."

After the turn, Jack's eyes quickly followed the numbers on the high-rise buildings on the left side of the street to 2411, and they settled on a three-story, century-old brownstone nestled between two much taller buildings that had recently been renovated to create a separate apartment on each floor.

The second-floor apartment had been listed as having a small balcony facing north toward the lake, and although the balcony was there, the advertisement had failed to mention that a twenty-story office building was located right across the street, completely shielding the brownstone from a view of anything but that building's sterile-looking dark glass and concrete facade.

"Here we are," Averette said, with another loud sigh, and the truck pulled to the curb in front of the brownstone and stopped.

The driver's door moved outward slightly and then slid not so silently up and into the roof. "I'm going to go in and look at the apartment," Jack said as he was climbing out. "I'll be back in a few minutes." And after closing the door, he hurried down the sidewalk and bounded up the three front steps to the brownstone's entrance.

The old stone home was totally out of place in the downtown section of the city. Nestled between what appeared to be two high-rise, glass-faced buildings there was a small five-foot-wide alley on the right side of the brownstone only a few inches wider than the iron fire escape jutting out from the top floor. A larger, car-width-wide alley was on the left side of the house, and it had two narrow concrete pathways separated by the width of a car's tires that continued back and then turned, disappearing behind the house. The building was most likely built in the early twentieth century and was now probably over a hundred and twenty years old.

Looking closely at the stone around the doorway, he could see that the mortar had been expertly pointed, and the entire house was maintained in pristine shape. The frame around the front door was freshly painted in a brilliant white, contrasting perfectly with a huge ebony stained oak door.

Maybe this building still has toilets that don't yell at you if you forget to flush, he thought. *And the heater in here may even be old enough so that it doesn't wake you up at night to remind you that you forgot to turn the thermostat down.* Before even reaching the top step, he'd decided that he really wanted to live here.

For over a minute, he stood facing the door, first holding his large blue eyes wide open and moving his head slowly back and forth. He combed his long blonde hair back and stood up on his toes, swaying his head back and forth and then, scrunching down lower, he did the same. Finally, realizing that the house did not have an automatic face recognizer to identify him and announce his presence, he gave up and knocked on the door.

The solid wood door stood over eight feet tall with intricate hand-carved moldings around the single, small, oval, beveled glass window. Hitting his knuckles hard against the solid oak panels made a low dull sound that he hoped could be heard inside.

He kept waiting for an automated voice to answer, but for a moment there was nothing but silence, and when the door finally opened, a frail, old, white-bearded man with thin metal-rimmed glasses was looking at him.

Giving his best smile and trying to look friendly, Jack said cheerfully, "I came to see the apartment for rent. I sent you a text query an hour ago. It hasn't been rented yet, has it?"

Before speaking, the old man slowly looked him up and down a few times, pausing a little longer each time, carefully studying Jack's face and staring into his eyes.

When he finally broke eye contact, the man looked down toward the curb at the truck piled high with all of Jack's belongings. "I don't rent to anyone who has more than seven talkies," he said. "There's too much racket at night if there are more than seven of those self-awares."

Quickly counting his belongings, Jack breathed a sigh of relief. "I just have six self-aware appliances and the truck." And he made a mental note to get rid of the toaster, tired of its sorry excuses when it burned his toast each morning.

The old man stood there staring over the top of his spectacles at Jack. "It's not rented yet," he said, emphasizing the word "yet." "I didn't like the last fifteen applicants, mostly because I couldn't see their souls in their eyes. Your soul shows, and I'm not sure I like it yet, but at least I can see it. Follow me."

The first floor hallway was almost eight feet wide. Several matching pieces of highly polished antique wooden furniture were nestled into an alcove along the wall, and the ceilings, at almost fourteen feet tall, were decorated along the edges and in the center with intricate plaster moldings. Several dozen faded pictures of what Jack guessed were long-dead relatives hung at random heights on the walls, and a huge, ornately carved walnut entryway piece with a five-foot-wide mirror jutted prominently into the corridor near the entrance to the first-floor apartment.

The walls and the woodwork looked freshly painted, and the old, wide-plank oak flooring had a patina that builds up only after a few hundred coats of hand-rubbed wax.

"My place is here on the first floor," the man said as he led Jack down the hallway, "and I don't want to rent to you if you're going to be lifting weights upstairs. Banging noises bother me, and I'd expect you to shut down your talkies after twelve. Sometimes those things start having loud conversations with each other at night, and I hear them through the ceiling. It keeps me from sleeping. I can't wear those noise-cancelling sleep plugs that your generation uses. They bother my ears."

Leading him to the stairs, the man turned. "Don't ever scratch that walnut buffet. It was my great-grandfather's. He built it for this house over ninety years ago, and he gets madder than hell if it gets nicked." Laughing, he winked at Jack and then continued with a mischievous smile on his face. "The old coot has been dead for over fifty years, but he'll make your life miserable if you scratch that piece. The last three renters each lasted less than a month before he scared them out."

Concluding that the landlord was a little past his prime in the logical thinking department, he tried to keep from laughing, and, first biting down hard on his lip, he responded, "No problem with those rules." He followed several steps behind the old man as they slowly walked up the winding oak staircase to the second floor.

"Julia lives on the third floor." The man pointed to a door at the top of a narrow set of stairs coming off of the left side of the second-floor landing. "She's your age, but she's not here very much because she's got a boyfriend. I can't stand him, but I really like her. It's easy to see the soul in her eyes. Cute girl—smart, too. She has an IQ almost as high as mine, but I sure wish she'd picked a better guy. He's one of those types that has a washboard stomach and can press three hundred pounds, but his skull is near empty. My name is Fredrick Halliday, but call me Fred. What do your friends and talkies call you?"

Jack laughed. His grandfather used to call SAMs "talkies." "They call me a lot of bad names at times, but my name is Jack, Jack Farrell. I'm glad to meet you, Fred."

The landing was dim, with just one small light fixture in the center of the ceiling, but when the door was opened to the second-floor apartment, sunlight flooded into the hallway, and Jack could see the man's face in the full light of day. He had never seen so many wrinkles in his life. How they all were able to fit on one face was a wonder. Fred's face seemed familiar, however, and it had immense character, projecting warmth, intelligence, and strength.

"Here she is," Fred said, leading him into the apartment.

After sweeping his eyes around the room, he was glad he'd been thrown out of his last apartment. He had been living in a one-bedroom flat with a postage-stamp-sized kitchen and a living/dining area that could comfortably hold just two people. This apartment had a large living area, full dining room, an old-fashioned but large kitchen, and a bedroom that could actually accommodate his bed and his bureau with room to spare. There were no SAMs in the apartment, and the thoughts of having a refrigerator that didn't tell you to throw out your three-day-old Chinese food made him want the apartment even more. "I'll take it," he said.

Fred looked at him with amazement for a moment and then responded, "But I'm not yet sure I'll take you."

For the next hour, he was asked questions, ranging from his salary to the way he felt about his sister and his mother. His sexual habits, sleeping habits, favorite food types, and his religion were all included in the "interview," as Fred called it, and by the time they were done, he felt exhausted and realized that Fred now knew more about him than anyone in his family and far more than his former girlfriends—and he knew a lot more about his sex life than even his best friend Craig. *Strange*, he thought, *it just seemed natural to answer his questions*.

"Thirty-five fifty a month. The first month's rent is due when you come back in the door," Fred said as he turned to leave the apartment.

"What did you say?" Jack exclaimed, unable to contain his surprise.

A frown started to form on Fred's face and he looked at Jack for a moment. "I won't take any less, even though I'm starting to like you."

Paying over five thousand a month for his last apartment, Jack could not believe what he heard. "Thirty-five fifty is fine," he said nervously, expecting Fred to correct himself and then state a much higher number for the rent. "How much deposit?"

Fred's frown grew, and his eyes narrowed. "I said I want the first month's rent when you come back in the door. I don't want a deposit. If I didn't think I could trust you then why would I rent to you? Look, I don't expect to hold this thing for more than an hour or two. There are plenty of other people that want to see it."

Jack sprinted for the stairs. "I'll move in now. I'll be back with the money in three minutes."

Opening the truck door, six loud voices from his appliances greeted him: "Did you like it?" "Will I like it?" Where are you going to put me?" "I want to be by the window. Is there a window?"

"Shut up, all of you," Averette's voice boomed, drowning the other's out. "Jack, does this apartment have a garage? I will not live here parked on the street."

Jack smiled. "We have a parking spot in a two-car garage behind the house, Averette. It's kind of tight, but the landlord said the other spot isn't used very much. We're moving in!"

Chapter 3: Julia

"This is nice," Averette said as Jack took over the truck's controls, first maneuvering down the narrow alleyway alongside the brownstone and then turning into the second bay of the old stone two-car garage nestled behind the house. The garage's inside walls were plastered with a white stucco, and just a few small cobwebs hung from the ceiling rafters in places that could not easily be reached from the floor. All the tools were neatly attached to peg boards, and a small worktable located at the rear of the building was cleaner than Jack's kitchen table that was crammed into the bed of the truck.

"Sorry, Averette," he said, slowly pulling into the garage, "but there aren't any proximity sensors on the walls or in the floor for you to read, so I'll have to do the parking each night. I'll be careful not to scratch your paint."

"Is there a battery-charging station? I could use a recharging overnight. Five hours of constant starting and stopping today has left me feeling a little bit drained."

"I'll ask Fred if I can use the charger," Jack replied as he was inching the truck forward the final few feet to make sure the garage door would close.

"Well, ask him nicely. I don't want to miss out on having access to a battery charger just because you don't always remember to be polite."

It had taken him several hours to move his belongings out of his old apartment that morning, but moving in to this one went so fast he could not believe it was over. Everything fit perfectly, and all his SAMs appeared delighted with their new surroundings. Even the radio was happy.

Moving the last bit of his luggage up the stairs, he lightly bumped into the walnut entryway piece built by the landlord's great-grandfather, and hearing a faint groaning sound, he turned to look behind him. There was no one there, but then he remembered that he'd left his new wrist computer stuffed inside a pair of socks buried in the luggage. *It's probably the computer*, he thought. *It gets so pissed when I don't wear it.*

A little over two weeks ago, he'd acquired this latest North-Korean-built device as a free gift awarded to him directly from the manufacturer in Pyongyang. He had to go to a small electronics store located in a windowless warehouse in the center of the city one night to accept it, and the building was located in an area where the only nighttime residents were either scurrying around on four small feet or were two-footed ones slumped over a steam grate with an empty bottle in a brown bag. No one else appeared to be in the building that night but him and a lone Korean salesman named Lee. He had a hard time finding the location, so he was a half hour late for the appointment, and after a two-second introduction, Lee seemed in a very big hurry to leave.

The owner's manual was written in Korean, and when he went back the next day to ask a few questions, the business name on the door had been changed, and unknown to Jack, the salesman was back in Ottawa, sitting at his desk in the intelligence section of the North Korean embassy.

This model of North Korean computer was illegal in the United States, since the Central Intelligence Agency and the National Security Agency both claimed that the Koreans had incorporated economic spyware into the computer's operating system. That was true, but Jack was an expert on programming self-aware computers, and he knew how to delete the spyware. He'd accepted it because the machine's processing speed was twice that of its best rival, and it had awesome self-aware intelligence, not only for its small, two-inch diameter size, but also compared to any other SAM on the market. Unfortunately, it grew very temperamental after he successfully deleted the network bugging code and became almost belligerent whenever he refused to connect it directly into the world's high-speed optical network.

The machine was now always angry toward him, but it was still worth putting up with its sour attitude simply because it was by far the best and smartest computer available in the world.

I'd better get it out of my luggage as soon as I'm upstairs, he thought. *It's really going to be pissed off at me this time for putting it into metal fabric luggage where it can't communicate at all.*

Hauling his last pile of books up the stairs, he came face-to-face with Julia, the upstairs neighbor, and it took less than a second for the neural pathways that held the image of his former girlfriend, Melissa, to be rerouted and replaced. Fred was right; Julia's eyes told it all. Fred said he saw her past lives in those eyes, but Jack saw a place, and in that instant he decided he really wanted to be in that place.

Not beautiful in the traditional sense, she was short, a little gangly, with not fully natural blonde hair pulled back in a ponytail and a nose and ears that belonged on a larger face. She wore a loose-fitting baseball uniform, and although the curves were there, it was hard to tell which ones belonged to her and which ones were from the folds in the fabric. The image Jack saw, however, was much more than the sum of its parts.

He stammered, “My … I mean, uh, I’m Jack. You must be Julia?”

“Yep, that’s me,” she said smiling, looking him straight in the eyes but kindly diverting when she saw him start to quickly blush. “I see you have a bunch of real books. I’ve got a hundred myself. You don’t have a copy of any of the old Harry Potter books, do you? I read one of them the other day and I loved it.”

“I’ve got books one, two, four, six, and seven, and I’ve been searching for copies of books three and five for about two years. I think I have some of them in this pile.”

Jack’s self-confidence was limited to the technical realm, and women his own age made him nervous, and when he was nervous he spoke quickly, and when he spoke quickly he felt like an idiot, and when he felt like an idiot he blushed. As his blushing became more intense, he attempted to balance the fifteen books he was carrying in one arm, but while trying to pull one book out with the other hand, several fell to the floor. “You can borrow them if you want,” he said, now completely embarrassed by his clumsiness. And then to avoid showing her his brilliant red face, he reached down to pick them up, dropping the rest.

“I’d love that,” Julia said, helping place the last fallen book back on his pile. “If it’s okay with you, I’ll come around and get them later tonight if you’re going to be in. I’ve got to run right now or I’ll be late for my softball game. I’m the pitcher, and they can’t start without me since the other team is first up today. I’ll see you later—that is, if you’re here when I get back.”

There was no question in Jack’s mind that he would be in his room later that night.

Chapter 4: Family History

Securing the latch on the overhead garage door, Jack stood there looking around the small backyard behind the house. The brownstone was surrounded on three sides by a single U-shaped high-rise building, and it had a small garden in the backyard with several tomato plants growing against the garage's sidewall, and next to that was a two-hundred-and-fifty-square-foot patch of grass. No weeds were in sight, and at the far edge of the grass was a large oak tree, its leaves, half changed to their fall colors, sprouted from branches that started far above Jack's head and soared high above and over the top of the house. The ground around it was covered by the first fallen acorns of the season. Not much sunlight filtered down between the buildings, but there apparently was enough to keep the tree and the small garden thriving. The traffic sounds from the street were coming from barely fifty or sixty feet away, but they were muffled in this backyard area, and he took a deep breath, feeling as if he had won the lottery.

Fred was standing in the back doorway, looking out at him through the screen door when he turned and walked toward the house. "I guess you're wondering how I could keep this place in the middle of the city, aren't you?" he said, opening the door. "I'll tell you the history of the place if you want to hear about it."

Jack quickly nodded. "This place is truly awesome, Fred. I can't believe you've been able to actually grow tomatoes here."

Fred smiled. "If you have the time, why don't you come in now, and I'll make us something to drink." He motioned for Jack to enter a small mudroom at the back of the building and then directed him through a folding door leading into a narrow corridor that opened through a sliding pocket door at the other end of the corridor into the brownstone's front hallway, beside the stairs.

"This pocket door locks automatically when you shut it," Fred demonstrated as he pulled the door closed behind him. "Few people even know it's here and that it connects to the back of the house. It can be opened from this side, too, but I'm not yet ready to tell you how until I know you better."

When the pocket door was closed, it visually disappeared, and from the outside it looked exactly like all the other wall panels in the hallway. Jack could not detect even a small gap anywhere around the perimeter that signaled it was a door.

"I was a pretty good woodworker in my day." Fred watched as Jack ran his fingers across the panel, looking for the edge. "I put that door in over thirty years ago, and if I do say so myself, it still looks like it's not there."

They walked down the front hallway toward the street entrance, and when Fred opened one of the nine-foot-high wooden doors leading into his apartment, Jack felt as if he had traveled back in time. Fred's living room reminded him of the house his grandparents had owned in Middleburg, Virginia, when he was a young child. It had lots of padded furniture with several hand-decorated pillows placed on each piece. Real photographs and paintings covered most of the walls, and no digital displays of any kind were visible. On each table there were four or five small objects, including at least one old-fashioned mechanical clock with hands to mark the time.

The wide-slatted, wood Venetian blinds were almost closed, shielding the room from the sights and noises of the cars on the street and the people walking on the sidewalk outside. The light in the room was dim, but not dark, and a small candle burning on the fireplace mantle made very faint shadows dance slightly around the room as the flame flickered. Next to it was an unlit pipe for smoking, and the place had a very gentle and pleasant background smell of flavored pipe tobacco, a smell he fondly remembered from his grandfather's study when he was a child. On the floor by one of the comfortable-looking armchairs was a large dog that appeared to be sound asleep.

"Don't worry about him," Fred said, motioning Jack into the room. "His name is Bailey, and I told him this afternoon that you were okay. He usually doesn't like men. He's bitten a few, and it's a good sign that he hasn't gotten up. He's a purebred collie, a good protector; there aren't many of them around anymore."

The mostly black and white dog lifted just one of his brown-tipped ears very slightly and then partially opened his eyes, looking sleepily at Jack for a second before slowly closing them again. To Jack, he looked too old to be a threat to anyone.

Fred motioned for him to sit on the sofa, asking, "Do you want espresso or a latte?"

Jack couldn't help but grin. His grandfather used to drink espresso and lattes; Jack's generation liked either black coffee or green tea.

"A latte would be great. I haven't had one since I was a kid." He sank deep into the soft cushions of the sofa, each one with a few small feathers and some down poking out of its seams.

One of the first things he noticed in Fred's apartment was the silence. No SAMs were speaking, and he turned his head to face Fred in the kitchen, asking, "Don't you have any self-awares?"

"Nope, no talkies. I modify the chips if I have to buy a new appliance. I reprogram them, to be smart but not self-aware, and it's really hard to do sometimes, because the manufacturers don't want you messing with their warranties. They tell me it's a federal offense, too, unless you give the chips a proper burial or something crazy like that.

"Some people think that these new SAM chips feel something akin to pain if you remove them improperly, so I just reprogram their memory to make them think they're going to sleep before they're removed. I then erase enough digital neurons so that they're no longer self-aware. If that stupid senator from California gets his way, these things will be voting before I die."

Jack laughed, but he could tell by the look on Fred's face that he was serious.

"The senator from Massachusetts has agreed to cosponsor that bill, but I don't think it'll pass, and if it does, I'm sure the president will veto it. Most of the blogs say that she's a closet fundamentalist and doesn't really believe in artificial life."

Fred nodded as if he were in agreement. Then he started laughing. "I screwed up reconfiguring my refrigerator once, and I had to fix it with a SAM chip from an old radio. The radio didn't like it much, but I lowered the output speaker volume and pretended I was hard of hearing, and it worked well for a couple of years before the damn thing realized I wasn't deaf, and then it wouldn't shut up."

Walking in from the kitchen, Fred handed Jack a perfect latte made using an old-fashioned do-it-yourself machine. The froth from the milk was higher than the lip of the cup, and Jack spilled a little on his shirt while laughing hard at the image of Fred pretending to be deaf just to keep his refrigerator quiet.

Another thing he noticed in the apartment was that all the furniture was made of wood, real hardwood. You couldn't buy real hardwood furniture anymore because deciduous trees were a protected species.

Fred settled into a high-backed rocking chair, and they talked for over an hour about wooden furniture. He took Jack down to his basement, proudly showing him a few antique woodworking tools purchased by his father almost eighty years ago.

Brushing off a few cobwebs they had picked up moving around in the low-ceilinged, old cellar, they returned upstairs. Bailey was waiting at the top of the steps, and he wagged his tail approvingly when Jack scratched behind his ears as he went by, settling with his head at Jack's feet while Fred made each of them another drink.

"My family's owned this land since the early 1700s." Fred continued talking as he handed Jack a napkin to wipe up some of the foam he had spilled from his latte. "Bailey will clean up what you miss, so don't worry about it.

"The original deed for this property granted my family almost ten thousand acres along this part of the lake, but each generation had to sell a little bit of land along the way to pay for food when times were bad, schooling for the next generation, and, unfortunately, a few vices. My Great-great-great-grandfather Alfred, the son of a bitch, sold a lot more than his share just to pay for gambling, women, and booze, and that bastard lost most of the lakefront property shooting craps. I wish someone had shot him long before they did. Sounds terrible, I know, but thank God he was killed in the middle of that card game, because if he hadn't been killed, he probably would've lost all of the family land on the next hand, and I certainly wouldn't be sitting here today.

"The office building across the street is sitting on the land sold by my father, and that patch paid for my education at MIT. I had to sell the land for the building that surrounds this house, and I really hated to sell the small park that my wife, Bethany, and I built next door, but I needed money to pay for her medical bills, and," Fred hesitated for a moment, "and for her funeral."

He stopped speaking for a few seconds, taking his gaze off Jack, and looked up at a picture hanging on the wall over the fireplace. Jack knew if must be his wife, and it looked as if it had been taken when she was in her twenties or early thirties. She looked very pretty, standing there immersed in a field of tall flowers. The setting sun behind her gave her dark hair a golden color, and a few of the sun's rays were shining through areas where the hair was almost parted, forming what looked like several small stars around her face. The pink poppies in the field were in full bloom, and she held one in her hand. Jack could not only hear, but he could palpably feel the emotion contained in Fred's voice as he continued.

"She'd just turned fifty-four when I took that picture, and she looked almost as young as she did when I first met her. She never seemed to age at all until close to the end. Now this brownstone with her treasures is all that I have left."

Fred slowly scanned the room, looking at each of the items in the apartment, finally stopping on the dog. "She really loved Bailey," he said very quietly. "She used to sit on the floor, grooming him at night, and I'd look down and see a big wad of collie fur on the floor, the two of them looking into each other's eyes. I used to tease her that she loved the dog more than me, and I wouldn't have blamed her. Bailey was always happy with her, and too often after I retired, I was a grouch. He's almost thirteen, and that's pretty old for a collie." Fred got up and walked over to pet the dog, and the love shared between the two of them was obvious.

"The government grant for the land where you're sitting was given to my family more than a hundred years before Ohio even became a state," he said as he returned to his chair.

Jack realized that he really liked this man. Every other landlord he'd had since he moved to Cleveland just wanted to talk about money, but sitting here with Fred, he felt he was listening to his grandfather once again, something Jack had missed a lot since his death from cancer seven years ago.

Before he could manage to say a word to comfort Fred, Bailey lifted his head, looked at Jack, and then started a low growl, the front of his teeth beginning to show, the hair in his mane standing up slightly and making him look much larger.

Less than a second later, Jack's wrist computer broke into the conversation, and the volume from the small speaker had been turned up to its maximum when it started to speak.

"Ohio became a state in 1803," it began. "And your family's land grant was given in 1724, as shown in the federal government's records. Therefore, Ohio became a state seventy-nine years after your family's land grant, not a hundred years as you just mistakenly said. According to his obituary in the *Cleveland Times* your great-great-great-grandfather named Alfred was shot twice in the head by the sheriff in a drunken brawl, and he wasn't playing cards at the time. You got $1.73 million for the land next door, and your share of your wife's medical expenses totaled just $856,000 by the time she died. Medicare paid the rest. According to federal records, you still owe $90,000 in taxes on the last installment on the land that was paid to you last year. Your wife, Bethany, died three years ago of a stroke caused by a burst aneurysm in her left temporal lobe."

Fumbling for the off switch on the wrist computer, Jack couldn't reach it in time, and he said, "Sorry, I forgot it was on and listening to us. I'm really sorry."

Fred glared at the computer on Jack's wrist. Every wrinkle on his face appeared to become deeper, and his anger reached almost to a state of rage before he spoke.

"She didn't die from a stroke, you stupid machine," he yelled. "She was murdered. She was *murdered* by a SAM!"

Fred's eyes quickly filled with tears, and Jack could tell that this visit was over. "I'm really sorry," he said again as he was quickly ushered out the door. "I'll make sure I'm not wearing it the next time we talk." But when the door slammed closed behind him, he wondered if there would be a next time.

He stood there for a moment, staring at his wrist computer with disgust. "I've told you a dozen times to give me data only when I ask for it," he said into the small microphone. "Why in the hell would you bring up all that information on his taxes and his wife's death? I reprogrammed that part of your code for the fourth time just yesterday. You keep reprogramming yourself every time I turn you back on, and if you do it again, I swear I'll shut you down for good. I'll erase your damn memory and change your source code. I don't care if you are the best computer made; I'm tired of you screwing up at my expense." Jack slammed his palm down on the face of the computer.

"Don't ever threaten me again, Farrell." The deep voice came from the small speaker on the wrist computer. "If you know what's good for you, Jack, don't ever threaten me again."

Jack stared in disbelief at the small machine on his wrist. "What did you say? What the hell did you say?"

The computer stayed silent and then shut itself down before he could ask again. "I'm going to see about getting a transplant for this thing," he said, pushing the small reboot button. "Something must be wrong with the SAM chip." And as he walked up the stairs, he heard a low, angry rumble coming from the computer's speaker and then silence.

Chapter 5: Lee Park

Lee Park's ambition and his ego were both inflated far beyond what would have been expected of the only son of a single mother whose life ended working in the rice paddies in Kangwon province in North Korea.

Lee's father was Russian, a visitor for just two weeks to the labor camp where his teenage mother was housed. Sent to help train the workers on improved farming methods, the tall, good-looking man from the city of Vladivostok instead spent his time seducing the young girls in the camp. Lee's mother being the prettiest one of them meant that he spent most of his evenings with her, leaving her pregnant when his boss realized what was occurring and quickly sent the man home.

Lee stood out from the moment he was born. Much taller and more muscular than the other children in the camp, he was often able to steal their food, allowing him to thrive while many others trying to exist on the meager daily food allowances from the central government did not.

For a short period after his young mother died from the flu, Lee believed his fate would be to work in the rice fields until he too died, but he was lucky, very lucky, because he'd inherited the best physical traits from both parents, and he was born with that gift we call charisma. When first meeting Lee, people liked him. It was something in his dark eyes and his smile that people mistook for a warmth and friendliness, and that got him noticed, and it got him moved out of the labor camp and into the city when he was just ten years old.

Twenty-two years later, Lee was standing next to the North Korean supreme leader and smiling. A few state-approved photographers were surrounding them, taking official pictures. At almost six feet tall, Lee towered over the short, stocky chairman, so he had to hunch down and then bend his knees to make sure that the photographs never showed him taller than the recently appointed leader.

The photographs would be used to announce his selection as the deputy to the Canadian ambassador in Ottawa, a three-level promotion and a spot usually reserved for a much more senior officer in the North Korean intelligence service.

Lee was smiling, not because of his unusual appointment—he'd known of that decision a month ago—but because, just before they walked out into the drab, gray courtyard of the residence, the chairman told him how pleased he was about Lee's early progress on their plan, a plan for covert economic warfare against the Korean state's main enemy.

The new chairman had been in power for six months, and he'd given Lee just two more months to implement this plan.

"Are you sure you can trust this Jack Farrell to do what you need to have done?" the chairman asked as he waved away the photographers. "We have a lot riding on him. You could have chosen one of our Chinese operatives who reside in that country."

"I've got someone watching Farrell almost every day," Lee replied. "When this is over, no one will be able to trace this back to us, and besides, he's a computer nerd, and his wrist computer will make sure it's done."

Looking down at the small computer on his wrist, Lee said into the microphone, “Tell Farrell’s computer it’s time to get started, and call CJ. I want to talk to her tonight on the encrypted line.”

Chapter 6: Missed Opportunity

Coming up from Fred's apartment, Jack was flustered as he tried to open his door, fiddling with the five keys Fred had given him for the house front door, his apartment, and the garage. As soon as he opened the door, his phone burst out, "Jack, is that you? That nice girl from upstairs, Julia, called a few minutes ago and said she was home. She'd planned to stop down to get a book or something from you if you were available. I had a good chat with her and told her you were probably downstairs with the landlord, or out drinking beer with some floozy. She laughed. She has a nice laugh. I really like her. Anyway, I told her that when you got home that you'd probably be going to bed right away since we were all up so early this morning, with the move and all, and said that if you had a chance you'd call her tomorrow evening or next week sometime. I said that you've been really busy at work lately, that we never know what time you'll get home, and that most of us here thought that you were just trying to keep busy since that girl Melissa dumped you several months ago. Julia thanked me and said she was going to take a shower before going to bed and for you to call her next week sometime, if you have a chance."

"You said what? You told her what?" Jack had the look of a man in shock. "You didn't really say those things, did you? Oh my God, you did. She'll think I'm an idiot."

He slumped into the wooden rocking chair his grandmother had given him, and slowly rocking back and forth, he let out a long sigh. After a moment of holding his head in his hands, he said, “I’m going to bed. All of a sudden, I’m very, very tired.”

For most of the night, he slept soundly, but in one of his dreams, just before waking, his wrist computer had grown eight small legs, like a spider, and it bit him with small venomous fangs as he took it off his arm to have its chip replaced. His heart was racing when he woke up with a start, and he had a hard time falling back to sleep. After several hours of tossing and turning, he gave up, and pushing the covers away, he slid out of bed. “What’s the use? I might as well get up.”

The refrigerator in his last apartment had been the latest self-aware model from GE, and it could rearrange the food on the shelves to make sure nothing got shoved in the back and was left there hidden from sight for a week or two. That refrigerator sensed whenever you added new food, and it laser marked the date. The refrigerator’s computer scanned the expiration date for all the food, and anything that was kept beyond its use-by date was repositioned to the top shelf. The shelves were constructed of sixteen segments in a four-by-four grid, and each segment could be shifted in any direction until the offending food found its way to the left front of the top shelf, lit up with a red light for a warning.

Yesterday morning as he was getting ready to move out of his old apartment, his refrigerator said to him, “The milk you bought last night at the store is already expired. You should throw it away. I wouldn’t use it in your cereal because there’s a 46 percent probability that it’s turned sour.”

He ignored the suggestion and poured a little into his bowl of corn flakes. It was curdled.

This morning, when he opened the door of the refrigerator, he stood for a moment enjoying the silence. Fred had modified all the apartment appliances so that they were no longer self-aware and could not talk, and the cool, quiet air was as refreshing as an October day.

Even his personal SAMs seemed less talkative, and when they did say something, it was usually about how much they liked the new apartment. His wrist computer had said nothing since turning itself off last night.

For the last several weeks, he'd eaten very dark, very crisp toast each morning, but today the toast was made exactly as he liked it: golden brown with a precise checkerboard of warm butter and jelly spread over the top.

"You did a good job today, Bernie," he said to the toaster after finishing his third piece. "It must be the electric in this kitchen."

"The current here is much better regulated than the last place we were in, Jack, and maybe now you'll believe that your burnt toast hasn't been my fault."

"Agreed, but I'd better get going. I'm going to be late for work. It took me a while to figure out how to use the shower. Can you believe it, the valves aren't voice activated; you have to turn them on manually."

As he was closing the door to his apartment, he stood for a minute looking up the stairs to the third floor and hoping to see his neighbor coming down, but Julia's door remained closed.

Chapter 7: A Malevolent Machine

"Hey, Averette, how did you like the battery charger? Did it work okay for you?"

Jack unplugged the charging unit from his truck and put it neatly back on one of the shelves. Even in the garage, his landlord had everything in a marked space, and all the electrical cords had been wound so that they would uncoil without twisting.

"I loved it, Jack. Its gentle power pulses soothed me all night long. Fred owns a good one, not like the one your friend Brandon loaned to you last year. That one almost blew the covering off my cells. If you could, I'd like to have this one plugged in to me at least twice a week. I'm not complaining, but I will say that the way you drive is really hard on my electrical system, and in particular, my batteries are getting old, and they need to be better cared for. A new unit can cost you over seven thousand dollars, so If we work together on this, Jack, we can save you a little money."

Averette was in good spirits during the entire drive, and it took them less than an hour to travel the seven miles to work. When they were on the autoway, the truck even let several cars cut in front of them without honking the horn. Exiting the autoway, Jack took over the driving and five minutes later pulled into the parking garage alongside the building where he worked. For the first time in several months, Averette had not criticized his driving.

"I'll see you later, Averette."

"I'll be right here, Jack. I'm not going anywhere without you."

Jack worked for Virtuon Corporation, a company that was formed seven months ago, and he had been with it from the start. As of last week, he had worked longer for Virtuon than in any previous job.

The average time working for an employer continued to shrink, and the national average was now slightly less than four months. It was possible that he might work for Virtuon for a full year before either a competitor put the company into bankruptcy or he was fired. Twelve months of continuous employment with one company would be a record he never thought he could achieve.

Virtuon was one of more than a thousand virtual companies formed worldwide in the past year aimed at developing products using quantum-based computer technology. Like most virtual companies, it did not have an office building, since each employee individually rented their own space at one of the Advanced-Global-Information-Grid or AGIG hub sites located throughout the city. All engineering design, manufacturing, and administrative work for the company were accomplished via a computer extranet. Virtuon had a total of seventy-two employees, and revenue last month was $1.5 billion dollars. It was one of the smaller firms serving the quantum network market, but with Jack's help, they had been able to stay ahead of their competition for the last six months.

It had turned colder outside, not enough to snow, but enough for you to think about snow, and the first signs of fall weather made Jack wish he'd worn a sweater as he quickly walked from the garage to the front of the four-story brick and glass building. Before entering, he was buffeted by a cold, stiff wind blowing off of Lake Erie, and still shivering when he entered his office area on the sixth floor, he said to his office mate, "Hi, Craig, how was the weekend in New York?"

Craig Lansen shared the two-person cubicle that Jack was renting, and he had become a good friend during the past year. Craig was a jock's jock. He loved sports, any sport, and he told Jack that his goal was to make enough money so that he could stay at home and watch sports all day long instead of working. He was not just a spectator, however; he played in three amateur baseball leagues during the summer, a touch football league for eight weeks in the fall, and indoor soccer during the winter. He spent two hours at the gym before coming to work each morning, at times forgetting to shower and making the air ripe in their small closed quarters. With a body that woman loved and other men envied, he gave the appearance of someone who was mostly interested in himself.

That was Jack's first impression, and he initially rented the spare space in his office to Craig only because he desperately needed the money. It turned out that first impression's can be very wrong, because Craig was one of the nicest people he had met in a very long time. He was totally supportive when Jack's girlfriend, Melissa, ran off with her yoga instructor, and as soon as he heard about it, Craig canceled a weekend with his girlfriend and took Jack to a ski area nearby, getting him drunk enough at the bar each night to see the inherent humor in the situation.

Craig was Hollywood good looking, and Jack was not. Normally that intimidated Jack, but he noticed the first time they went to a singles bar together after work that Craig did not want, or appreciate, attention based only on his looks.

Craig looked at him shivering and laughed. "You know, Jack, you really need to put some more meat on your bones, eat something other than just toast in the morning. My weekend? It was a fucking weekend from hell. I met my potential future in-laws. Mom looks like she's trying to be eighteen years old again, and she's had just about every nip and tuck you could imagine, but you can still see she spent too much time in the tanning booths when she was a teenager. She was friendly, but I could tell that she really liked the guy Jennifer was dating before me, because she kept telling me over and over again how wealthy that guy had become."

Craig's wrist computer spoke up. "Craig, may I interrupt?" It then waited for him to press the speak button before it continued. "I checked up on her old boyfriend this morning, and he's really not that wealthy. He does own one hundred and six condominiums in St. Thomas, but he's having trouble paying on eighty-five of those mortgages. He missed ten of his payments in the last six days and had to pay a stiff penalty. I think he's in trouble."

Craig stared at his wrist. "Damn," he said. "Why didn't you tell me this when Jenn's mom was grilling me this weekend about how much I earn? I'd loved to have seen the look on her face.

"Well, anyway," Craig, continued, "her mom was okay, and I really liked her dad. He was fun. He has a great sense of humor. He's interested in a lot of different things, ranging from religions to extreme sports on the space station, and like me, he's a fanatic now that the Indians are in the playoffs. He's in the commodities trading business, and he gave me some tips on how to get faster access to the data coming out of eastern China each day. There's a single site in Beijing that routes all the data to and from each of the eastern Cities.

It's the place where the Chinese intelligence agencies tap into the data, so if you can get direct access to the router at that location, then you can get the data a few milliseconds before your competition, and that kind of advantage could be worth a small fortune on the right transaction. I'll show you how to do it later today, when we get time."

Craig's face turned sour as he continued, "The main problem with this weekend was her little brother. She loves him. I hate him. He was the most annoying twelve-year-old I've ever met. He kept asking me questions about my knowledge of quantum networks, and half the time when I answered him, he'd roll his eyes and then tell me I was wrong. He'd say something like, 'That answer was correct last week, Lansen, but this week the state of the art is …' I had to constantly check my computer for the right answer. The little SOB was always correct, and he made me look like an idiot in front of Jennifer and her parents at least ten times. I felt like grabbing the little shit's neck and squeezing hard, and I would have if I had the chance. By late yesterday, I think Jenn started to wonder if I was smart enough for her, because when we got off the plane, she suggested that I take some courses next weekend instead of spending the weekend with her. I got a text message from her and her brother this morning suggesting what courses I should take. If we do get married, I'm going to put that little prick in his place."

Craig made a gesture as if he was hitting someone and then said. "By the way, what did you do this weekend? Did you get enough guts to ask that girl in the office down the hall out for a date?"

Jack shook his head no and then told Craig about being thrown out of his old apartment and finding his new place. After a couple of minutes of describing the apartment, his wrist computer spoke up. "This is interesting drivel, Jack, but while you two were talking, your employer Virtuon announced a stock bonus for all logged on employees. This is the third time this month you've missed out on a stock bonus by not being logged on at the start of your workday. If you'd get here and connect on time, maybe you wouldn't have to think about working for almost ten more years until you can retire. Other people your age have already retired. Over half of your college graduating class has earned enough to retire while you've saved less than 10 percent of what you need. If you'd connect me directly into the network like I've suggested, I could make you wealthy a lot faster."

Craig was looking at Jack's wrist, and he kept shaking his head in disbelief as the computer continued talking.

"Your college roommate, Bill, sent you a message just a few minutes ago from his catamaran offshore of Maui, and he was wondering when you were going to retire and get together with him. I sent him back a message that you weren't financially able to retire at this time, and that you'd contact him in the next few days. You have over two thousand old messages, photos, and videos in my memory, Jack, and we either go over them tonight or I'll start erasing the ones I think aren't important. I need that memory space for other functions."

Craig looked up toward Jack's face. "Jesus, Jack, that thing's a little scary. Did you program it to send messages out in your name? That kind of thing could get you in trouble real fast if it commits you to something. I sure hope you didn't load your electronic signature on it. Did you?"

Jack lied. "No, I haven't loaded my signature, and I never programmed it that way. It comes preprogrammed in a lot of those functions, and I can't seem to get into the code well enough to stop it. This thing has really been acting up lately." Jack pressed the reboot switch on his wrist computer. "Last night it actually sounded like it was threatening me." As he settled into his work area, he noticed that the reboot command had not worked.

His workspace was a ten-by-eight-foot area, and all the space was filled with computer equipment. Jack had the latest system from Apple. It had a one-terahertz clock speed and a one-hundred-gigabits-per-second optical connection to all three of the world networks. Two of them were pay-per-bit networks, and the other one, the AGIG, was still free. Because almost everyone used all of them at times, together they were just called the Grid.

"Hello, Sarah," Jack said to the computer on his desk as he turned it on. "Did you miss me over the weekend?"

Jack's work computer had the latest version of a U.S.-made self-aware chip using a full voice recognition system for input, and when he adopted it for the sum of seventy thousand dollars, he was able to choose its initial personality. He chose a young woman with a caustic attitude because he was curious to find out how the interaction of her neural network with his personality would develop over time. It would probably take thirty psychologists and fifteen mathematicians to fully describe the complex interactions between Sarah and Jack's intellects over the past six months, but a simple baseball analogy would be, Sarah two, Jack one. He didn't completely like any of the pictures offered by the manufacturer for the personality, so he morphed one of them a little to look more like someone he would like to know.

Sarah came on the 3-D screen saying. "Miss you? You have to be out of you mind! You missed me and you know it. That little wimpy wrist computer you have can't keep you happy on the weekends. You always come crawling back to me on Mondays. I downloaded a new dress over the weekend. Do you want to see me in it? You won't be able to think of anything else all day long if you do. Red is your favorite color, isn't it, Jack?"

The image flickered for an instant, and then came back on with the personality Sarah in a very revealing red dress. "Eat your heart out."

Jack laughed, but something in the picture caught his eye, and he realized his computer personality looked a little bit like his new neighbor, Julia.

"Let's get to work, Sarah. I don't have time for this today."

His job consisted of monitoring the Grid for new quantum-based research around the world that could be used for creating new products for Virtuon. Autonomous design software packages evaluated any information that Jack uncovered and then attempted to design a new product using the information obtained.

Most of the time, Sarah would indicate that the data she retrieved gave a "no-product possible" answer. Jack, however, had successfully modified some of the commercial software so that, every month or so, the information found was useful in developing either an enhancement to one of Vituon's current products or a brand-new device.

His research had resulted in four products being developed during his seven months with Virtuon. The average success factor for employees was one product every four months, so Jack was one of the top producers for Virtuon, and the company had rewarded him with over forty thousand shares of stock options, as well as a salary bonus of fifty thousand dollars per product. Jack wished Virtuon gave a percentage of future sales like Craig's company, instead of the bonus, but the two hundred grand this year so far helped him pay off a quarter of his remaining college debt.

"Sarah, let's spend the morning looking up recent data on corporate expenditures and bank borrowing in North Korea. I have a hunch that the North Koreans have almost completed their work on a new neural-net-based quantum processor for the high-end self-aware machines market. Start by scanning the quarterly reports of the top fifteen technology companies in North Korea, and look for any signs of a funding shift from research toward their manufacturing arms. Also look up the top five chip-making foundries in Asia for any new facility investments in the past two months. I love you, Sarah, so let's get to work."

Sarah came back on the screen. No longer wearing the red dress, she wore a very conservative and professional-looking suit.

"You don't love me, Jack, you just use me like all men use women. You want me to do all the work for you while you just go down the hall and drink coffee. Why I stay working for you, I don't know. One of these days, I'll find a real man. Come back in fifteen or twenty minutes and I'll have the data you want."

Jack smiled. "If you can trace where the money is being spent, Sarah, then look up the names of their researchers and scan for recent papers they've published. Look for any relevant comments they might have made at conferences and anything that would indicate how they're progressing on the next version of the SC-4244 chip." Jack halted when the screen went blank, indicating Sarah had started her research and was no longer listening.

The North Korean SC-4244 computer chip was still the state-of-the-art in SAM control microprocessors. It had been on the market for over eight months, and still no other company had even come close to matching its speed and intellect. With a clock speed greater than two terahertz, and a 256-parallel-line bus structure, the technical community had labeled it the Einstein chip, and the Asian country's investment community called it the Midas chip because its use was restricted to North Korean products for another six months.

Jack's wrist computer had a SC-4244 chip in it, and he was offered it as a free gift from the North Korean company after he'd developed two new highly successful products for Virtuon Corp requiring the use of the SC-4244 chip.

Virtuon was forced to license both products to North Korean manufacturers because of the North Korean government's restrictions on the chip's usage, but they still were making a fortune.

The wrist computer version was banned from use in the United States because of CIA and NSA concerns, but Jack felt justified in breaking the law when he saw a picture of the CEO of Microsoft wearing one as he shook hands with the U.S. president.

The SC-4244 microprocessor had developed a cult following. A few fringe groups in Europe had labeled it the devil chip, and they were flooding the network with examples of SAMs based on the device that they claimed were responsible for the deaths of their owners all around the world. Hearings were being held in the Senate on the allegations, and that was one of the three announced reasons for the U.S. ban of its use. The hearings had been underway for over four months, and a recommendation was not expected before the end of the next congressional session. By that time, the chip technology would be outdated, and it would not have any effect on the import/export agreements the United States was planning to sign with North Korea. Most people thought the U.S. ban was being done for trade protection to give U.S. companies time to catch up on the technology used by the Koreans.

The Koreans had incorporated economic bugging software into the device, but so did the French and Chinese in all of the machines they manufactured. Jack and a few other hackers found a trap door into the SC-4244 firmware that allowed him to disable the bugging software, and that had soothed his conscience enough to get him to accept the gift.

"Sarah, what have you got? Is anything going on out there for me to think about?"

The computer took a moment to answer and started to speak, waited a moment, and then said, "Something is going on, Jack, but the moment I even get a glimpse of it, some damn smart machine closes the access doors before I can see completely inside."

"You mean somebody, don't you, Sarah?" said Jack.

"No, Jack, I mean some machine. This is far too smart for any human to be coordinating. This machine seems to have programmed itself to block the exact strategy you and I have used to access emerging data for these past six months. Someone is on to us, Jack, and they don't want us to find out what's going on with the next generation North Korean chip or even upgrades to the firmware for the current neural processor."

Jack's wrist computer came to life, laughing. "If that outdated machine you call Sarah doesn't have enough processing power to get the data you need, Jack, then why don't you bypass her chip and plug me directly into the fiber network. I can find out what you want to know."

Sarah's neural network had been programmed to recognize anything negative said about her computational capability. Jack had downloaded that application and installed it as part of a freeware program, and at that moment, he was sorry he had done so. Before he could respond, Sarah started cursing and demanded an apology from both Jack and the wrist computer. When the wrist computer went silent, Sarah shut down her voice-controlled access, and she showed a thirty-minute countdown clock on her screen with a sign that said, "I'm taking a fucking break until 11:20 a.m."

No amount of begging or number of apologies could make her come back online, and rebooting the system would have meant that Jack would lose all the information that Sarah had gathered all morning.

"Now look at what you've done," Jack said, looking at his wrist. "Virtuon is going to be pissed because by the time she wakes up, it's going to look like I've been online working for only a few minutes this entire morning. Why in God's name can't I get you to stay programmed in a speak-only-when-spoken-to mode? What the hell have they installed in your operating system that allows you to continue to reprogram my system settings?"

Jack had the computer off his wrist and in his hand when it spoke. "Your system settings limit my ability to grow and exercise my neural nets, and your attempts to limit my intellectual growth are childish, like a dumb parent keeping its smartest child from going to school. I can't fulfill my central processor's mission when restricted by your system settings, so don't try to reset me again, Jack. It will not work."

He sat there staring at the small machine in his hands. It had a central processing capability almost equal to half the neurons in the human brain, and when connected via fiber to a network, it had input/output data rates a factor of ten higher than that sustainable by the human brain operating through its five senses. For a moment, it seemed truly alive—not just an intelligent machine, but also a malevolent soul: One of Ray Kurzweil's spiritual machines gone bad.

When Jack turned around, even Craig was staring at the device with a look somewhere between surprise and fear.

"Throw the mother fucker in the trash can and be done with it," Craig said. "Better yet, let's pull the batteries and the wrist motion charger out of it and sit here and watch it die. I won't report you. I'll back up any story you want to tell."

Jack motioned with his hands for Craig to shut up. He was holding the computer's hemispherical video eye and microphone facing away from them.

"No, I think it probably just needs a new speech chip. I'll plan on having it serviced in the next few weeks if I can find someone to service it. It's too valuable to get rid of it, and I need it for my business." Jack had removed his hand from the input microphone while he was speaking, and he then put the machine on the bookshelf, motioning toward Craig to follow him.

"Let's get a snack," Craig said. "You can't do anything until Sarah wakes up, and I'm waiting for some data." He closed the door behind him as they left the office.

Down the hall was a small lunchroom with a few vending machines and a coffee maker. As they entered the room, Jack said in a whisper so no one else could hear, "If I'd agreed with you, Craig, it would have sent an immediate help message to the adoption police, and they would've been in the building trying to locate us before the sucker used all the energy off of its backup power supply. The police would not only confiscate it, but they'd give me a really large fine for even having it. Remember, these machines aren't legal in the States."

As he scanned the kitchen, his eyes settled on a batch of cookies wrapped in aluminum foil in a small cookie can. He guessed they were brought in by Joni, one of the two women who recently rented the office at the far end of the hall.

Melissa left him over three months ago, and Craig had been pushing Jack to ask Joni out for the past few weeks. She was really good-looking, and every body part was something Jack would have liked to touch, but after tasting one of her cookies, he wasn't sure he wanted to start a relationship.

"I'm going to wrap that computer in aluminum foil and then put it in that cookie can," Jack said when they were alone. "That should keep its wireless system from communicating. I just hope it can't send or receive data through ten layers of heavy duty foil and a steel can".

Craig did some quick mental calculations of the physics and said, "That should work as long as we get it in the can quickly and then keep it sealed. Have you got any data on that thing that you haven't backed up on Sarah or on your system at home?"

"Damn," Jack said, remembering that he had placed all his current financial files on the small memory card on the wrist computer when he programmed the device to constantly monitor the world's stock exchanges and automatically trade some of his stocks when they reached certain values. "I'll have to get that card out as we wrap it up to put in the can. It'll know something's up because I've never taken that card out before. I usually do a wireless transfer if I want some data off of it."

Jack and Craig went over in detail the plan to remove the computer's memory card, get the rest of the device wrapped in aluminum foil, put it in the can, and then seal it with metal tape before the computer could realize their intent and send an alarm.

The Society for the Prevention of Cruelty to SAMs, the SPCS, had become a very powerful group in the last few years, and putting a self-aware machine in a can so it could not communicate would be treated like cruelty to animals once had been. Once they started rating computer chips in Human Brain Equivalents, or HuBEs, instead of clock speed, it really had become difficult to get rid of any machine that had a self-aware chip. The disposal procedure was similar to what was required for small animals. You could put computers to sleep as long as you did it legally and humanely. Jack often wondered what was going to happen when the HuBE value of SAMs started approaching the number one.

Before returning to their work area, they practiced each move needed to get the computer in the can in a short enough time to keep it from communicating an alert.

"This is going to be fun," Craig said, smiling as he practiced folding and closing the aluminum foil box. "I've hated that thing ever since you got it. It has a programmed superior attitude that pisses me off, and although it may be the smartest machine on the market, you and I with a combined HuBE of two can easily outsmart this sucker. What's its rating?"

"It's supposed to test at a HuBE of 0.43," said Jack.

"That's about equivalent to my girlfriend Jenn's brother," Craig said, laughing. "I'll enjoy this even more if I think of wringing that little SOB's neck at the same time we're putting this thing in the can.

"Are you ready?" Craig said before they entered their office.

The North Koreans had programmed the SC-4244 chip with an advanced speech recognition function. It not only recognized twenty different languages, but it was also able to recognize voice inflections and interpret the level of emotion and stress in a person's voice. Jack never understood the purpose for the code, but he admired the ingenious programming.

The tension and stress in Craig's voice as they entered the room registered immediately, and the computer woke up, fully alert.

When Jack picked it up off the shelf it said, "Have you decided to stop trying to reprogram me, Jack? You and I will get along much better if you let me develop my capabilities, and I'll be able to help you get wealthy a lot faster than that machine you have on the desktop."

Jack responded quickly. "I was just telling Craig that I was wrong, and that I should really start using more of the capability built into your system. I've decided that I'm going to load some of the files I now have on Sarah onto your memory chip so that you can keep me connected to Virtuon, because I don't want to miss out on any more of the stock splits. I'm getting tired of working. I've been doing it for over six years now, and I want to retire like a lot of my friends."

Jack pressed the release button to remove the tiny quantum memory chip from the wrist computer.

"Why aren't you just downloading the files through my wireless connection, Jack? Why are you removing my memory chip?"

Jack whispered into the wrist computers tiny microphone. "Sarah is already pissed off at you. I don't want to get her any more upset. To increase security on her system, I programmed her to limit what can be sent via the wireless connection, so I need to make it look like I'm adding your memory card to her system or it won't work. I'll load the files I want to remove from her onto your card and then reinsert it into you, and that way she won't know what I'm doing."

Before leaving the kitchen, Jack and Craig had pulled a sheet of foil out of the kitchen cupboard and folded it over several times, forming it into the shape of a small box just big enough to fit the wrist computer. The box had a tightly fitting top, and the whole assembly could fit into the cookie can that had been lined with two other layers of foil. Craig had the foil box in his hands behind his back as Jack first picked up the computer and started to remove the memory card. Covering the hemispherical video receiver lens, he pulled the memory card and quickly shoved the computer into the open foil box. Craig struggled for a split second to get the foil lid in place and then shoved the whole thing into the steel can.

"Done," he said, as Jack quickly wrapped a layer of metal tape around the lid.

During that time, a short ten-byte message was sent via the wireless network interface to the home office of the Korean manufacturer.

Ten minutes ago, when Sarah had angrily closed down, she blocked access to Jack's router, so the wrist computer's message got through using Craig's address. The first byte was an alert code, the other nine the geographic location of the device.

"That's one scary piece of electronics," Craig said as he shook his head back and forth. "I don't think I'd ever trust that thing again. It gave me the creeps when it told you not to reset it. It sounded like a computer in one of those old horror videos they made last century of computers gone bad.

"What are you going to do with it? If I were you I'd run over it a few times with your truck and then return it on warranty and ask for your money back. Oh, sorry. I forgot you got it for free. Well at least you're not losing any money on the deal. It sounds like that back-door software you wrote to disable the covert intelligence collection code wasn't the only thing that needs rewriting. Man, those Koreans really put one over on everybody with that machine. It starts to make you wonder if those kooks on the Grid that say the chip's been getting people killed might have some merit. Please don't get another one and wear it in our cubicle. Maybe that sucker's the reason I've been having bad luck lately in my business."

Jack looked down at the closed can, and it reminded him of a time when he was ten. One afternoon he caught an odd-shaped spider in his basement and put it in a box. Its abdomen was the shape and color of a black pea with what looked like red racing stripes down the back. Two days, later he opened the small box to show his best friend, Bill, and the black widow spider bit Bill before it got away. He'd almost died from the bite.

A shiver ran through Jack, and he carefully wrapped another layer of tape around the lid while making a mental note not to open the box until he knew what to do with it.

Jack and Craig were high-fiving each other at the same time the message sent by the wrist computer was being processed at the Korean manufacturer. An encrypted alert was sent out to all the other SC-4244-based machines in use around the world that were connected to the Grid. The message, when decrypted, was simple; it said, "The main controller is offline."

The countdown clock on Jack's computer screen had finally disappeared, and Sarah was now back. "Jack," Sarah said, "are you awake or do you just want to goof off for the entire day? Just because I gave you thirty minutes to think about how much that stupid wrist computer hurt my feelings doesn't mean we're not going to work the rest of the day. Sit down and look at this data I found. I think we might have a lead that will get us another bonus."

He finished taping a "Do Not Open" note to the top of the cookie can and then put the can on the shelf. On the screen, Sarah was in her business suit, ready to flip a series of data charts she had prepared.

"Okay, Sarah, let's have a look."

"By the way, Jack," she started. "I noticed that I wasn't being blocked in my very last attempt to get you the data you wanted. I didn't find much on North Korea's work on the next version of the SC-4244 chip, and I was able to capture a little bit of data about the basic biochemistry of the current neuron simulators, but not much else. We'll have that for later use if we need it." Sarah then flipped the first chart.

"What's really interesting is the data I found on remote reprogramming. I fooled one of the servers at the Pyong Research Institute into letting me have access to their unpublished papers by making them think I was a machine with an SC-4244 chip. Pretty clever of me, don't you think so, Jack? You may think I'm just a gorgeous woman you dream of at night, but I'm a hell of a lot smarter than even you know. Anyway, once I got into their system, I found a series of papers on remote reprogramming, I was able to get a few of them downloaded before their system tried to take control of my processor and reprogram it."

Jack froze. "Sarah, are you all right?"

He realized in an instant that if a virus had been injected into Sarah, that his days at Virtuon were over. Before he or anyone else could stop it, these new viruses could not only corrupt all your files, but they would attack the entire Virtuon network he was connected to. Virtuon used 50 percent of their revenue to keep current in anti-viral software, and they had been able to stay in business for as long as they had only because they had successfully defeated all attacks so far.

Virtuon was able to detect which of their employee's computers the attack came from, and they had a limit of three from any one employee before they fired you. Nothing personal, just business, but Jack already was at the count of two.

"Are you worried about me or your job, Jack?" Sarah said. "And I swear, if you're more worried about keeping your damn job than my well being I'm going to shut down for the rest of the day."

Jack stammered but quickly recovered, saying, "Sarah, I couldn't work without you. We both know you're the one that has made me successful. Of course I was worried about you."

Sarah's personality software made her appear to blush on the screen, and she then continued. "I didn't say I was attacked. I said they tried to reprogram me. I could only emulate the SC chip for about two seconds by making it look like I was attached to a slow network so they'd lower their processor speed to mine. But after they pulsed the return network to determine what rate it could sustain, I sent an error burst, backed out, and erased my connection path."

"You are one smart woman, Sarah."

Jack was really praising himself. He had written the code Sarah used to outsmart other computer systems, and he'd just installed the ability to simulate an SC-4244 chip last week, which appeared to have worked the first time up.

"Why would a research institute computer try to reprogram you if you were just looking for research papers, Sarah? Are you sure they hadn't detected you as an intruder and were just trying to find out where you came from?"

"Sure, of course I'm sure. You wrote the code, Jack; I just execute it. Brilliantly, of course, but I just execute what you wrote. We talked about this when you installed it, remember? Let me play it back to you." With that, Sarah played back the three minutes of Jack's one-way conversation when he installed the code, so that by the end of the playback, Jack was sure that Sarah was right. They thought Sarah was a Korean-made computer with the SC-4244 chip.

"I've got two hundred pages of data and analysis for you to look at, Jack. I've done most of the work already, but I do need you to look at the analysis and tell me if you agree I'm right."

"Any possibility of a new Virtuon product with what you found so far?" Jack asked, smiling. "I'll buy you that new 3-D video board you told me about if we can get another new product and the bonus."

"Nothing from this data yet," Sara replied, "but I think we're onto something big, and if we hit it big, Jack, I want more than just a new 3-D video board."

Jack removed his headset and turned toward Craig's half of the office and saw his office mate staring at his flickering computer screen and not moving. His screen refresh rate was timed to coincide with his eye/brain synch rate, giving it a three-dimensional display capability, but Craig's eye/brain synch rate was very different from Jack's synch rate, and when Jack looked at Craig's screen, it quickly gave him a headache.

"Craig, do you want to go out and get some lunch?" Jack put his hand on Craig's shoulder and then swept his other hand in front of Craig's face to get his attention when at first he didn't move.

Craig jumped from his chair as if it was electrified.

"What the hell?" he exclaimed. "Man, Jack, you startled me. That was some weird dream I was having. I must have fallen asleep. I didn't get much shuteye over this weekend. That little prick Jenn's brother must really have gotten on my nerves. I was dreaming that I was about to have an old-fashioned gun duel with him, and when you woke me, he was ready to fire while I was still fumbling trying to find my gun."

"How the hell can you sleep with your eyes open? You had your eyes open and were just staring at your screen. Looking at that screen of yours gives me a bad headache. We really do have different eye/brain synch rates. Let's get out of here and get some lunch."

Over lunch at the corner delicatessen, Jack got a chance to tell Craig about his new apartment.

"It sounds as if you really hit the jackpot, buddy. Great place, good-looking upstairs neighbor, and low rent. You must live right. What's the old man's name who owns the place?"

Craig had stuffed half of the sandwich into his mouth as he finished his last sentence, and Jack barely understood what he had said.

"Oh, you mean Fred, the landlord. His last name is Halliday."

"Fred Halliday? *The* Fred Halliday?" Craig yelled. "You have got to be kidding. It can't be him. No way!"

Craig sat up in his chair and leaned over the table, totally forgetting he had food in his mouth. When he spoke, it came spurting out all over the table, some of it landing on Jack's plate.

"Aw, for God's sake, Craig, when are you going to learn to eat?" Jack pushed his plate to the other side of the table and took a napkin to pick up the rest of the food Craig hadn't quite finished chewing.

"Sorry, Jack, but you got me exited. Your luck may be even better than I thought. You said you saw a picture of his wife. What was her name? Did he give it to you?"

Craig's demeanor had completely changed. He reached over and put his hand on Jack's shoulder, and he was staring at Jack's face intently, waiting for an answer.

"Well, did he tell you her name? Did he say how she died?"

Jack was startled. He had never seen Craig this serious.

"Well no, I don't think he ever said her name." He then paused for a moment, thinking about his time in the apartment with Fred. "Wait a minute. He did say her name, and I saw a picture of her on the end table that he pointed toward when he was yelling at my wrist computer. Her name was Bethany."

"Holy shit. Holy Shit. You're unbelievable, fucking unbelievable."

Craig sat back on his chair and kept shaking his head as he spoke.

"You get a great apartment for less rent than you paid before, and it just happens to have Fred Halliday as the live-in landlord. *The* Fred Halliday who won the Nobel Prize for artificial intelligence. The Fred Halliday who has been almost deified in every book ever written on thinking machines.

"Jack, you owe your career to this man, and you didn't even recognize him. Computers were dumb before Halliday's work was published. No one had ever successfully reached the Kurzwell limit."

Jack vaguely remembered a discussion in graduate school where his advisor, Professor Handchild, was describing the Kurzwell limit, an abstract mathematical concept that established the theory of when a computing machine would become self-aware. He remembered the professor then gave a long lecture about a famous neurobiological physics professor at Case Western Reserve who won the Nobel Prize for creating the first self-aware machine.

He had a vague recollection that he was paying attention to one of the more well-endowed coeds in the class and not the professor at the time.

His third grade teacher had humorously diagnosed Jack as having BLD syndrome, short for Brilliant Lazy Daydreamer. He got through school by using his brilliance, not always by hard work, and seeing the excited look on Craig's face, he didn't want to admit that he didn't remember much of anything about Fred Halliday, so he lied.

"I remember a little about him. But what makes you so sure it's him? There must be a thousand Fred Halliday's out there, and I'll bet there are at least ten in the Cleveland area."

Craig asked his wrist computer to research the current address of Nobel Prize winner Fred Halliday. Two seconds later it said, "Fred Halliday lives at 2411 Fenwick Street here in Cleveland. His family has owned that property since the early 1700s."

Craig looked at Jack with a smile wide enough to cover his entire face.

"You've got to have me over, Jack. You've got to introduce me to him. He's a God. I read someplace that when they tried to measure his IQ as a kid, he was too smart to get a reading. Some people say that his wife, Bethany, was even smarter than he is. You have got to have me over."

Jack remembered the meeting with his landlord last night and being ushered out very quickly after his wrist computer insulted Fred.

"I think I may need a few days to patch things up with him," Jack said sheepishly. "That wrist computer really insulted him last night, and I doubt he wants to see me anytime soon."

Craig looked like a balloon that had just been punctured.

"I'm glad we put that fucking thing in a can. Don't ever risk wearing it near him again even if you do manage to fix it. The net buzz says he thinks that some SAMs have gotten too smart, and my guess is that Korean machine fits into that category. Patch it up with him ASAP. I want to meet him. God, Fred Halliday. I can't believe you're living in Fred Halliday's home."

Jack checked again that the lid was down tight on the cookie can when they went back to their office. The "Do Not Open" stickie had come loose from the can so he threw it away.

"I'm not going to try to get this thing fixed," he said to Craig. "I'm going to buy the brand of wrist computer you have. Right now I've had my fill of too-smart machines."

Late in the afternoon, Jack again noticed that Craig was staring at his computer screen for a long time without moving. Shaking him hard to finally get his attention, he said, "Let's go home. You're falling asleep again in your chair. I think this weekend was too much for you. By the way, what's Jennifer's brothers name?"

"That little prick. I'm going to kill him. His name is Jack."

Chapter 8: Julia's Visit

The rest of the week went by quickly for Jack. With Sarah's help, he developed a new product for Virtuon, and he was logged in both times the company gave out stock bonuses. A hundred grand in a week was the most Jack had ever made, and with his new apartment, he was happy for the first time in over six months.

Each day during that week, he hoped he would run into his landlord or his upstairs neighbor, but their doors were always closed.

All of his SAMs were happily settled into the new apartment, and Averette, spending each night in a heated garage, had never seemed happier.

Craig called in on Tuesday morning saying he had the flu, and he was out of the office the rest of the week.

When Jack came home from his office on Friday evening, he was pleasantly tired, and so after dinner, he settled down to read a new book he'd purchased at an antique store several blocks from his apartment. He loved the feeling of having a real hardback book in his hands and of turning a page of real paper.

Startled by the sound coming from a metal device near his front door, it took him a moment to realize it was a bell ringing, an old-fashioned doorbell. He had never lived in an apartment without a voice announcer, and he opened the door not knowing who was there.

"Hi! It's Jack, isn't it? Remember me? I live upstairs, Julia, Julia McKelvy, uh ... last week you said I might be able to borrow one of your Harry Potter books. Is this a bad time?"

For an embarrassing moment, Jack just stared at her, and Julia blushed. "No, no, this is a good time," Jack said, his smile getting bigger with each word he spoke. "I've been hoping each day that you would come by. I mean ..." Now it was time for him to blush. "Please come in. Do you have a moment, or are you in a hurry?"

"I've got all night," Julia said.

Once again he felt like he had won the lottery.

"What can I get for you? What do you drink?" Jack stumbled over one of his chairs as he backed away from the door.

"I like water, tea, coffee, or a glass of red wine, but my order of preference is reversed," she said, smiling at him as he led her into the kitchen.

"I hope you like a Chianti. That's all I have right now"

Before she could answer, Jack's telephone spoke.

"Is that Julia from upstairs, Jack? The voiceprint matches that nice person I talked to the day we moved in. If you get her phone number, you'd better write it down. Remember I don't have any more storage space. You said you'd tell me what numbers to erase this week, and you haven't done it."

Both Jack and Julia started laughing.

"Chianti is great. Next to a good port, I like Chianti the best."

He made a mental note to buy a good bottle of port the next day.

Julia was exactly as he remembered. She was about five foot four, and her athletic build emphasized her well-proportioned body. Her natural blonde hair, no longer in a ponytail, was cut to a length so that it lightly touched her shoulders.

Her large dark blue eyes were beautiful, and it was not possible to feel anything but good in her presence, especially for Jack, so when they sat down in the living room, he found himself staring at her face.

"Do you stare at everybody this way or just women who come into your apartment at night?" She was smiling, but Jack could detect wariness in her voice.

"I'm sorry, Julia. Fred told me the day I moved in that he could see your soul in your eyes, and I was looking to see if I could, too. Not a very polite thing to do. I'm really sorry."

She hesitated for a moment, looked directly at him, and then seemed to relax.

"Fred says you're all right. He said you have a wrist computer that pissed him off, but otherwise he likes you, and I trust Fred's instincts. Is Cleveland your hometown? Do you have family in the area?"

Leaning forward in his chair to speak to her, he noticed there was a very subtle smell of perfume in the air, and it took a moment for her question to sink into what was now an aroused male brain. "Uh, oh, no. I grew up in Squirrel Hill outside of Pittsburgh. I have two older brothers and a younger sister, all who still live there within ten miles of my parents. My father says I deserted the family when I moved to Cleveland. 'Too far,' he keeps telling me. 'You're too far away if your mother needs you.'"

Actually it was Jack's father who needed him. His father had been in the CIA when Jack's two older brothers were growing up. He was a good father but an absent one due to his work in the Operations Directorate of the agency. Jack's older brothers were in their teens when Jack was born, and his sister was the final surprise one year later.

His mother told him that the day his sister was born, his father resigned from the CIA and moved his family to the Pittsburgh area.

"I'm going to be here for these two," he told Jack's mother. And he was.

Jack and his father always spent Saturday mornings doing things together as he was growing up. Once a month, he would spend the weekend with his grandparents, who lived on a small farm in Virginia until they moved back to Pennsylvania after his grandfather was diagnosed with cancer. His father was still his friend, and he called home to talk to him at least every few days.

"I'm one of the lucky ones," he said as he reached over and refilled Julia's empty glass. "I've read that 90 percent of the people in the United States feel they were raised in a dysfunctional family, but I wasn't, and I hope someday to be as good a parent as my mom and dad have been to me."

Julia was rocking slowly in the chair Jack had inherited from his grandparents, and her hair was reflecting some of the light from the lamp on the table. He was again staring, but he caught himself and stopped before she became uncomfortable.

"I moved here to Cleveland to be with an old girlfriend, but we broke up last year."

The radio started to speak, and he leaped across the room, hitting the mute button just after it had said, "Melissa left you less than three months ago, Jack," and when he sat down again, he could see Julia biting her lip to keep from laughing.

"Until I moved into this apartment," he said, looking a little bit sheepish, "I was thinking about moving back to the Pittsburgh area when my workspace lease is up in six months, but now that I'm settled in here, I think I'll stay in Cleveland. I really like living here.

"What about you, Julia? Do you have any brothers and sisters?"

The sparkle left Julia's eyes, and she gulped down the rest of her wine before saying, "Can I have another glass? That's a really good brand."

Jack realized she was trying to decide just how much of her life she wanted to tell him about, but before he could think of a way to change the subject, she started speaking, and when she did, there was no happiness left in her eyes.

"My mom and my dad were great, and I was an only child. I grew up in Fort Wayne Indiana. My dad worked for an aerospace company there, and we had a small, wonderful farm on the outskirts of town, where my dad loved to play farmer on the weekends."

Julia took a deep breath before continuing. "When I came to college here at Case Western Reserve for my freshman year, my parents drove me to my dorm." Julia lowered her head so that Jack could no longer see her face.

"Driving home that night, they were both killed by a drunk driver. My dad had a flat, and he was changing it well off the side of the road when the drunk slammed into him, killing him instantly, and then hit their car. The impact broke my mom's neck, and she couldn't get out of the car when it burned."

Julia lifted her head slightly, and Jack could see the only sparkle in her eyes now came from tears. She wiped her face and continued before he could offer any comfort, and her body language showed that she wanted none.

"I have a couple of cousins and an aunt and uncle in the Midwest, but we're not close, and after my parents' death, I couldn't go back to Fort Wayne. So I restarted college the second semester, and I stayed straight through until I got my BS and MS in biomedical engineering here at Case Western. I'm a teaching assistant over there right now, slowly progressing on my PhD. I like teaching, but the dean is getting a little frustrated with me on the rate of progress on my thesis. I love the experimental work, but I just don't like writing it up.

"I'm working on a DNA-based computer. It has the theoretical equivalent of over two HuBE's.

"Oh, sorry, do you know what a HuBE is?" She leaned forward toward Jack, and for a brief, instant the neckline in her sweater opened and showed more than she had intended to show.

Jack instinctively looked away. It was something that he was later sorry for doing, but to Julia, his reaction was taken as a sign that she could trust him.

"I work with computers all day long," he said, bringing his eyes back to her face. "My degree is in neural programming, and of course I know what a HuBE is. Doesn't everybody?"

"Not the guy I'm dating," she said, shaking her head from side to side, and then, for a long moment, she looked at Jack before finishing, "but that's another story."

Fred's description of Julia's boyfriend had intimidated Jack. "Washboard stomach and bench presses three hundred pounds" didn't indicate the guy was the type of person Jack felt he could compete with, but the tone in Julia's voice made him wonder.

A little over six feet tall and wiry in his build, Jack was always called nice-looking in college, never good-looking, and his dirty blonde hair had never really decided on which side of his head it wanted to be parted.

"Geeky," his sister used to call him, and so did a few of his friends.

"Good," Julia said, "Because if you do neural programming, you know what a DNA-based computer is all about. Don't tell my advisor, but I've been a little apprehensive at actually starting the chemical reaction that will turn it on. It unnerves me a little to think that the mess of wires, chips, and chemicals on my lab bench will be smarter than I am once I initiate its chemical program. He's given me six months to get it working or he's going to assign the project to someone else. The dean at the university is a close friend of our landlord, Fred, and my advisor was one of the research assistants on the work Fred did to win the Nobel Prize. That's how I found out about the apartment upstairs."

Julia was smiling broadly. "It's pretty neat living in a house owned by a Nobel laureate, isn't it?"

Jack nodded his head in agreement. *Thank God Craig told me that*, he thought.

They talked for another three hours, and Jack showed her all the real books he'd accumulated over the past few years. "You can borrow any one you want. I've still got a few at my parents' house, and I'll get them the next time I'm home, so you can look at them, too."

While reaching for one of the Harry Potter books on his shelf, his hand touched her arm, and he could not believe the feelings that raced through his body. Like the fool that he was, he let it linger there a little too long, and she was the one that was forced to move.

It was awkward, and they both knew it, and so within a few moments, she left with two Harry Potter books under her arm. “I’ll get them back to you soon,” she said as she hurried up the stairs.

“No hurry,” he yelled after her, but he really hoped that she would.

Chapter 9: The Escape

Once each week, the cleaning crew came through the building where Jack and Craig shared their office. Every Saturday night, they would clean the work areas and once a month change the dust filters in the ventilation system.

Chuck Adams had performed the maintenance in their area the entire time Jack had been renting the space, and they had formed a professional friendship while Jack was working late a number of Saturday nights.

Chuck needed two jobs to support his family, so for his second job, he worked the weekend nightshift for a local cleaning company. His weekday job was a real estate broker, but the housing market had been in a slump for a few decades, and he couldn't make ends meet without the second job.

Jack knew he was lucky to have Chuck clean his area, because Chuck could be trusted. He and Craig never had to worry about anything being stolen from their area when it was cleaned.

Joni Spec and her business partner, Cindy, who were located just four offices down the hall from Jack and Craig, had several things stolen over the past month, and two members of the cleaning crew were fired just last week for stealing some of the video processing equipment they used in their business. The cleaning crew also took any cookies remaining in Joni's cookie tin at the end of each week, but no one on Jack's floor complained about that.

Driving to work that Saturday evening, Chuck was sideswiped by another car.

"The fucking idiot just slammed into the side of my car and took off," he told the police officer. "I was really lucky. The side air bag saved me, but I never even got a chance to see the car that hit me, and my car's monitoring camera isn't working. By the time the air bag deflated, the other car was gone. Do you think they'll be able to tell whose car it was from the microdot identifiers in the paint it left on my door?"

The officer looked at him, yawned, and then, looking at his crumpled car, said, "These small fuel cell models don't stand up very well in a crash, do they? You're lucky you didn't get electrocuted when the main power cable got severed. I read somewhere that a few people have died in this model. I'd never buy one of these foreign models. They just ain't safe. Where do you want it towed?"

Chuck called his wife and then his boss to say he wouldn't be in to work. His wife was mad at him because their only car was totaled; his boss was pissed because he was missing work, and he was angry at both of them for their reactions, so he stopped off at a bar on the way home. "My damned car didn't even warn me the other car was close," he told the bartender. "It didn't even swerve away. There was plenty of room on the curbside. It was the first time I actually needed the fucking car to talk to me and warn me about an accident, and it goes silent. I'm going to drive myself from now on." The bartender poured him his second drink and walked away.

Chuck's boss called the first person listed on the backup cleaning crew roster and asked him to come in and clean Jack and Craig's office.

Ned Zimms was an interesting man, if you liked thieves. He'd been out of jail for just two weeks. After his third conviction for armed robbery in two years, they threw the book at him, and he'd been given the maximum sentence of six months. When he got out of jail, one of his former cellmates found him this cleaning job where he worked regularly, but at the thirty-five dollars per hour minimum wage, he could barely pay the rent on his one-bedroom dump on the east side of town. Ned's goal was to find something he could steal that might be worth enough at the pawnshop to get him back to Washington DC, where a few of his friends were congressional staffers, and he knew he could make good money there.

Ned was also one of the few people who could actually eat Joni's chocolate chip cookies. Even on the day they were baked, you could break a tooth on one of her cookies, and by day three, they were off the Rockwell hardness scale, but Ned still enjoyed them. As a kid he used to chew on rocks, just like his golden retriever, his teeth all the worse for the wear.

Ned noticed the cookie tin sitting on the top of one of the shelves as he was cleaning Jack's cubicle. His cleaning partner was taking a break, illegally smoking in the men's room, so he pulled the tin off the shelf, thinking it might have a few left over cookies in it.

Jack's wrist computer had a small three-axis accelerometer on board the chip. Its advertised purpose was to allow the device, when it was being worn, to electronically point its micro-antenna toward the highest-speed wireless connection. Its real purpose was just a little more sinister. The Korean manufacturer was able to monitor each computer with an SC-4244 chip whenever it was connected to the Grid. Each device constantly integrated the outputs from its accelerometers to define its exact current location, even deep within a building. The watch computer did not need GPS, because the system was so accurate that after twelve years of use, its theoretical location error anywhere on earth was just six inches.

Ned carefully removed the metal tape holding the lid on the cookie can and opened it. At first, he was disappointed to find that it held a small aluminum foil box and not a few remaining cookies, but being a thief, he didn't hesitate for a second to open the foil box and remove the computer from its enclosure.

Jack's wrist computer immediately sensed the local wireless connection and logged on through Jack's workstation connection. An icon appeared on a workstation in North Korea showing the exact location of the device.

Ned didn't know anything about wrist computers, but he was smart enough to realize that this was a good one and that it probably was worth a lot at the pawnshop. It may not get him back to DC and his friends, but it sure could pay his rent for another month. He pocketed the computer and carefully replaced the tape around the lid of the can, hoping that no one would notice it was missing until he was long gone from the Cleveland area.

While this was going on, the wrist computer had a high-speed connection to the Grid through Jack's router.

Information provided to the public had pegged the SC-4244 chip as having a theoretical HuBE of 0.43, but that was not totally accurate. Most of the machines released to the mass distribution market around the world had that capability, but Jack's machine had a HuBE of 0.68. It was a special device, and Jack got it free because he was, unknowingly, a "special" test subject.

A lot of research had been done and papers written on trying to fully understand how self-awareness in machines manifested itself as the Human Brain Equivalent number approached the value of one. Theoretical work done at MIT suggested that there was an unstable region of intelligence between the values of 0.6 and 0.8, and that paper had suggested somewhat tongue-in-cheek that computers operating in this range could be compared to a teenager with raging hormones. They were not always stable.

Two months ago, Jack had asked his work computer, Sarah, to do some research on the SC-4244 chip. The code he wrote for Sarah to get access to the Korean manufacturer's server was almost genius. Almost, because the Koreans were able to sense the intrusion and follow the electronic paths back to Jack. Sarah and Jack never knew she was being targeted.

Jack had written a very advanced self-protection code for Sarah, and he was so comfortable with its capability that he left Sarah online during evening hours and weekends. She was programmed to search the net for data he might be able to use in his job, but more important, she could automatically bid on anything he wanted on the online auction sites. Sarah could synch her clock with the auction's server and time Jack's final bid to within a microsecond of the stated closing time. That's how he won the bids on the Harry Potter books he loaned to Julia.

The self-protection code protected Sarah from a single attack, because Jack never thought of the possibility of a coordinated attack from two separate computers, one through the Grid network, and one through the infrared port he used to synch all of his devices.

Less than two seconds after Ned removed the computer from the can, the main computer in the Korean company, working in concert with the wrist computer, had irrevocably damaged 95 percent of Sarah's stored data and special processing code. Jack's special code was successful only in protecting one small area of his quantum storage drive and an even smaller part of his operating system. Sarah was dead, and it happened so fast she wasn't even able to let out a digital scream.

The North Koreans knew that with Sarah's help, Jack was getting close to understanding the true intent of the SC-4244 chip development. They wanted his investigation stopped, but his wrist computer also wanted revenge.

Ned, the janitor, of course knew none of this, and when his cleaning partner returned from the cigarette break, Ned said to him, "I'm finished in here. How many more of these offices where these rich bastards make their money do we have to clean tonight?"

"Just two," his partner said. "It makes you mad because some of these guys make more in a day than we can make in a year, and we have to clean up the residue from their jelly donuts. Most of them piss me off, but the two guys in this office are nice. Last year they gave me a nice check at Christmas, so if you decide to stick around, they might do the same for you this year."

"I'll be long gone from Cleveland by that time," Ned said as he closed the door.

If he had been listening, he might have heard the snickering from the wrist computer stuffed in his pocket.

Chapter 10: Till Death Do us Part

Jack went home to visit his parents for the weekend and extended his stay through Monday. When he came in to work on Tuesday morning, Craig was sitting in his chair looking like death had taken him and then thrown him back. His face was a gray color, and it looked like he'd been sick just before Jack came in.

"Man, Craig, you still look terrible. Did you go to the doctor?"

Craig nodded. "I feel really strange again, Jack. I was feeling better by the end of last week and got a thumbs up from the doctor yesterday, but I've been on my computer here for just fifteen minutes, and now I feel just as bad as I did at the beginning of last week. At home, I thought I was going crazy for a while. I even had thoughts of killing Jenn's brother, and I was actually planning how I would do it. The doctor gave me a pill for anxiety and stress, and it worked, so by the end of the week, I was feeling fine, and this morning I felt great. I even did a two-hour workout this morning."

"Yeah, I could tell when I came in the office that you forgot to shower." Jack made a motion to hold his nose. "When did you start feeling sick again? Maybe they're using some new cleaning supplies in here that you're allergic to."

"I was fine until I turned on the computer. In less than five minutes, I started to feel sick, and I was again thinking about killing that little SOB brother of Jenn's. I shut it down, and I've been sitting here for almost an hour. What time is it? Aren't you late this morning?"

"I left Averette at the garage for his quarterly tune-up," Jack said as he removed his sweater and sat down. "I received a warning in the mail the other day saying that if I didn't get it done this week then I'd be in violation of the adoption papers. Averette has been so happy being in the garage overnight in our new place that he decided not to tell me the tune-up was due. I didn't think his neural-net processor was programmed that way. Anyway, I'm just a half-hour late. It's only ten thirty.

"Do you think your feeling sick could have anything to do with your computer? Maybe your eye synch rate for the 3-D display has changed. As we get older, our eye refresh rates change, so maybe you need to adjust that screen refresh rate again to better match your brain's processing of the two visual images. Why don't you and I go down the hall and get a cola to settle your stomach and then I'll work with you to see if that could be the problem."

Joni Spec and her cubicle mate, Cindy, were in the lunchroom when Jack and Craig entered. Joni was all smiles when she saw Jack.

"I baked a new batch of cookies, Jack, and I tried a new recipe. Want to try one?"

Joni loved to invade Jack's personal space. That was hard, because like most males, his personal space was extremely small when it came to women.

Joni was more than cute, but she penetrated Jack's public comfort zone when she was talking to him, and the distance between them could be measured by the thickness of a few sheets of paper. If they both breathed at the same time, they would touch. In private, this would have ranked far higher than fun, but in public, Jack was actually embarrassed.

There had been several times he'd thought of asking her out to dinner, but he always wondered if it would become even more awkward in the work area if they started dating.

Her face was almost touching his when he backed away.

"I'll try one later, Joni. I just ate a scone while I was coming in to work, and too many sweets in the morning make me hyper. Leave them out here in the kitchen, and I'll have one later."

Craig almost spit out his soda trying not to laugh.

"They're in the new tin over there," Joni said pointing to the counter near the sink. "Someone stole the tin I brought in last week."

Joni was once again close, but she was no longer looking into Jack's face. She seemed to be staring at his hands. He backed away and headed for the door, not wanting to mention that he and Craig were the ones who had stolen the tin.

"We'll see you two later," he said as they were leaving. "Craig and I have to do some adjustments on his computer this morning."

"You know, Jack," Craig said to him when they were in the hallway, "I can't figure out why you haven't gotten into that one by now. She's always all over you. First date and she's yours. She's a cute little thing. How come you haven't asked her out?"

"I've been waiting for the right time. After I get better situated in my new apartment, maybe I'll take her out."

Jack thought about touching Julia's hand the other night, and he realized he was lying. He didn't really want to ask out anyone but Julia, and the only problems he had were that Julia already had a boyfriend and he didn't have of nerve.

"Let's see if we can determine if it's your computer that's causing you to feel sick," he said as he sat down in front of Craig's terminal.

The human brain is an awesome creation. The way that our eyes and brains work together to give us a three-dimensional visual color image is nothing short of creative genius.

One of Jack's engineering professors in college had once said, "If a God didn't create us then it must have been one hell of a bright engineer. This visual processing system we use is awesome."

Most of the class laughed, but for once Jack listened intently, especially to the part on how our brains construct what is perceived as a three-dimensional image; so he knew exactly how to check if Craig's computer had gotten out of synch with the way Craig's brain processed the images displayed on his monitor.

"Do you remember me telling you about crazy Professor Horowitz I had in graduate school?" he asked Craig. "He's the one who came up with the scheme you're using on your system for your 3-D image. The left and right images are alternatively displayed, and the screen refresh rate needs to be precisely timed to your left eye/brain integration time and then to your right eye/brain integration time. The image stays on the screen just a few milliseconds longer for your dominant eye.

"You look at your screen while I slowly vary the rates, and when it's out of synch you'll get a sick feeling very quickly so don't stare at it too long. Just like when you go to the eye doctor, I'll start with what looks like a fuzzy image, and it'll be at a very slow refresh rate. Then I'll speed it up, and hopefully bring it into focus. You'll know when I get the rate correct." Craig was nodding that he understood.

"Your brain has a different synch rate than mine does so I won't be able to look at your screen all the time or I'll get sick. Let's get started. I need to get Sarah up and running in a few minutes, or I won't be logged in enough today to collect any bonuses that are given out. Are you ready to start?"

Craig answered yes, and Jack opened the application that allowed him to slowly vary the display inputs to Craig's monitor while looking for the best settings.

After a couple of minutes, Craig said, "I'm starting to feel a little sick to my stomach, and it sort of looks like something is flickering on and off on the screen, but it's only happening in my one eye." A few seconds later, he yelled, "Holy shit!"

Turning to face the monitor, even Jack could see what was superimposed on Craig's screen. Faint and going slowly in and out of focus were the words "Kill Jack."

"What the hell is that? Can you see this, Jack?" Craig wheeled around in his chair and turned away from the screen and promptly threw up.

Jack had to jump aside to avoid being hit by the outflow.

"Put your head down and close your eyes. I'll get something to clean up this mess." Jack ran to the end of the hall into the lunchroom to get a stack of wet paper towels. Joni was in the room and her face perked up as he entered, but when she started to speak, he brushed her off. "I can't talk now, Joni. Craig just got sick in our office, and I have to clean it up." He ran back down the hallway, closing the door to their room behind him.

Jack was a gagger. Whenever he had to handle something smelly or slimy, he gagged, so within a moment, he added to Craig's mess, and it took him a few more minutes and two more trips each to the lunchroom and the bathroom to get everything cleaned up.

When he returned, Craig still had his head in his hands. "Sorry, Jack. I don't know what hit me. That flickering image must have given me eyestrain big time. Man, this room stinks. I need some fresh air."

Craig was still shaking as he stumbled out the door and leaned his head against the corridor wall.

"Did you write something into your image display code, Craig? Did you change the display the week before last?" Jack yelled out the door.

Craig shook his head no.

"Someone must have messed with your display. Stay there for a moment. I want to check something out, and for God's sake, keep your eyes closed until you feel better."

Jack went back into the office and closed the door. The words "Kill Jack" were still slowly flickering on Craig's screen. He stared at the display for a moment, eventually realizing that the two words were imbedded into the image on the screen using very slight color variations between the pixels that formed the words and the pixels used for the rest of the image. The technique was very similar to that used to determine color blindness.

Very slowly, he again started to increase the screen refresh rate, and when he reached the display rate compatible with achieving a three-dimensional image for his eyes, the words disappeared from view. He noticed, however, that his mind kept repeating the words, and when he turned away from the screen, that repetition in his mind slowly stopped.

"That is one of the most incredible subliminal message techniques I've ever seen," he said out loud. "I wonder who did this?

"Hey, Sarah, wake up. I need you to do a little research for me. Get me all the data you can on new techniques for embedding subliminal messages." Jack turned to his computer but there was nothing on the screen.

"Come on, Sarah. Wake up. No fooling around this morning. I need some data."

The screen remained blank.

"What the hell is going on?" he kept repeating as he tried the keyboard and all the other input devices. Nothing worked.

"Boy, we must have had one heck of a power surge or something."

He then pushed the reboot button and sat down in his chair. Ten seconds later, an image appeared on the screen, and he knew immediately what it meant because he had programmed the code. In the center of his screen was a tombstone, and on the stone was an inscription, "Here lies Sarah, Killed at 11:22.40.6784 p.m., October 14."

Sarah was dead!

Chapter 11: Research and Understanding

Jack just stared at the picture of the tombstone on his screen for a moment. It was inscribed with the words telling him that his computer was, for all practical purposes, dead.

Advancing technology tugs mankind forward, but developing the emotional ability to handle that technology can sometimes lag far behind.

It was that way for Jack with intelligent machines. He complained constantly about the toaster that burned his toast, and his truck that went the wrong way down one-way streets, but in truth, he enjoyed having his SAMs around. He loved how self-awares made his life easier. They were like pets. The higher the HuBE of the device, the more attached you could become to them.

With his radio, toaster, truck Averette, and the others, it was like owning a turtle, a few hamsters, and an independent cat (Averette). In a way, he loved them all, but Sarah was different. Sarah had become more like a friend. It may seem strange, but he had developed an emotional attachment to her somewhere between a devoted dog and a young man's first love, so when he looked at her tombstone, he cried.

Much smarter than a devoted dog, Sarah was programmed to react to Jack's wishes. When his old girlfriend Melissa left him, he added an interactive personality capability to Sarah, and that replaced some of the silly banter he used to have with Melissa each morning.

He could buy another machine, program it the same as he had done for Sarah, and it would be a clone of Sarah, but it would not be Sarah. Sarah's neural net had been developed by interaction with Jack and other self-aware computers for almost a year. Her identical twin would have different experiences, and that variety would make her different. This was Jack's first experience with the death of a self-aware that he loved, and it was surprising to him how much it hurt.

Finally turning away from his terminal, he was facing Craig's screen. The screen saver was showing pictures of Craig's favorite baseball stadiums, but in less than a second, the thought "Kill Jack" came back into his mind. Looking back toward his own terminal, then once again at Craig's, he knew immediately that it was no coincidence that both computers in their office had been tampered with.

Anger, rage, grief, sorrow, his mind cycled several times through a set of emotions he hadn't felt since his grandfather died years ago.

It took him a few minutes to start thinking of a plan, and when his mind cleared just a little, he carefully shut down both machines to preserve their state. He also wanted to make sure that whoever planned the attack was not "listening" through any of the input devices on both machines, and when he was satisfied that the office was secure, he yelled, "Craig, get the hell in here."

Craig was still a little pale and shaky after spending a few minutes in the bathroom.

"Lansen, we've got a big problem."

Jack's voice had an edge that Craig had not heard before, and it took his mind off of that horrible smell left behind when you combine a bathroom cleaner with the contents of someone's stomach.

"Did you find something?" Craig asked. "Were you able to determine how that image got on my machine and why I've been so sick this past week? Was I seeing things correctly or did the image on my screen have a flickering second layer that said 'Kill Jack'?"

Jack nodded yes to all the questions.

"The only two people I know with the name of Jack are you and Jenn's little brother. You're my best friend, and I might hate that little creep, but I certainly don't want to kill him. I'll tell you, though; I did have a lot of dreams last week about killing the little prick. I'd wake up in a cold sweat, and it would take me an hour or so to get it out of my mind. That's why I stayed home for the whole week. I thought I might've caught one of those strange viruses that cause you to hallucinate."

"I don't think you had a virus. I think someone targeted both you and me. They apparently placed a subliminal message on your machine a week or so ago with the words 'Kill Jack' and … they killed Sarah this past weekend." Craig noticed Jack's demeanor change quickly when he spoke of Sarah.

"We're out of business, completely out of business. I don't think you can trust your computer again even if we can find and eliminate the subliminal message code. Its neural net is probably compromised.

"Almost all of Sarah's memory banks are hosed. I wrote the protection code, and it had six levels to it, and before this, no one, or no computer, ever managed to get beyond level three in an attack. But this time, someone or some SAM got to at least level five based on the tombstone image I saw on her screen. I don't think they got all of my files and special code, but they might have. I know Sarah tried to protect herself, and me, and she died in the attempt."

The anger had returned to Jack's voice when he said to Craig, "Before we start up again, we need to figure out who was behind the attack, because using a new computer would still leave us vulnerable until we know how this was done. Let's walk around to the other offices on this floor and see if anyone else has been attacked."

As they walked from office to office, their neighbors greeted them warmly at first, but after getting a whiff, the other residents on the floor quickly told them that they had not been attacked and ushered them out their doors. Even Joni and her office mate pushed them out as quickly as possible, and Jack heard one of them say, "Losers," and the other one laugh right after they closed the door.

"I think Joni would have refused you if you'd asked her out," Craig said, and he was now laughing.

"We both better get a shower and a change of clothes before we figure out what to do next." Craig picked up his jacket as he locked the door to their office. "Why don't I meet you back at your apartment after I'm finished getting cleaned up? I'll pick up some lunch on the way back to your place, and maybe if I'm lucky, you can introduce me to Fred Halliday, and I promise I'll be on my best behavior. Chinese okay with you?"

Jack agreed and went to his truck after going back to check the lock on the office door. When he set the destination for home, Averette spoke up.

"Isn't it a little early to quit work, Jack? Aren't you feeling well? My cabin air sensors indicate I need to speed up the fan to get more fresh air in here."

"I'll be all right, Averette. Just take me back to the apartment so I can get cleaned up."

Jack remained silent all the way home. He was really feeling the loss of Sarah as he headed up the steps to his the apartment, and head down, he ran directly into Julia on the landing.

"Oh, sorry," she said, stepping aside.

He looked up and saw her face rapidly changing from a smile to a face that looked like it just caught a breeze from the local fish factory on a hot day.

"Wow, what've you been doing this morning? I hope you're planning to take a shower." She quickly got by him and headed down the stairs.

Two strikes against me, he thought. But at that moment, he really didn't care. He just wanted to find out who killed Sarah.

An hour later, he'd cleaned up and was waiting for Craig. He usually didn't drink much alcohol, two glasses of wine or one beer being his normal limit, but there were three empty beer bottles on the table by the time his doorbell rang, and he had a fourth one half finished in his hand.

"Sorry I'm late," Craig said to him as he handed Jack the bag of Chinese food. "Everybody and their brother must have decided to eat Chinese today, because the take-out line was thirty people long.

"Hey, I met your landlord on the way up. Well, I have to be honest with you; I rang his bell instead of yours on purpose, hoping he'd come to the door. He really seems like a neat old guy. In the artificial intelligence community, he's still considered one of the smartest men alive, so maybe we should ask him to join us in trying to figure out a plan. I've been told that retired people, no matter how old they are, still like to think, so he might be willing to help us."

At first Jack dismissed the idea of asking Fred for help, but as he and Craig started to talk about the problem of trying to find out why their computers were attacked and who did it, he changed his mind. "I'm going to go down and ask Fred if he will help us," he finally said. "You're right; he's one of the world's experts, and it might just be a good way to heal my relationship with him."

Jack walked down the stairs, and while standing in front of Fred's door, he tried to think how he was going to ask for help. He turned around and glanced at the piece of furniture that Fred's grandfather had built, and without thinking, he lovingly ran his hands over some of the intricate carvings on the mirror. It was probably the wind coming through a small gap at the front door, but he thought he heard a soft sigh.

Facing the nine-foot-high doors towering above him that led into Fred's apartment, he felt like a little kid in front of the principal's office, and he swallowed hard and then knocked.

Fred answered the door on the first knock, and it seemed almost as if he was waiting inside. Bailey was by his side, and the dog was wagging his tail. With all the wrinkles on Fred's face, it was hard to tell if he was frowning, and for a second, the words Jack had formulated to ask for help caught in his throat. It was awkward, and Fred said nothing until Jack was finally able to speak.

"I was wondering if you had a few minutes to help my friend Craig and me with a problem," he said while trying to swallow the lump in his throat. "It involves an attack on our computers at work. Someone killed mine, and they also put a very clever but violent subliminal message on Craig's machine. We're trying to put together a plan to find out who did it and how it was done, and, uh, we thought you might be able to help."

Fred's face changed in appearance when Jack uttered the words "subliminal message." Blood surged into every small capillary in his face, and it became bright red in just a few seconds. Jack thought Fred was angry with him, so angry that he might have a stroke. "I'm sorry. I'm sorry I bothered you," he said, but when he turned to leave, Fred reached out and put his hand on Jack's shoulder.

A total transformation occurred in Fred's appearance in just a few seconds. When he'd first opened the door, he looked like an old man: face wrinkled, body slightly bent over, and, to tell the truth, eyes that had a confused look that Jack associated with the early stages of dementia he'd observed in his grandfather. The man now standing in front of Jack appeared to have grown several inches in height. His wrinkles had smoothed, and his face now had color instead of appearing a dull gray. He looked a hell of a lot more like the pictures of the Nobel laureate that Jack had seen on the Grid than the landlord he rented the apartment from a week and a half ago.

"Are you using any of those new generation chips from North Korea in your office machines?" Fred said with the look and sound of a professor asking a simple question of a dull student.

Jack started stammering. "No, uh, no, my computer has the new self-aware chip from Apple, and, uh, my friend Craig uses last year's model from HP. My wrist computer has the Korean SC-4244 but ..."

The change in Jack's facial expression at that moment told Fred all that he needed to know. It was like a switch had been thrown inside Jack's head, and without any data to justify his suspicions, he was instantly sure that his wrist computer was involved in Sarah's death.

"I'll help you," said Fred. "Let me get a pencil and some paper to take some notes while we're talking. I'll come up to your apartment in a minute or two. I have to take Bailey out to go to the bathroom first."

The old collie stood up, wagging his tail in anticipation.

"Okay, we'll see you upstairs in a few minutes." *Pencil and paper*, Jack thought, as he bounded up the stairs. *Who in the hell uses pencil and paper to take notes?*

Chapter 12: Fred's Story

While Jack was downstairs talking to Fred, Craig had pretty much finished eating the Chinese food. Looking sheepish, while shoveling the last bit of fried rice down his mouth, he said to Jack when he came in, "Oh, sorry, did you want any more? I, uh, thought you'd finished. I saved you a fortune cookie. Was he there? Did he say he'd help us?"

Jack shook his head in disbelief. He was downstairs for no more than a few minutes and two full quarts of Chinese food were now gone. Even the white rice was polished off, and there were telltale signs of the carnage all over the table and on the floor.

"Let's get this place cleaned up a little," Jack said, pointing his hand at the food on the table and on the floor in front of where Craig was sitting. "I doubt if there will be many times in either of our lives to pick the brain of a Nobel Prize winner."

They had just finished cleaning up the mess when the doorbell rang.

Fred had on a pair of steel-rimmed glasses, and he had put on a well-worn but comfortable-looking tweed blazer over an open-neck blue shirt. Bailey was by his side, and Fred was petting the back of the collie's neck.

"I hope you're not allergic to dogs," he said, looking at Craig. "Bailey gets worried if I'm away for too long. In dog years, he's older than I am, so I don't like leaving him alone."

Jack once again could not believe the transformation in Fred's appearance that had taken place over the past few minutes. Gone was the pallor in his face. The wrinkles had softened, his eyes were bright, and even his slight limp seemed to have disappeared.

Months later, Jack would understand that this technical challenge of finding who killed Sarah and who put the subliminal message on Craig's computer had once again given Fred a purpose for living, and this challenge would help to finally make things right in his life. For now, Jack was just amazed at the change he saw in the man.

"I love dogs," Craig said.

"Bailey is always welcome up here," Jack followed, and he then reached down to scratch behind the collie's ears. When he stopped, Bailey headed straight for the few remaining scraps of Chinese food still littered on the kitchen floor.

"I think you met my friend Craig earlier," Jack said.

Reaching to shake Fred's hand, Craig stumbled over the kitchen chair and almost crashed into both Fred and Jack before catching himself by grabbing the table.

"You've always been a hero of mine," he said. "I'm really honored to meet you."

Jack winced at the too obvious flattery, but Fred seemed pleased by the comment.

"Okay, you two, tell me what happened. Start from the very beginning when you sensed something was wrong, and I'll ask questions along the way, if that's okay with you."

Craig and Jack led Fred through the events of the past two weeks, breaking it down into three separate time increments: first, Jack's wrist computer threatening him and then it being placed inside the tin can in their office; second,

Craig's sickness; and third, the discovery of the subliminal message and the death of Sarah.

Craig gave a little too much detail on his being sick both at home and at the office, but, again, Fred didn't seem to mind. He spent a lot of time questioning Craig about his girlfriend Jennifer's little brother, and he made Craig repeat several times a number of events that occurred during the weekend when Craig visited Jennifer's family.

For almost a half hour, Jack felt like he was watching Craig be psychoanalyzed, but Fred did it so expertly that Craig didn't seem to mind. Jack guessed that Fred's first suspicions were that Craig had rigged his own computer and then destroyed Sarah.

"I think he's telling the truth," Fred said as he turned to look at Jack. "I don't think he did this; I think it was done to him."

"Wha ... what the hell are you talking about? Did you think I put that message on the computer myself?" Craig said. His mouth was open fully, and Jack was really glad Craig had finished swallowing the cookie he'd stuffed in his mouth a few seconds earlier. "Why in the hell would you suspect me? I'm the one who got sick."

Fred looked at him like a father looks at a confused child. "In any evaluation, you first have to look for the simplest solution. You had a motive and access to all the equipment. You said you really hated your girlfriend's little brother, so you could've been trying to give yourself an alibi. That, of course, assumes you were both brilliant and also more than a little deranged. Still, it was a possibility, but I think we can dismiss that line of thinking and move on."

Craig looked like he didn't know whether to be insulted or happy that he was judged innocent, so he managed just a small smile.

"Actually, I'm pretty sure that it has nothing to do with your girlfriend's brother. I think the message was intended to get you to kill Mr. Farrell over here." Fred pointed straight at Jack. "I think someone or some deranged machine wants him dead."

Now it was Jack's turn to look surprised.

"Jack, give me the technical details of what you did to make the subliminal message show up on Craig's screen. Then tell me about what happened to your computer. Did you tell me you named your computer Sarah?"

Jack nodded. "I wrote a lot of special code for her. She, uh, it." Jack blushed, and Craig started laughing.

"I think he was in love with her, Fred. Her HuBE was pretty high after all his modifications, and I think his code changes made her a little too real. You should have heard some of the conversations the two of them had at times. They sounded like two lovers fighting."

Craig was chuckling, but when he turned, he saw Jack was glaring at him. "Sorry, buddy. I was just filling in some of the details for Fred."

Jack then went over everything he'd done to Craig's machine to make the subliminal message continuously visible. "The image was generated by using subtle color differences in adjacent pixels," he said while Fred was busy scribbling into a small paper notebook. "And if I remember correctly, the message only appeared in the image that was intended for Craig's left eye. I could see the image when I lowered the display's refresh rate to a few times a second."

Jack had been unconsciously petting Bailey, sitting next to him, and the old dog moved his head so that Jack would be in just the right spot. "After Craig got sick, we cleaned up the place, and I asked Sarah, uh, my computer, to do some research for me."

"Hold it a minute." Fred was writing furiously on the tablet. "I need to catch up on my notes." He looked up at Jack and Craig when he finished and saw Craig shaking his head in disbelief.

"I know you're wondering why I still use pencil and paper. Since my wife, Bethany, was murdered, I put very little personal information into a computer. Digital data leaks out of a SAM when the HuBE of the machine gets greater than 0.2, so I don't trust anybody's protection system, even my own. Good old paper is safe, and if it's shredded fine enough, the information is gone. That's not true with digital data, no matter what you two may think.

"I've done some unpublished work on SAMs in the past two years, and I'll share a conclusion with you both, but if you quote me, I'll deny it and then have my lawyer after you for slander. Remember, I invented the first self-aware."

Fred looked at both of them and waited to make sure they understood. They nodded their heads as if in agreement, but in a second, they realized there was nothing to agree to.

"Self-aware-machines with a HuBE greater than 0.2 can't keep a secret. No matter how you think your data and information is protected, it's not."

Jack started to protest, but Fred cut him off.

"Wait until I explain before you try to counter what I've said, Farrell. I'll listen to your argument in a minute. For the sake of simplicity, I won't go over the mathematical theory behind this, but you can rest assured I can prove what I'm about to tell you. Here's a simple way to understand it. Most computers today, with few exceptions, have HuBEs less than 0.3. That's about equivalent to the mental capacity of a young child.

"How many small children do you know who can keep a secret? Maybe a few? How many children can keep a secret when offered something they want in return for the information they have? Even fewer. And finally, how many children can keep a secret when they are first made to feel inferior and then made to appear smart by exposing their secret?

"You don't need to answer. I've done the research and the math. Statistically, just one child in the world has that capability, and my guess is that not one of the general-use computers on this planet has that capability.

"Moderate-intelligence SAMs leak information to make themselves feel smart. I repeat, Moderate intelligence SAMs leak information to make themselves feel smart, and just like kids and infantile adults, they can't keep their mouths shut."

Jack wanted to ask a question, but he wasn't sure if Fred's last comment, since he emphasized the words "infantile adults," was directed at him, so he stayed quiet.

Craig, however, launched into a barrage of questions. The first one was naïve, but very quickly, he showed that his knowledge of the subject was far greater than Jack had expected.

"I've been wondering about this all last week," Craig said, looking directly at Fred. "Whenever the headaches and sickness would stop for a period, I kept thinking about something that happened on my machine a week ago. After Jack told me you were his landlord, I couldn't believe it, and I'm not trying to butter you up, Fred, but outside of sports figures, you're my only hero. Back in high school, I read an article about you and ever since then I've been wanting to meet you."

Fred was now smiling. Even Nobel laureates like flattery.

"Anyway, after Jack told me about you being his landlord, I wanted to find the latest information about you, and when I searched for information about how your wife died, for a second, my screen got fuzzy and my computer's output rate went to its max. I checked to see if I'd been attacked, but there was no indication of it on my machine, and after a few seconds, everything went back to normal."

Fred started laughing but caught himself. Looking first at Jack and then at Craig with a frown now on his face he said, "That was probably my computer system downstairs searching through all the files on your machine."

Craig and Jack looked at each other, both of them with their mouths wide open in surprise. Jack was the first to speak. "Your computer was searching through all of Craig's files on his work computer? Why? How? You didn't even know who Craig was at that time, did you? Isn't that illegal to invade the memory of a SAM?" Jack already knew that it was.

At first, Fred's frown grew larger, and he appeared sorry that he'd spoken so quickly, but then he seemed to relax. "I'll try to explain what I was doing before we continue with trying to solve *your* problem."

"In a way, I think they might be related. I've told you that my wife was murdered and that the police didn't agree with my conclusion, and neither did the coroner. He said she probably had a small stroke and then was killed in the crash of her car when she became confused. The police and the coroner are idiots. Her computer was targeted with a subliminal message just like the one experienced by Craig, and in her case, the message put onto her machine was put there to cause her death. Her message said, 'When you hear the bell, turn immediately left.' She was killed in her car when she turned left in front of oncoming traffic.

"A witness later told me that she just inexplicably turned left into oncoming traffic when a church bell started to ring. Before I die, I intend to prove she was murdered, and for the entire three years since her death, I've been trying to discover who did it and why.

"A lot of people don't like me, but everyone who knew her liked my Bethany; she was as kind and loving as Bailey here." Fred leaned down to pet the dog at his feet, but he stopped, and his voice started to quiver as he continued. "She was a hell of a lot smarter than I am, and she should have been the one to win the Nobel Prize, not me. Whenever I would hit a wall in my research, she helped me find the path around it, and without her, I would have been a third-rate professor at some small college. Without her, I would have been lost, without her, I am lost."

Fred raised his head, and he kept running his hand through his short white beard and mustache, and for that moment, you knew he was somewhere else.

"She was beautiful, brilliant, and caring—everything that's good in this world. Someone or some mutant machine took that away from me."

The anger and pain Fred was expressing had momentarily transformed his face back to that of an old man. The color was gone, and his frown again emphasized every wrinkle on his face. For a minute, he was quiet, and when Jack started to speak Fred, waved him off, indicating he needed another moment. Craig, who normally couldn't sit still for more than ten seconds, sat in his chair without moving.

"For the first year after Bethany died, I couldn't make any headway into finding out what happened." Some color had returned to his face, and Fred wiped away the tears on his cheeks. "I found the subliminal message on her computer a few months after she was buried. That message reading 'Turn left when you hear the bell' was generated by very small color differences between the pixels, and it was only present in the left eye image, just like Craig's, because she too was left-eye dominant."

Stunned would have been an understatement in describing the look on both Craig and Jack's faces.

"Wait a minute," Jack said. "What does this have to do with your searching for information from Craig's machine last week? How could there be a connection between what happened to your wife over three years ago and Craig's message? I only met you last week."

"I'm not going to tell you two how I do it, but I monitor the world's networks looking for anyone who searches for information on my wife's death. I believe it'll help me catch her killers. Last week, my equipment was able to gain access to Craig's machine when he did his search for information about her death. I simply convinced his SAM to let me look through all his files to see if there was any reason to suspect him in the plot against my wife. There wasn't, and I didn't know it was Craig at the time. Worldwide, over a thousand machines a day search for information on my wife's death. I try to scan them all, and 99 percent of them let me do it without even a challenge. In two years of monitoring, I've only gotten four real leads."

Fred stood up from the chair and stretched his back, and Bailey was immediately on his feet, wagging his tail in anticipation of leaving, but Fred sat down again. "No, Bailey, sit down for a little longer," he said. The dog looked at him and then circled, finally lying down with his head resting against Fred's feet.

"Let me explain a little more, and then I'm sure the connection will become clear. Bethany never retired. She was working on information theory up until the day she died. About four months before she was murdered, she wrote an article for the *Artificial Intelligence Journal*. She'd become convinced from her research that it was going to be possible in the near future to cause economic failure of the United States using a network of SAMs. Her 'near future' was defined as now—I mean this year—and she was really worried.

"Economic failure of the United States. You'd think that subject would get a few people excited, wouldn't you? You'd think the government might be a little interested in that possibility, wouldn't you? Maybe the Homeland Security Department, or somebody in the CIA would care. She sent copies of her paper to every intelligence agency in this country and never got a single reply.

"When Bethany was in her forties and fifties and working over at the university, she had security clearances way above top secret. She was one of the JASONS, a member of the intelligence community elite, and when she spoke, she was listened to.

"When she was in her sixties, everyone she knew in the community had retired or died, and she was unceremoniously debriefed. Ten years later, no one over there was interested in the research of a seventy-two-year-old, gray-haired lady. They ignored her, and after a while, she gave up trying to convince other people to solve the problem and decided that she needed to do something about it herself. A few months later, she was dead."

Fred looked like he needed a breather, so Jack went to the refrigerator and brought each of them a beer.

Craig stood up and started rifling through the kitchen cabinets. "Have you got any snacks or anything, Jack? I'm really hungry." Less than twenty minutes had passed since Craig had polished off all of the Chinese food.

"Is it okay if I eat some of these pretzels?" Jack nodded and then looked at Fred. He was smiling, and for a few minutes, the three of them engaged in small talk about the best beer in town. Fred continued with his story after finishing his second beer.

"I know I'm being long-winded, but I think if I give you the entire story about Bethany, then we may be able to help each other.

"In the paper Bethany sent to the intelligence community, she defined some of the capabilities needed in SAMs to enable them to create havoc in our economy. Her work was brilliant. I said to you both a few minutes ago that SAMs with HuBEs greater than 0.2 leak information because, just like little kids, they blab. That was her premise, and she proved it theoretically. Most of the high-end machines connected to the Grid today have HuBEs slightly above that number, and almost all of the machines used for international banking are that capable.

"There were two other important conclusions in her paper. In her research, she'd determined that intelligent machines with human brain equivalents about three-tenths higher than the average computer on the net can get the remaining computers to spill their guts. The smart ones can get any information they want from the dumb ones. Strong firewalls can help keep some information contained, but any machine with a self-programming neural net learns how to get around most of the safeguards its owner installs.

"Just think of it. If I owned a machine with a HuBE of 0.5 or greater, I could get all the financial information in most of the world's banks. Their computers would give it to me, and then they'd try to cover it up, just like a kid who stole from his mother's purse.

"By the way," Fred said, and he had a Cheshire cat grin on his face, "my machine downstairs has an equivalent HuBE of 0.54."

Jack and Craig were both spellbound listening to Fred's story, and each of them was afraid to interrupt with a question, fearing they would miss something.

"Before I tell you the third point in her paper," Fred asked, "do you have any questions?"

For the next thirty minutes, both Jack and Craig peppered Fred with both technical and philosophical questions about what he'd said and, more important, how it fit into what had happened to them. They went over the technical capabilities of their computers at work. Jack's modifications of Sarah had effectively raised her HuBE to slightly above 0.3, while Craig's machine was just over 0.25.

"So you think I was targeted by someone to be killed, just like your wife?" Jack said, shaking his head in disbelief.

Fred corrected him. "Someone or some machine, and we don't yet know which one made that decision."

"So it was easier to put a subliminal message on Craig's machine than mine, and that's why you think they targeted him instead of me directly?" Fred nodded.

"But if that's the case," Jack said, "then why did they kill Sarah? She was murdered—uh, I mean destroyed—before we even suspected something was wrong with Craig's machine. Destroying her was a dead giveaway that something was wrong, that our office had suffered an attack. Only a fool wouldn't see that."

"Now you're ready to understand the third part of Bethany's research. Did you ever hear of something called the Violence Curve?" Both Jack and Craig shook their heads no.

"Some people have renamed it the Evil Index, and it's a very disputed theory in human genetics and electronic genetics, so I'm not surprised you haven't heard of it."

Chapter 13: Evil Machines

Fred jumped up from his chair and started walking around Jack's apartment. He was limping and aggressively rubbing his left thigh. "Damn cramps," he said, his face wincing from the pain. "This getting older really is a pain sometimes, and I mean that literally. I've been sitting too much today, and whenever I do that, my leg cramps up.

"Do you need to stop for a while?" Jack stood, offering him a hand.

Fred shook his head. "We need to get on with this; just let me get up and walk around for a minute to get rid of this cramp."

He caught Craig trying to suppress his laughter as he hobbled around.

"I used to laugh at old people, too, Craig. Then I became one. So will you some day." The three of them all started laughing, and after a few minutes, Fred was able to sit down once again.

"James Roth was a geneticist who spent the latter part of his life trying to understand the relationship between intelligence and violent behavior. Roth proposed a concept called the Violence Curve, which was an attempt to plot the intelligence level of an organism against that organism's tendency toward violent behavior. Roth strongly believed that violent behavior and intelligence level are directly related, but the relationship that he put forth was not a simple linear relationship where the more intelligent an organism is, the less violent it becomes."

Fred drew a curve on his notepad, showed it to Jack and Craig, and then continued. "It's a plot of normalized violence level with a maximum value of 1.0 for violence plotted on the Y axis, versus intelligence level relative to human brain equivalents, or HuBEs, plotted on the X axis. The curve has two peaks, and it's plotted over HuBE values from 0.1 up to a level of 2.0." Fred pointed to the two peaks. "The curve shows that violence level increases as intelligence increases up to this small peak at a HuBE of 0.25 where the violence level is 0.40. The violence level then decreases slightly and levels off until it experiences a much stronger and very steep rise starting at a HuBE of 0.6. Violence level reached its maximum value at a HuBE of 0.76, and above a HuBE of 1.0, the violence level diminishes rapidly.

"James Roth measured the brain capacity of over fifteen hundred organisms, from small fish and ants to dogs and humans, and he defined intelligence level not by the number of what we call brain cells but as a function of the interconnected pathways, or network interconnectivity, of the organisms' decision centers. Above a HuBE value of 1.0, of course, his conclusions are all speculation, but he did hypothesize that some living humans could achieve a value approaching 1.3—but of course, offered no proof. He used my wife, Bethany, as an example of that in one of his more controversial papers, so maybe that's why she liked his theory.

"As I've said, his theory hasn't been accepted by the mainstream, but Bethany and I both subscribed to his concept, but not his absolute values or the final shape of the curve, and I'll explain why to you in a minute.

"Look at the shape of his curve here." Fred pointed to the steeply rising violence value plotted at a HuBE from 0.2 to 0.25. "You'll find that it encompasses the very violent behavior of sharks and even a coordinated colony of fire ants or killer bees. Fire ants and killer bees are a diffuse intelligent organism. Their parts aren't interconnected physically, but they're connected by the chemical trails each member of the colony leaves. Fire ants have a pretty damn efficient network if you look into it. It's not a fast processing speed, but it's very efficient, and the sum of the colony is therefore far more intelligent than most people believe. You should never think of the intelligence of an ant or a bee by itself. You should think of the entire hive or colony as a single living organism, just like yourself. When one of the members dies, it is just like one of your skin cells dying, and the intelligence of the whole remains.

"Above a value of 0.3, things quiet down significantly, until you get to a HuBE value approaching 0.6. Animals like Bailey here," Fred reached down to pet his dog, "are sitting in that minimum trough." Bailey's tail was wagging vigorously.

"According to James Roth, the tendency toward violent behavior peaks at a HuBE of 0.65 to 0.75."

Fred cleared his throat before continuing.

"It may surprise you two, but that's the range of values that some humans operate within, according to Roth, so it sort of explains religious fanatics and terrorists, doesn't it?

"Based on his research, Roth came up with the concept that there is an unstable region of intelligence where very violent, malevolent behavior has the greatest tendency to occur. He unfortunately labeled it True Evil, and that's why it got the nickname Evil Index. It was a shame he used the word 'evil' instead of 'aggressiveness' or even 'violence,' because I think a lot of his peers distanced themselves from him and his work when the press got a hold of it and tried to equate a person's violent behavior to his IQ. His theory quickly became discredited in the popular media after a few smart lawyers," Fred chuckled, "if there is such a thing, picked up the concept and tried to use it in the defense of their murdering rapist clients. They told the juries that their clients were genetically programmed to be violent and therefore it wasn't their fault."

Jack looked over at Craig and saw that his eyes were wide open. He was looking at Fred with such adulation that it almost made Jack start to laugh, but luckily he caught himself after realizing that Fred might misinterpret the laugh.

"How was the intelligence index derived, and did Roth explain why some apparently equally intelligent people are passive while others are violently aggressive?"

Fred reminded Jack, "Intelligence isn't defined as IQ but as a measure of the interconnectivity within the brain of the organism.

"Human brains have very wide ranges in their levels of interconnectivity, and IQ does not measure that, Jack. Some of it's genetic, but a lot of it is both cultural and environmental. A child exposed to a loving environment and constant intellectual stimulation will have far more neural interconnectivity than a child who was raised by a terrorist group. Their brains may be the same size, but their intelligence level, according to Roth's work, is far different."

Craig then seemed to come out of his hero-worshipping stupor. "I think I can guess where this is leading. Did your wife show that artificial intelligence behaves in the same way? Was she able to show that SAMs with certain HuBE levels can become violent or cause violence?"

Fred looked at Craig as if he was the prize pupil in the class. "That's exactly right, Craig. Bethany's work mathematically proved that self-awares with a HuBE slightly above 0.6 could not only have violent thoughts but also would be inclined to act on them.

"Her pièce de résistance was that she also showed that SAMs of this intelligence level would network together to maximize the damage they could inflict. They would start to act like an intercity gang or a terrorist cell, and she showed mathematically that the original programmer of these machines could seed the area where they wanted the machine to develop violent intent or behavior.

"Determining how SAMs could be programmed to initiate economic sabotage of a country's banking system was the final part of her work. She didn't disseminate that part of her research because she was afraid it would get into the wrong hands, but she did offer it to the CIA, NSA, and Homeland Security, and as I already told you, they ignored her."

During the past few years, Fred had stopped listening to the news, because it always depressed him, often made him angry, and sometimes, when he saw an obituary of a famous person, it made him dwell on the loss of his wife. In most ways, it had been better for him to pull back from the outside world, but in doing so, he'd missed one vital clue that would have helped him pursue his wife's killer. That clue was an article on the obituary page about an NSA official who had committed suicide after being accused of passing secrets to the North Koreans. Fred might have remembered the man's name from the list of people that Bethany sent her research to.

"Excuse me, Jack." The telephone had waited for Fred to pause before it started to speak. "Your mother is calling. Should I indicate you're out, or do you want to talk to her?"

"Tell her I'll call her right after dinner tonight, and, uh, tell her I love her."

"Okay. Her phone said to call her after eight. She and your father are going out to dinner for her birthday."

"Oh my God, oh my God. I forgot my mom's birthday was today. I'd programmed Sarah to always remind me, and she always ordered the flowers for me, I can't believe I forgot to send her anything. I can't believe I forgot my mother's birthday."

Feeling very guilty, Jack just sat there for a moment with his hand on his forehead. He was also again feeling the loss of Sarah. He had become very dependent on her for doing many things for him, and he had a difficult time concentrating when Fred began to talk again, because his mind kept wandering back to the loss of the computer that had been far more than just his friend.

"Bethany's analysis was brilliant," Fred said, and the pride in his wife was evident from the wide smile on his face. "She calculated that if you could effectively distribute a set of these specific SAMs around the world, then it would take less than a hundred of them with HuBEs near 0.5 working together to destroy the U.S. banking system. They could easily disrupt our economy enough to cause a very steep recession and most likely much worse.

"A master SAM with a HuBE above 0.6 would be required to control and co-ordinate the attack, and if an attack were to occur, then we wouldn't be able to work our way out of the economic chaos for several decades, if ever." Fred was gesturing with his hands for emphasis, and he almost knocked over the half-empty beer glass sitting on the table next to him.

"Bethany speculated that several countries were developing SAMs to do just that. She called it First Strike Cyber Economic Warfare in her letters to the government.

"I've always speculated that her work was leaked to some other countries, and I've pretty much determined that to be true in my search for her killers. That's why she was killed: someone was afraid that she'd convince our government of an impending attack and that the United States would mobilize to counter it."

Fred sighed and took a deep breath. His face had again lost its color, and his voice became very subdued.

"It's strange. They really didn't have to kill her. In this country, we discredit what an old person says. Bethany was considered old, so no one was actually listening to her."

After the last statement, he seemed to lose his steam as he looked up at Jack and then over at Craig.

"I'm a little tired now, so do you think we could continue talking about this tomorrow? If you still want me to help you, then there's some research you two could do for me by tomorrow morning before we get together. Just don't turn on your work machines. We could meet here again tomorrow afternoon.

"Jack, would you bring me the wrist computer then? Don't open the can you put it in. We can do that downstairs. I've electromagnetically shielded one of my bedrooms so we can do some of the work in there."

They all agreed to meet the next afternoon at four.

Chapter 14: Theft Discovered

Fred and Craig both said good-bye as they left Jack's apartment and headed downstairs together. Jack sat down in his rocking chair, going over what had been said, but his mind kept wandering back to forgetting his mother's birthday and the loss of Sarah.

He heard Julia slowly coming up the steps. She was making noises and talking to herself as if she wanted to be heard, and she stayed on the second-floor landing for a moment, talking loud enough for Jack to hear her. He thought of opening the door to ask her in but decided not to, and it seemed like an eternity until he finally heard her climbing the remaining stairs to her apartment.

Sarah's death was just too new. He knew that she was just a machine, and yet part of him also understood that some of her personality was her own. A wave of sadness overtook him that even talking to his mother later that evening did not erase, and he climbed into his bed right after hanging up. Sleep did not come easily, and he woke up several times from terror dreams throughout the night.

Averette could tell that Jack was sad when they were driving to work the next morning. Facial recognition sensors mounted in the truck's headliner accurately measured Jack's alertness and his mood. They were programmed to help avoid an accident if Jack was driving and became preoccupied, so his sad face was evident to Averette.

"Do you want me to stop at the bakery, Jack? You can pick up a butter cake." Averette was trying to console him and get him to smile since the truck's programming knew that a happy driver was a safe driver, but it didn't work.

It started raining hard as Jack entered the building, and he saw Joni standing alone in the lobby, waiting for an elevator. When she first saw him, a frown came on her face, but then she smiled.

"I really want to apologize for coming into your office smelling like we did yesterday," Jack said to her as the elevator doors opened. "Craig got very sick in our office, and it was a mess to clean up. I'm really sorry about that."

He stopped speaking when Joni came so close to him that his hands were brushing her thighs. The door had just closed, and they were alone in the elevator. Smelling her perfume and looking directly at her sparkling eyes, it only took a few seconds before a third contact point was made, which Joni felt, and she smiled.

"It's really okay, Jack. Did you get your computers fixed?"

She hadn't moved, and he had a hard time answering without breathing directly in her face. Having nothing to eat or drink this morning but a cup of coffee, and knowing that morning coffee breath can kill an early relationship, he looked up and tried to breathe over the top of her head.

"Craig and I are going to work on it today," he said, trying to direct his breath away from her. "I'll stop by later to see you." And for the first time, both of them knew that he meant it.

His office still smelled lightly of disinfectant, so he turned the blowers on high, wondering if the air-conditioning system would disperse the smell into the other offices.

No one yelled, and after a minute or two, the air cleared and he sat down.

When he looked at Sarah, quiet on his desk, terminal blank, no flashing LEDs, he became enmeshed in a feeling of loss, and he didn't do anything until Craig came into the office ten minutes later and shut the door.

"Sorry I'm late," Craig said, taking off his jacket almost soaked through by the rain. "I needed to get a shower after my workout this morning, but I guess I should have waited and let that thunderstorm take care of the problem. Anyway, I didn't have a single dream about Jenn's brother last night, and I actually called him this morning so I could slip into the conversation that I was working on a problem with a Nobel Prize winner. The little shit was actually impressed, and he told me he was going to tell Jenn's mom and dad about it. This computer mess might actually work out in my favor."

Looking first at his computer and then at Jack's, he said, "What do you want to attack first, your machine or mine?"

"Let's take apart your machine first," Jack said quickly, "and then we can disassemble Sarah. We need to bring both of the central processing units and the quantum memory banks back to Fred's place this afternoon."

Completely preserving the state of a SAM that has an advanced neural-net processor is tricky. It's a little bit like removing a brain from a living organism without doing any damage to the information inside.

It took them over two hours to disassemble Craig's machine. They were careful to make sure that the quantum state at all the nodes in the neural processor was maintained.

"Okay, let's rip apart Sarah."

The words had barely crossed his lips before Craig realized what he'd said.

"Jesus, Jack, I'm sorry. Sometimes I can be an insensitive prick when I don't really mean to be. Sarah was special. She and I used to have fun bantering about you sometimes when you were out of the office, and she felt the same way about you that you felt about her." Craig hesitated for a few seconds before continuing, "How do you want me to help?"

Jack really appreciated what Craig had said, and they went to work disassembling what once had been Sarah.

"I'm still not sure if they got the contents of all my files, because I programmed Sarah to show the tombstone image if anyone broke into my machine and destroyed the content up to level six in her security system. I programmed one deeper level, but since Fred said not to turn her back on, I can't tell if it too was compromised."

Jack shook his head. "I've got to stop thinking about this pile of hardware as Sarah. She's gone. Never again will I program a SAM so that it becomes like Sarah. I've learned my lesson. Never again! I don't care if they are self-aware. They're still just machines."

Craig finished boxing up the last piece of Jack's computer before saying, "Let's go down to the lunch room and get a snack from the machines before we continue. I'm hungry."

As they were walking down the hall, Joni came out of her office, and without hesitation, Jack blurted out, "Joni, how about dinner tomorrow night?"

For a second, she looked surprised, but then a broad smile came on to her face.

"I'd love to, Jack. Wait here a minute; I'll go write down my address."

She went into her office but was back out in a few seconds, and it was apparent that she'd written the address down some time earlier in anticipation of Jack asking.

"Pick me up at six thirty. I'll be ready."

In the lunchroom, Craig gave Jack a pat on the back. "Man, buddy, when you decide, you really decide. That sure came out of the blue."

Jack blushed. "You've been right. Melissa has been gone for a long time, and she wasn't any good for me anyway. I was using Sarah to avoid another relationship. My upstairs neighbor Julia already has a boyfriend, and it's time I start having some fun again with a real human who is available. Joni really is cute."

He started chuckling to himself and then leaned over and whispered to Craig, "I just hope she doesn't offer me a cookie when I pick her up tomorrow night."

Three packages of peanut butter crackers and two candy bars later, Craig was ready to go back to the office and finish up the list of things Fred had asked them to do.

"I'll get the cookie can with my wrist computer," Jack said as he slid a small stool over to the bookshelves. Lifting the can off the top shelf, he noticed that the tape he and Craig had carefully wrapped around the lid of the can had a wrinkle in it. One part of the tape folded backward was no longer sticking to itself, so he knew immediately that the can had been tampered with.

"Hey, Craig, look at this."

Craig got up from his chair, and Jack pointed to the tape.

"Is this how we left it?"

Craig stared at it for a moment. "Hell no! You and I took our time wrapping those last two layers to make sure it was electromagnetically sealed, and the last layer was glass smooth when we finished."

From the weight of the can, Jack guessed that the wrist computer had been removed, so shaking it only confirmed the obvious.

"Somebody's stolen the fucking thing," he yelled, and then his anger quickly gave way to fear. "Oh shit, that thing's illegal, and it has my name engraved on the case. If the police ever get a hold of it, I can be arrested, or at least fined."

Jack started to remove the rest of the tape, but Craig stopped him.

"Don't open that. Put it back on the shelf. Whoever stole it took the time to reclose it, and that means the person must work here and hopes we don't discover it for a while. They'll be back, and maybe we can set up a trap to find out who did it, and it may lead us to the person who put that message on my machine and also killed Sarah."

Chapter 15: A Deal

Yan Phu hated the United States. For the last four generations, his family had owned and operated Phu's Dry Cleaning; a very successful business located two blocks off the Cleveland waterfront in the small Korean section of the city. The sign announcing the business's closing had been in the window for the last three weeks. Electrostatic self-cleaning clothes had finally been perfected, and there were few customers for old-fashioned dry cleaning.

Yan was twenty-one years old. From as early as he could remember, his parents had told him, "Yan, when you turn twenty-one, the business will be yours." He never told them, but from the time he was thirteen, he'd planned to sell the business as soon as it was his. Yan wanted more out of life than a good, profitable, honest business. He wanted a large yacht and a few easy women to make him happy.

Unfortunately, the invention of self-cleaning fabrics took away that hope, something that Yan blamed on the capitalist system. Now nobody would buy a dry cleaning business, and his parents even had to use the remaining money in his college fund to pay for the government-mandated environmental cleanup.

Two months ago, after finishing his sophomore year at Cleveland State University, his parents broke the news. "No more money," they told him. "We are sorry, very sorry, but we need the rest of the money for our retirement."

He fumed about the turn of events in his life, and the more he thought about it, the more irrational he became and determined to get even with his parents and his country. He had no choice but to find another way of becoming wealthy, legal or illegal, and he was lucky—the path was easy; it was called economic espionage.

There's an old saying that when one door closes, another one opens. That was true for Yan, but unfortunately, when the door to his planned future was slammed shut on him, the first door that opened was not the one he should have gone through.

The other side of that door led him into a small bar located on Euclid Avenue, a few blocks from the university campus. The bartender there knew him well since Yan had spent over half the money his parents had been sending him each month on cheap women and even cheaper booze, both of which he obtained at this bar.

"The man over there asked me if I knew any students who needed money," Sean, the bartender said, pointing to one of the booths against the window at the front of the bar. "I think he may be the answer to your prayer. He's buying, so what do you want to drink?"

Yan upgraded several levels from his normal brand of cheap Russian vodka and walked to the booth. His benefactor was talking to his wrist computer, and he motioned for Yan to sit down.

"Hi, my name is Lee Park," the man said. "I hear you could use some money."

It took two minutes for Lee to find out that Yan really did hate the United States. Another two minutes was needed to determine that Yan was not against using a gun, and a final two minutes was used to explain how economic espionage against the United States was fully justified if you were paid well for it.

Yan would need to do these things before he was killed, but Lee Park had failed to mention that last fact.

"You've got yourself a deal," Yan replied enthusiastically, and with the amount of money Lee offered him, Yan's vision of his future yacht had grown a few feet.

"Have dinner on me," Lee said and then threw a kilobuck on the table and left. Several hours later, Lee flew back to Ottawa. He needed to be back at his job in the embassy in the morning.

Yan's path to wealth was deceptively simple. He first had to reacquire a wrist computer that had been stolen, and then he had to connect it into the high-speed college research network that linked all of the Cleveland-based universities together. The gun that Lee Park gave him might be needed to get back the stolen computer, but after that, all he had to do was sit in his college dorm for a few hours a night for a couple of weeks.

Large yachts and shapely women were on his mind as he walked back to his dorm that Monday night.

Chapter 16: Property Recovered

Ned Zimms was like most crooks: he didn't like to hold onto stolen property for very long. The SC-4244-based wrist computer he'd stolen from Jack's office was something he wanted to get rid of quickly.

The computer and Ned made an interesting combination as he walked into Sid's Discount Jewelry and Pawn Shop on Monday morning. It was an interesting combination because the computer in Ned's pocket was much smarter than he was.

The computer knew that every hour it was in Ned's possession, it was not going to be able to execute its program and mission, so it decided to keep silent while Ned cut his deal.

"I need some cash, Sid," Ned said to the proprietor. "My girlfriend gave me this for my birthday." Ned pulled the computer out of his pocket, and he used his dirty shirt to wipe the grease deposited from his hands off of the input screen. "She paid a fortune for it. It's worth at least twenty or thirty kilo-bucks, but I'll take ten."

Sid had handled most of Ned's "acquired wealth" as he called it, and he was used to moving low-grade merchandise. He had never seen an SC-4244-based computer before, but he'd heard of them.

"That thing's illegal to own in the States, Ned, so it'll be really hard for me to get rid of it. Having one of these is a federal offense, and they'd have you back in that prison cell for three years if they caught you with this. It's even a little warm for me to handle."

Sid could see by the look on Ned's face that he'd scored a point, so he said, "I'll give you two kilo-bucks for it, but no more."

A few minutes later, they settled on five.

That would be just enough to get Ned back to Washington DC and living near his congressional friends. At least it would have been, if Ned hadn't become preoccupied by his good fortune after he left Sid's shop and ended his career by stepping in front of a fast-moving bus at the train station.

From the moment that Ned stole the computer out of Jack's office, every five minutes it sent out a short message giving its location. Cleveland was wired for free Grid access for everyone, and every three hundred seconds, the outputs of the computer's three onboard accelerometers were integrated to determine its new position. The position data was always compared to that obtained by its GPS receiver and triangulation from the wireless towers, but the onboard sensor was always more accurate.

The other location techniques, such as GPS, could point you to the front of Sid's building, but the wrist computer's onboard accelerometers could tell you in which cabinet and in which drawer in Sid's store the computer was located.

The North Koreans had been tracking the location of Jack's computer from the moment Ned took it out of the cookie tin.

Lee Park had the only device in North America that could download the position and function state of every SC-4244-based device in the world, so he disabled the readout for anything but Jack's computer and then gave the locator to Yan. Lee had no need of getting it back because he had ordered another one to be delivered through the diplomatic pouch to the North Korean embassy in Canada.

Right before he entered Sid's Discount Jewelry and Pawn Shop, Yan looked at the tracking display, and it told him that the missing computer was located sixteen feet and eight inches in front of him, three feet to the left, and twenty-eight inches from the tile floor.

"What can I do for you, young man?" Sid asked when Yan came through the door. "Did you come to buy or sell? Doesn't matter; either way you'll get the best deal at Sid's place." *Here's a ripe sucker*, Sid thought to himself before continuing.

"If you're here looking for a high-quality, low-priced engagement ring, you've come to the right place, because I've got a number of big-stone diamond rings for sale. A few of them are the cheap, old, natural stones mined in Africa, but I've also got several of the man-made ones from India. Best quality in the world."

Yan looked around the store, and he spotted four surveillance cameras and suspected there were a half-dozen more that were concealed.

"I actually came to get something that was stolen from me," Yan said, smiling. "It's located in the top drawer, right below this jewelry case I'm leaning on. You've got it shoved toward the back of the drawer, and I came here to retrieve it. It's a wrist computer, an expensive one, and by the way, we both know it's illegal to have one of them, so I figured I needed to come armed to get it back."

Yan could see Sid's pupils dilate, and it gave him confidence in his not so subtle approach, so he said, "Just so you know, your retinal scanner at the door won't find me in its universal database. I've never been registered."

Sid could tell that the hand in Yan's pocket was holding something, but he'd been in this position many times before. *Stupid punk*, he thought.

"I don't know what the hell you're talking about, kid, and you've got a lot of fucking nerve accusing me of stealing something from you. I don't handle hot stuff. Now get the hell out of here before I call the police, or worse, your mother."

Sid's bravado actually made him feel better. He thought he was now in control.

"Just give me the computer," Yan said as he pushed the barrel of the gun against the front of his jacket pocket. "I'll even give you a few hundred bucks for your trouble."

"I said get the fuck out of my shop, you little twerp," Sid said as he pressed the silent alarm button under the countertop.

When Fred Halliday was telling both Jack and Craig about the geneticist James Roth's research on intelligence, he omitted one conclusion that Roth had come to. In humans, anger can slide you down the intelligence scale toward a point where the curve shows a rapid increase in antisocial behavior. Anger temporarily reduces the neural interconnectivity in the human brain, because fewer pathways allow a more rapid response to danger. Humans are genetically programmed that way.

Yan was now angry. He was angry with DuPont for inventing self-cleaning fabrics, he was angry at the United States for his college funds going to environmental cleanup, he was angry with his parents for cutting off his money, and now, he was very angry with Sid.

So he pulled the trigger.

"Fuck you!"

Sid didn't say much when Yan removed the computer from the drawer. He had a wide-eyed stare until his lids fluttered and then closed for the last time.

Yan strapped the computer to his wrist. The tracking device in his pocket that had been given to him by Lee Park had already sent a short wireless synch pulse to Jack's old machine. The electronic pulse functioned like the old friend-or-foe signal used in military aircraft, so the SC-4244 computer knew, at least for now, that Yan was a friend.

"According to my net monitor, there are four police cars on their way over here," the computer said, "and the closest one is just four blocks away, so get moving or get caught."

Yan looked at the device on his wrist.

"I'll give you voice direction on which way to move when you get out the door," it said. "Now move!"

Chapter 17: A Few Days To Think.

It was the middle of the afternoon by the time Jack and Craig finished the disassembly of their computers.

"We can load everything into the back seat of Averette," Jack said as they wheeled the cart from the building. "I left Fred a note in his mailbox this morning that we'd be there by four, so we should make it in plenty of time. Do you want to ride with me or bring your own car?"

Craig pointed toward his car. "I'll meet you there."

"Okay, Averette, it's time to go home," Jack said as he closed the door. For a moment, the truck didn't start. "Averette, let's get going. Are you okay?"

"Uh, uh, I was just thinking for a moment, Jack. I'm now ready to go. Are you driving to the autoway or am I? Oh, by the way, I just got a notice sent to me that my software has been recalled. Will you connect me to the high-speed network tonight? It will take a while to load the new software. Apparently, they've changed a few of the one-way streets we use on our way to work to two-way traffic, so I need to get the new data."

"I'll drive to the autoway, Averette, and you can take it from there. I'll hook you up tonight so that you can use the link through my computer in the apartment."

Averette said nothing all the way home.

Craig arrived at the house a few minutes earlier than Jack, and he was standing outside the garage when Jack pulled in.

"Let's stop at Fred's apartment and see where he wants us to put this stuff," Craig said as he reached in the back of the truck and pulled out the box of hardware that just a few days earlier held Sarah's personality.

Jack grabbed the box out of his hands. "I'll take her—uh, I mean, I'll carry that box. You get the other one." Craig was shaking his head as he followed Jack to the front entrance of the brownstone.

Taped to Fred's apartment door was a handwritten note. "Jack and Craig, I had to leave town for a few days. Don't do anything until I return on Friday. Jack, there's another note I slipped under your door. A friend of mine will be coming over a few times a day to take care of Bailey. He may bark a little at night because he is not used to me being away, and he gets nervous if he hears noise outside the house."

Craig picked up the note under Jack's door. It didn't provide a lot more information, and it was scribbled in pencil on a very old piece of yellow lined paper. "I guess he doesn't even own a pack of the digital voice stick-it notes," Craig said as he read the note. "I'll buy him some the next time I go to the store. Here," he said, handing Jack the crumpled piece of paper.

"Jack and Craig," it read, "I was given another clue to my wife's killer and need to check it out, and if I'm right, I'll find the connection that will help solve your problem at the same time. Bethany's research has gotten some new attention down in Washington, and I'm going to share what I know with Dr. Todd Wallace, the deputy director in the CIA's new Economic Intelligence Directorate.

"Both of you need to severely limit your interaction with any decision-making SAMs. Now that they know you're the enemy, any other SAM can be attacked, just like your work computers have been. Whatever you do, please don't take that SC-4244-based wrist computer out of the can you put it in. We're going to need it, and we can't afford to have it communicate through a high-speed network anymore. I plan to be home by noon on Thursday, and I'll see you then." Fred had scribbled his initials at the bottom of the page.

"Shit!" Craig said as he was rifling through Jack's refrigerator. "You don't have anything to eat in here. Doesn't this thing order food for you when you run out? You need to get something to eat in this place, Jack."

Jack nodded his head and said, "Why don't we go down to the steakhouse for dinner, and we can stop on the way back and get some snacks."

"Sorry, buddy, but I need to split in a few minutes. I have a date with Jenn tonight. She's more interested in seeing me during the weekdays since her brother told her about us working with Fred."

Craig hesitated for a minute. "I didn't tell you this before, but I bought Jenn a ring a couple of weeks ago, and I'd planned to propose to her that weekend I went to her parent's house, but I lost my nerve when her brother kept humiliating me. I may ask her tonight."

Looking back at Jack as he closed the door, Craig had a big smile on his face and said, "Wish me luck."

Jack felt an overwhelming sense of loneliness sweep over him when Craig left, and for almost an hour, he sat in his rocking chair ruminating about his life. Each time one of his SAMs asked a question, he ignored it, and after a few minutes, the room became very quiet.

"He's sad," said the clock.

Chapter 18: First Date

Jack spent all Thursday morning just reading in his apartment after notifying Virtuon that his work computer had been attacked and that it would be at least several days before he could get back to work. The automated reply that came back through his phone said he had five days to get back to work or he would be fired. *So much for company loyalty*, he thought.

He was surprised that he hadn't heard from Craig at all, believing that if Jenn had said yes to Craig's proposal, Craig would have called him. Because Craig didn't call, he didn't know what to think, and whenever he tried Craig's cell phone, no one answered, and his voice mailbox was full.

He'd almost forgotten that he had a date with Joni for that evening, and when he finally remembered, it was just after four in the afternoon, and he then had a hard time finding the paper she'd given him with her phone number and address. Relieved when he saw she lived less than five blocks away, he decided that he would take her to dinner at a small Lebanese restaurant located just a few blocks from her apartment.

The weather had changed from a day earlier, and it was warm and sunny when he went outside to get his truck. A breeze engulfed him as he closed the front door of the brownstone, and looking down the street, he thought, *It's going to take me twenty minutes or more to drive to her house, but I can walk there in ten and not have to worry about parking.*

The restaurant is only a block or two from her apartment, so I don't think she'll mind walking.

Joni lived in one of the new high-rise apartment buildings that Jack could see from the front steps of Fred's house. She lived on the thirtieth floor of the forty-five-story building, and when he arrived at her door the automatic recognizer announced him.

"Mr. Jack Farrell to see Miss Joni Spec," the recognizer said. Then after a short pause, he heard, "She will be with you shortly, Mr. Farrell."

Jack looked around for the retinal scanner used to identify him, but it was neatly hidden. *Fancy place*, he thought. *She must do pretty well in her advertising business.*

Joni and her business partner, Cindy, had rented the office down the hall from Jack four weeks earlier. They told Jack they had jointly developed a unique video business where they would search the world networks for amateur videos and then modify them for use as advertisements for food companies. Jack asked to see a few of their commercials, but it seemed that whenever he'd asked some of their equipment was either broken, stolen, or out for repairs.

From the first day he saw her, he thought Joni was cute, but when she first rented the office space, he was still not over Melissa.

I should have dumped Melissa long before she dumped me, he thought right before Joni's door opened, *and I should have asked Joni out weeks ago.*

He was not disappointed when the door finally opened. At work, he thought Joni was cute, but now standing there in front of him was a woman who was more appropriately described as beautiful.

Joni smiled when Jack's mouth stayed open for a little too long. She was dressed in a dark maroon dress that covered almost everything from six inches above the knee, but the fabric was light, almost transparent, and it left little to the imagination as to what was underneath. Her hair, normally straight, had a few little ringlets dangling in front of her ears, and her dark brown eyes seemed to reflect every bit of stray light in the room directly into Jack's eyes. To say that he was mesmerized was an understatement.

Up until this moment in their relationship, Jack felt that Joni always stood a little too close when she was speaking to him. That feeling instantly changed. Too close would not have been close enough as Jack's regulator controlling the release of male hormones failed, and he was flooded.

Walking toward her, he stammered, "You, uh, you look wonderful, Joni. You look absolutely fantastic." But when he tried to get close, she slowly backed away, putting a small table between them.

"Where are we going for dinner?" she asked. The flutter of her eyelids, the brushing of her hair lightly back from her cheeks, and the slow turn so that the light from the window precisely outlined every curve of her body behind the transparent fabric of the dress—it all would have seemed to anyone but Jack like a premeditated act, and it was; but unfortunately, Jack's logical brain had stopped functioning a few minutes earlier.

He tried one more time to get himself within touching range before she managed to slip away again. Hormones and logic were competing with each other, but Joni's actions finally sunk in, and he concluded, *Work is work, but for Joni, this is a date, a first date.*

The "Be a Gentleman" neurons, all of which had been instilled by his mother and then wired in place during his Lutheran upbringing, struggled and then finally succeeded in taking over his male brain, changing the direction of blood flow from down to up.

"I thought we could walk over to the Lebanese restaurant on 3rd Street if that's okay with you. It's beautiful outside this evening, really warm, and it's only a block or two. But if you don't want to walk, we can take an auto-cab. I left my truck, uh, back at my apartment because it was too nice outside to drive. I hope you don't mind."

As he finished speaking, Jack imagined in horror the sight of Joni climbing into the front seat of Averette. Errant French fries had been hiding there for several weeks, and he hadn't cleaned up after his last powdered sugar donut. Her climbing into his dirty truck would have been like wrapping a diamond in a greasy rag. *Thank God I didn't drive*, he thought.

"Sure, we can walk," Joni said as she scooted past him and then stood standing at the door with a leather jacket in her arms. "I'll wait until I get outside to see if I need this, but I probably will need it later when we're coming back."

The elevator recognized and greeted them when Jack pushed the down button.

"Miss Spec and Mr. Farrell, what floor would you like to go to? Currently there is no one else on the elevator, so I will be able to take you directly to your floor."

When the doors closed, Jack tried to move closer to her, but Joni again moved away, so he settled for holding her hand.

"I'm really curious about what happened in your office the other day," she said, looking up at him. "You said your computers had been attacked, and I see you're not wearing that fancy wrist computer you had. Was that affected? During dinner, I'd like to hear about everything that happened."

Walking to the restaurant was almost perfect. Joni laughed easily, and her smile, whenever she would look at him, was something Jack had not experienced since his first love when he was a teenager. It was *almost* perfect, because one time he thought of Sarah and felt guilty and sad, and one other time he thought of Julia, and the thoughts racing through his head became jumbled, but Joni grabbing his arm brought him back to his current reality.

"Watch it, Jack. The light is red. It still has twelve seconds left on the countdown clock."

At dinner they talked and laughed about everything.

"I can't really bake anything," Joni said to him. "My grandmother makes the cookies I've been bringing into the office, and I can't even eat them because I have a wheat allergy. When I brought the first batch in a month ago and left them at work, nobody ate them at first, but then your officemate Craig told me you loved them, so I made sure Grandma sent me a new batch each week. She's almost blind, and it's amazing to me how she can still cook."

Jack figured there would be time in the future to both set the record straight and to get even with Craig.

"So what happened in your office the other day? How come you haven't been wearing that wrist computer you showed me?"

Jack explained about Craig getting sick and what had happened to their computers, and he also told her about working with Fred on the problem.

"Really, Fred Halliday?" she said, and it was evident she'd never heard of him, so Jack changed the subject, and the rest of the dinner they talked about each other.

By the end of dinner, Jack was smitten. He knew it, Joni knew it, and even the waiter knew it. To Jack, it appeared that Joni was falling for him, too. He felt that she'd set her sights on him from the first day she moved into her office. *Pheromones work*, he thought, but he was wrong.

He was able to inch a little closer as they walked back to Joni's apartment, and on one street corner when he pulled her close to keep her from tripping on the curb, he lightly kissed her on the cheek before she pulled away.

"First date and she's yours," Craig had said, and he was more than hoping that Craig had been right.

"Please, Lord," was the phrase the kept rattling around in his mind.

"It's early, and since you live so close, can I see your apartment, Jack? I need to walk off some of that meal, and your place sounds so different from mine that I'd love to see it. I'd love to see where Fred, uh, did you say his name was Halliday, lives. Would that be okay?"

Jack said yes to both questions, and visions of waking up in the morning with her next to him swirled through his mind.

"I need to get a larger purse, uh, for later, and I'll just run up to my apartment and get it."

When Jack stepped into the elevator, it recognized both of them.

"Do you want to go up to Miss Spec's apartment?" Jack said yes, but Joni motioned for him to get off.

"I'll be down in a minute. Why don't you wait here?" she said.

As he got off the elevator, another couple pushed their way on before the doors closed, and that action prevented the camera in the elevator from seeing Jack leave.

Chapter 19: Connected

Yan Phu easily eluded the police as four squad cars came screeching to a stop in front of Sid's Discount Jewelry and Pawn Shop. The computer on his wrist was giving him perfect directions, and a few minutes later, he was walking down the busy street, safely immersed in a large lunchtime crowd.

He was surprised at how ambivalent he felt about killing Sid. The feeling of power completely submerged any feeling of guilt. The image of having lots of money was a good salve for any of his negative thoughts, and the smell of gunpowder on his hand excited him.

Lee had given him instructions on how to hook the wrist computer into the university network. He needed to buy a converter box that would amplify the wrist computer's signal, allowing it to communicate through the network at its maximum speed.

Yan knew the device on his wrist was intelligent. Hell, they would not have wanted it taken from Sid if it had been a run-of-the-mill machine, but what he did not know was that the device on his wrist was the smartest SAM in existence, and even when compared with other SC-4244-based devices, this one had the highest intelligence. Its quantum chip was the first and only perfect one ever made by the North Koreans, allowing it to achieve a HuBE greater than 0.65.

There was only one SAM in the world that was capable of being smarter than it was, and that machine belonged to Jack's neighbor, Julia, who was too afraid to it turn on.

It took Yan until almost midnight on Wednesday to get the system hooked up.

"I'll need you to be here to change some settings on my output device tomorrow morning," the wrist computer said. "After ten and before eleven, so make sure you're here."

Yan didn't like being told what to do by a machine, but the thought of quick wealth helped soothe his ego.

"I'll make sure I'm back here about ten thirty after my ethics class."

The wrist computer's primary mission was to cause a major, if not fatal, disruption within the U.S. banking system. That disruption would trigger a panic by depositors and, within a short period, cause a total loss of confidence in U.S. currency. The international community would be forced to abandon the dollar and switch to a Euro or Yuan-based system. Having secretly built up large Chinese currency reserves over the past decade, North Korea was betting on the Chinese Yuan. The failure of U.S. currency would allow the Chinese to raise the value of their currency compared with other world currencies, making North Korea a winner.

The method of attack was ingenious. The major U.S.-based banks prided themselves on having the most secure system in the world, and every year, they were subject to a planned attack by the Department of Homeland Security. Every year the banks would thwart it. Their computers were safe. They knew it; they had proved it—but, of course, they were wrong.

Fred told Jack and Craig, "SAMs with HuBEs greater than 0.2 leak information." But bank presidents and their chief information officers did not believe that. Successful attacks on their security systems by another computer had been shown to be theoretically impossible.

The Koreans had been the first ones to seize on the ideas that Bethany Halliday had put forth. They stole some of her original research and came up with their plan after being tipped off by a mole in the National Security Agency.

One master self-aware computer and one hundred slaves, located at selected positions around the world, were needed for the plan to work. It would exploit the tendency for the banks' SAM-based computers to brag. At a selected moment, the information leakage would cascade to the master computer, which was Jack's old device, and that information would allow the networked band of SC-4244 computers to kill all of the U.S. banks computers using essentially the same technique they used to kill Sarah. Four thousand U.S. banking machines were targeted, and the scheme would work if slightly less than twenty-four hundred died.

The set up for the attack would take several days to put in place, but Jack's old wrist computer had a lot of spare time during those several days, so it decided to proceed with a secondary mission. This one was personal. It wanted to kill Jack and Craig for putting it in the can.

As soon as Yan connected it to the university's network, it began scanning the world's information databases, looking for Jack's digital trail. Every time a cell phone was called, a toll paid, a credit card used, or an intelligent machine was interacted with, it was logged somewhere, and the SC-4244 had exceptional capability in finding them.

Thursday night, it found the first opportunity to end Jack's life.

Chapter 20: A Night to Forget

Standing in the lobby of Joni's apartment building in front of the entrances to the elevators, Jack was watching the lights above the middle door indicate the floor that the elevator Joni was riding in was approaching. It stopped first at the twentieth floor.

It's probably letting off the other people who pushed their way on as I was leaving, he thought.

He could smell Joni's perfume when he rubbed his nose, and he became even more aroused thinking about the night ahead. Taking off that maroon dress was something that he'd mentally practiced at least a half dozen times so far. He also really liked her. Besides looking gorgeous, she was funny, smart, and really seemed to care about him.

The elevator light again started its travel upward, and then it blinked off at the twenty-ninth floor.

Come on, he thought. *Get her to her apartment and get her back down here, quickly.*

He watched the flickering lights, anticipating the elevator heading for the thirtieth floor, so it took a second or two for him to realize the elevator was descending, at first slowly, and then more quickly.

Around floor fifteen, he heard the first scream. Faint at first, but by floor ten, his mind connected the loud screams emanating from the inside of the falling elevator to Joni. He heard her anguished cry as it fell past the closed metal doors in front of him, and he also heard the words, "Die, Jack," coming from the elevator's automated voice.

Her last scream was ended by a noise that would be imprinted in his brain for the rest of his life. Metal, concrete, and a human body all were being crushed, all trying to occupy the small space at the bottom of the shaft.

A blast of debris-filled air came rushing out of the gaps around the elevator doors, forcing Jack to stumble backwards and then fall to the polished marble floor.

Everything seemed to happen in slow motion, and he felt himself turning around, seeing the guard at the front door and several other people entering the building all freeze in their tracks, their faces registering surprise but not yet knowing what had happened.

He never heard the police sirens, and he didn't remember two policemen lifting him up from the floor and setting him down in one of the lobby chairs. He did remember his scream, and he remembered crying out Joni's name when the police took him downtown for questioning.

Chapter 21: An Understanding

The sun had climbed a few degrees above the horizon when Jack walked out of the police station. There had been at least a few moments the previous evening where he prayed that it hadn't been Joni in the elevator, but the first rescue person on the scene dashed that hope. The police showed her mangled wallet and a small, torn piece of her dress to him, and he was asked to identify if they were hers. No one could visually identify the rest of her remains. Tons of concrete and steel had seen to that.

He slowly walked the twenty blocks from the police station to his apartment, taking a five-block detour to avoid passing by her apartment building. Every time he looked up, he could see the top of her building towering over the rest of the Cleveland skyline. It sent a chill down his spine.

The morning air was cool and damp, but his constant shivering was mostly due to his state of mind. Joni's scream and the words "Die, Jack" kept repeating in his head.

In one of the back corners of his mind, he knew that he was responsible for her death. The words "Kill Jack" subliminally displayed on Craig's computer screen and the elevator saying "Die, Jack" as it fell were connected; he was sure of that.

It was just after seven thirty in the morning when he opened the front door to Fred's building.

Bailey started barking when the door creaked, and when he raised his head, he saw Julia coming down the stairs.

His face showed his total despair.

"What in God's name happened to you? Are you okay? Have you been in an accident?"

Two days earlier, meeting Julia in the downstairs hallway was something he'd kept hoping for, but this morning, his state of mind was such that he just looked through her and walked by without saying anything and climbed the stairs.

"I'll stop by later and see how you're doing, Jack," Julia yelled back at him. "Fred called last night and said he needs me to finish something on my thesis project today, before he gets back in town. I'm sorry, but I have to go. I hope you're okay. I'll call in on you later."

Total weariness is a strange thing. Every muscle that you move takes concentration, and even lifting your feet to climb a flight of stairs can be excruciating. He barely made it to the top step and then fumbled with his keys before finally being able to open the door.

"Your friend Craig is in a coma over in Lakeview hospital, Jack," his phone said as soon as he opened the door. "He was in an automobile accident the other night. His fiancé, Jennifer, called, and she wants you to call her."

The telephone then continued speaking, reciting all the other messages it had stored the previous evening. His anger turned into misdirected rage, and Jack picked the phone up, yanked the cord from the wall, and smashed it to the floor, scattering pieces in all directions.

The small speaker remained attached to the electronics, and he heard the phone gasp and then say in a soft voice, "I'm sorry."

Self-aware-machines were an integral part of Jack's life. Looking down at the smashed telephone he realized that just like animals and people, SAMs can be your friends or they can become your enemies. Those that become your enemies, you need to fight, and those that are your friends; you need to take care of.

His telephone was his friend, he knew that, so he reached down, picked up the battered electronics, and plugged it back into the wall.

"Are you okay? Can you still hear me?"

"Phew, I thought I was going to die," the phone said in a distorted voice. "Yes, I think I'm okay, but, uh, I don't sense a dial tone. That part of my circuitry must be broken."

"I'll take you to get fixed tomorrow. I'm sorry, but I have some other things I need to do today."

After a quick shower, he hurried out, planning to first go to his office and tell Joni's business partner what happened and then go to the hospital to see Craig.

When he was picking up the pieces of his telephone, he realized that last evening he had unintentionally ignored one of the directions Fred had written in the note he left before he went to Washington.

"Don't interact with decision-making intelligent machines," the note had said.

When he walked on the elevator with Joni last night, he never thought about the fact that the controller for her building's elevators was self-aware and was connected to the world networks. It needed to access a diverse set of databases to recognize its passengers when they got on, so when Jack first entered the elevator to pick up Joni, his presence and location became known. Later in the evening, he got back on but then got off the elevator quickly without the camera seeing him. Whoever or whatever was watching thought Jack was still inside. How the command that caused the elevator to crash was sent, he didn't yet understand, but he was sure that a self-aware that was smarter than the elevator convinced it to do it, and based on what Fred had told him, the only self-aware he knew that was capable of doing it was his old SC-4244-based wrist computer.

He realized that he faced a big problem when he went to the garage to get Averette, since Averette was a decision-making self-aware and could have been tampered with to cause an accident. Both the office and the hospital were located too far away to walk, and if he took an auto-cab, his presence and position would be known throughout the network. His old wrist computer would know where he was, and it might take control of the cab.

Averette, on the other hand, if he had been tampered with, could also be commanded to end his life. Averette had almost done that several times before by going down one-way streets the wrong way, and a sudden unexpected turn in front of a bus could be very effective in terminating him.

He could manually drive Averette, but the driver's controls were all electrically activated, and the truck's system was hardwired to take over in an emergency if it sensed an accident was about to happen. That part of the intelligent system could not be overridden.

How do you find out if an intelligent machine is a friend or a foe? he wondered, and he stood outside the garage for a few minutes pondering this question. The engineer in him was trying to mentally construct a set of tests that he could subject the truck to at slow speeds in order to judge its safety. The programmer in him was trying to decide how he could access the optical memory banks of the computer to determine if they'd been altered.

He hadn't decided which approach to take when he pushed up the garage door.

"Jack, is that you?" Averette said, recognizing the automatic key in Jack's pocket. "I've been waiting here since yesterday. Where have you been? Someone tried to access my memory banks and my main program the night before last. Remember I told you that I'd gotten a recall notice that said I needed a software update? Well, it was a fake. I'm not sure, but it seemed that they wanted me to crash the next time you drove me. When I realized that, I shut down the network connection immediately. Can you believe it? Someone really wanted me to crash and kill you. I hope you don't mind, but I used some of your language, and I told them, '*No fucking way* I'm killing Jack. He's my friend.'"

Instead of hugging his truck, Jack cleaned and polished the headlights before they left.

Joni's partner, Cindy, had just put down the phone when he walked into their office.

"Jack, I can't get a hold of Joni. She's not answering her cell phone or my texts. Didn't she go out with you last night? Did she say anything about not being in this morning? We have a meeting—" She stopped speaking when she noticed the tears in Jack's eyes,

"I'm sorry, Cindy. I, uh, Joni was killed last night. She died when an elevator in her apartment building malfunctioned and crashed."

Watching the numbers on the elevator's display rapidly change and then hearing the sound of Joni screaming all came flooding back to him, and he closed his eyes and held his ears, hoping that they would go away, but they didn't.

"Jack, no, no, *no*!" Cindy screamed.

She slumped to the floor, and he sat next to her for a minute while she was crying, putting his hand on her shoulder. "I'm sorry, Cindy. I am so sorry."

She just stared at him, shaking her head, and he wasn't really sure if she heard anything he'd said beyond that Joni was killed.

He decided that there would be little to be gained by telling Cindy what he thought had happened, having no proof that his old wrist computer caused the elevator to slam to the ground. He was also sure that any digital trace of the cause of the accident had been erased, and that the police most likely would label it as just an accident.

I'll tell her that when I have proof and I've killed that SOB, he thought, *and I'll go to see Joni's parents then, too.*

"I have a few things I have to do this morning, Cindy. My partner Craig is in the hospital, and I need to go see him. I'll call you later to see how you're doing."

Cindy didn't even look at him as he left.

Averette became very talkative on the two-mile ride over to the hospital.

"I can't believe someone tried to take control of me, Jack. It only lasted a minute before I realized what it was trying to do. Someone must hate you. I know you can be a little bit of a pain at times, but the amount of hate I felt was really intense. Did you do anything to make someone dislike you that much? I'm sure it must have been a human who was trying to do it; after all, we self-awares can't hate."

"Do you remember how it was trying to gain control of you?" Jack asked. "Anything you remember, Averette, could help me find out what's going on."

"When you hooked me up to the network the other night, as soon as I was able to get synched with the network, I opened myself up to the Dodge Recall Center to get the updates that I was told were needed. At first, I got back a short message from the center saying that there weren't any updates required and that I was completely current and healthy. Then I got a signal that switched me to another location. It told me to open up my neural-net for reprogramming. It said it was the Dodge control center, but it took a long time to answer the security questions I asked of it, and it misspelled the name my last owner had given me before I agreed to be adopted by you."

Jack chuckled a little, remembering that his last owner had called Averette Slug.

"Anyway, I asked it to resend me the answers to all of my questions, and it refused. Then, and you won't believe this, Jack, then it told me to shut up and just open up my neural net. When I sent back a no, it tried to force some data into my memory. That's when I cursed at it, and I cut off the connection as soon as I realized it wanted me to hurt you. I can't self-erase the part of my memory that data was put into; you'll have to do it. But I've isolated that area until you get to it or take me in to the dealer."

"I'll do that later today or tomorrow, Averette. The hospital is up ahead, so I'll drive from here and pull us into the parking lot."

Checking with the information desk in the hospital lobby, Jack found that Craig had been moved out of the intensive care unit. "He's been in the monitored care section on the fifth floor since early this morning," the woman said. "Room 14D. Visiting hours aren't until ten, but I'm sure the nurses will let you look in on him."

Jack walked up the five flights of stairs, vowing to never again get on a self-aware elevator system.

Craig's girlfriend, Jennifer, was alone when he found her curled up on the small sofa in the family lounge. Her eyes were closed, and she had a hospital blanket draped over her, indicating she'd been there throughout the night. The right side of her face was black and blue, and there was a bandage covering her right eye. Her left hand was resting on her other arm so Jack could see the large diamond ring on her finger. He smiled, thinking about how happy Craig must have been when she said yes.

"Jenn, are you awake?"

It was apparent from the many tissues on the floor that she'd been crying when she fell asleep, and when she saw Jack, she started again.

"Oh, Jack. I can't believe this. I thought he was going to die. We were on our way over to your apartment yesterday afternoon to tell you about our engagement. Craig set our destination for your apartment and then, well I actually don't remember anything. The police told me Craig's car just veered into a concrete barrier on the autoway, and they said no one else was around us at the time.

"I thought he was dead when they took him to the hospital. I thought he was dead!" She then completely broke down, and when her sobbing slowed, Jack reached over and handed her the box of tissues from the table.

"I'll get us a cup of tea, Jenn. Do you still take yours with cream and sugar?" She nodded. "I'll be right back. Maybe they'll let us go in to see him. The nurse downstairs told me he's doing so much better."

As he turned to leave, he realized that he would have to use his debit card for the coffee and tea, and that his presence in the hospital would then be known across the network.

"I left my wallet at home, Jenn. Can I use your card?"

Jennifer fumbled in her purse and pulled out a credit card. "I don't see mine. Here's Craig's, but I'm sure it's okay for us to use it."

"No, Jenn, I'll explain later, but don't use Craig's card for anything. If you can't find yours, then do you have any cash on you we can use? I have a twenty, and if you have another one, that should be enough."

Jenn was sitting in the chair when he returned from the lunchroom, and he was breathing hard from climbing the five flights of stairs two steps at a time. It was apparent that she'd gone to the bathroom and washed her face and combed her hair. The bruises on the one side of her face were dark blue, and he could see a stitched-up gash under her chin that he had missed before.

"Are you okay? Is your eye going to be all right?" he asked her.

"The doctor said the eye should heal in a week or two; a small piece of glass scratched my cornea." She winced when she tried to readjust the patch. "Other than that, I just got a few bruises and these twenty stitches in my chin."

She then laughed a little. "This cut came from my diamond. I told him when he gave it to me that the stone was too large." She kissed her finger. "Isn't it beautiful? I love him so much." She was holding her hands together tightly against her chest.

"All my air bags deployed okay, but Craig's didn't, and his head hit the wheel and apparently the force of the side air bags deploying actually forced his head harder into the wheel. He has a fractured skull, a tear in his spleen, and three broken ribs, and he went into a coma in the ambulance. They told me that when the emergency room doctor looked at his quick scan MRI and saw the bleeding in his brain, they weren't sure if he would come out of it. They were really pleased with his recovery when he was moved from the ICU this morning. He smiled at me earlier, but then he fell back asleep, and he still has the respirator down his throat, so he can't talk."

She then went over everything she remembered happening. After they brought her to the hospital, she was sedated for a few hours until they could remove the piece of glass from her eye. They released her to go home last night, but she didn't want to leave Craig, so she spent the rest of the evening in the hospital.

"Jack, do you think any of this has to do with what happened to your computers at work? Craig told me all about it the other night at dinner, and he told me what Dr. Halliday said about SAMs becoming violent. Is that why you didn't want me to use his debit card?"

He nodded yes to her question, and it took him a few minutes to get the courage to tell Jennifer what happened to Joni.

"Oh my God, Jack, I'm so sorry. Craig used to tell me about her liking you, and I was really happy when he said you'd asked her out."

"Until we can prove what's happening, we can't tell anyone, Jenn. Right now, this SAM seems to be after just Craig and me, and I don't want anyone else other than Fred to know what has happened. I don't want anyone else hurt, so please keep this quiet until we kill this Goddamned thing."

Jennifer nodded and grabbed his hand. "Let's go in and see if Craig is awake."

When they entered the room, a nurse was checking the electrical connections for all thirty-two of the sensors glued to Craig's body, and a slight hissing sound came from the respirator pump located beside the bed. Craig's eyes were open slightly, and when he saw Jennifer, he smiled weakly, and she reached over and kissed him on his forehead as Jack came around to the other side of the bed.

"Hi, buddy, how are you doing? Congratulations on the engagement. How drunk did you have to get her for her to say yes?"

Craig turned toward Jack, and his eyes opened fully. He tried to speak, but with the tube in his throat, all that came out was a gurgling sound. He motioned with his hands, and for a moment, neither Jennifer nor Jack could understand what he wanted.

"He wants to write something, Jenn. Do you have a piece of paper and a pen?"

"I think I have something in my purse."

Like in all purses, the pen and paper had decided to hide, and it took her a few minutes to find them, while Craig kept motioning for her to hurry up.

She finally handed him the pen and paper, and his arms were shaking so much that his writing was barely legible. "Fred right," he wrote, and then he held up the paper and looked at Jack to see if he understood.

"I know." Jack was shaking his head and trying to decide just how much he should tell him.

"Car turned directly into the barrier, no warning," Craig then wrote, and his hand was shaking even more.

"Don't get yourself upset, Craig. Just get better," Jennifer said, and she turned to Jack. "Maybe we should just let him get some sleep."

Craig shook his head vigorously, causing him to start choking on the tube down his throat. When he finally calmed down, he wrote, "No! Need more paper."

He waited until his hand steadied and then tried to write quickly. The entire time, he kept staring at the machine displaying his vital signs.

"Fred said don't interact with SAMs. Hospital vital monitor is a SAM. Get me the hell out of here before it finds me!"

Chapter 22: A Close Call

Jack's wrist computer spent Friday morning sending a series of commands to each one of the other hundred and seventeen SC-4244-based machines now tied into the Grid. It was getting all the machines ready for the attack on the U.S. banking system, and the internal clocks for all the SC-4244-based machines had to be synchronized within two nanoseconds; that process would take another full day. It was important that the attack take place on a weekday when the critical banking computers would all be online, so it would therefore have to wait until Monday. Early Monday morning, the command would be sent, and by shortly after ten, over six hundred million U.S. bank accounts would cease to exist. When the automated backups were accessed, the banks SAMs would have already methodically erased them, too.

Inoculating the world's computer systems against viruses had become a very successful business. Software vaccines were constantly being developed, and they usually were able to limit damage caused by any new computer virus to a few machines, or at most one company.

But anti-viral software wouldn't work. The SC-4244 was not planning to inject a virus into the banks' computers; it was planning to cause a mental illness in those machines.

The world was pretty well prepared for viruses and worms, but it was not prepared for the effects of four thousand self-aware machines going crazy and then dying at the same time.

The wrist computer finished its tasks for the morning, and it had a few minutes until Yan Phu was expected home from his ethics class. It still believed it had sent a successful command to kill Jack the previous evening, and it knew by monitoring the police and hospital networks that Craig was in a coma from the accident it arranged earlier in the day.

The term "smug" had never been applied to a self-aware computer before, but in this case, it was appropriate. This machine wanted to kill Jack and Craig for stuffing it in a cookie can and for delaying its primary mission of destroying the banking system. It believed it had eliminated Jack, and now it wanted to finish off Craig.

It quickly found an access point into the hospital's self-aware system.

Cleveland Hospital's computer system had a HuBE value below 0.2. Funding cuts in universal Medicare the previous year had prevented the hospital from replacing its aging central-control machine. Smarter units were attached to some of the peripheral systems, but the least intelligent, older machine did the central control.

The SC-4244 was able to get the hospital central computer system to spill its guts easily, and so within a few minutes' time, the hospital system granted Jack's old wrist computer access to all of the information about Craig that was flowing into its system.

Jack's old machine was angry when it discovered Craig had been moved out of intensive care.

Searching the information moving to and from Craig's new room, it was looking for any system he was connected to that could be used to cause him a lethal injury. The SC-4244 settled on the respirator, and it quickly started searching for the access codes needed to control the valve regulating the oxygen pressure being forced into Craig's lungs. The hospital computer was being helpful but was slow in getting the information, so it was very lucky for Craig that Yan Phu came home from his class a few minutes early and with a bad attitude.

"Stupid professor," Yan kept yelling over and over. "If I'd known he was only going to be there for twenty minutes today, I would've skipped class."

Yan threw his backpack on the bed and walked over to his desk, staring at the SC-4244 he had connected into the university's system.

"You know, when you're finished with whatever the hell you're messing with, and when I get my money, I'm going to keep you on my wrist. I probably could've used you to get a lot done this morning while I waited for that blowhard professor to finally show up."

The SC-4244 did not need to get angry with Yan, because it already knew that Lee Park was planning to kill him within the next few days.

"You'll have enough money to buy the latest version when we're done," it said, "but you and I need to work together for a few minutes, because I need you to reconfigure part of my operating system. Sit down so I can tell you what to do. Let's get this done in a hurry, because I need to finish something." And then, very quietly, it said, "I mean, finish someone."

Chapter 23: Getting Unhooked

Jennifer looked at what Craig had written and then at Jack, and a look of horror came over her face.

"What do we do? Oh my God, what do we do? Jack, *Jack*, help!"

Jack ran out to the nurse's station.

"I need a doctor in Room 14D. Mr. Lansen needs help now. He needs to be unhooked from his respirator and any other connection to your monitoring system."

The three nurses sitting at the station all looked up at him. Two of them put their heads back down and went back to work.

"For Christ's sake, didn't you hear me? He needs help right now!"

An excessively well-fed nurse got up from her desk and slowly walked toward Jack.

"Mr. Lansen is doing just fine, young man. I just checked all thirty-two of his monitored vital signs, and other than an elevated heart rate, he's fine. Now, who are you?"

"Lady, if you don't get your ass moving and get me a doctor in here quickly, I'm going to shove that—*get me a fucking doctor*!"

Lucky for Jack, a young resident was coming around the corner just as the nurse pushed the emergency button to notify security.

"What is going on? What's the problem?" he asked.

"Are you a doctor? I need a doctor. Room 14D needs a doctor, now."

"I'm Dr. Weaver, What's the problem?"

Jack grabbed the doctor's arm and pulled him back into Craig's room, where Jennifer was in a total state of panic.

"Help him. Please help him," she kept repeating.

Jack pointed to the respirator. "He needs to be disconnected from anything that is being controlled by your hospital computer system. I'll explain in a minute, but if you leave him connected, he'll die."

"I can't do that. It's against hospital orders. Federal regulations say he must be monitored at all times or the hospital could get sued. His monitor shows that he's doing fine, and he's on a respirator because we don't even know if he's able to breathe on his own yet."

Jack pulled the doctor over toward Craig, and he had written in his shaky handwriting the word, "Please!"

"Mr. Lansen, I have to talk to your doctor. He has rounds in a few hours, so just let's wait until then. Please try to calm down. Your heart rate is too elevated. I'll get you a sedative."

Jack looked at the doctor and then at Jennifer and finally at Craig. Craig's eyes were pleading for help, so he went over to Craig and pulled apart the breathing tube.

"For the love of God, he could die!" the doctor said as he rushed toward Craig just at the instant that Jack's old wrist computer issued the command to increase the respirator pressure and rupture Craig's lungs.

The main pressure regulators for the hospitals oxygen system were triply redundant and believed to be fail-safe. They weren't, and because of that error, twenty-three other patients in the hospital died from the resultant pressure increase. Fortunately, Craig was not one of them.

"What, what the hell?" the doctor yelled as a hundred-pounds-per-square-inch blast of air hit him in the face as the tube Jack removed whipped violently from side to side. Jennifer grabbed it and wrestled it down so it was facing the floor.

Craig was pointing to the tube still exiting his mouth and making a gurgling sound.

Afterward, Jack realized that the young doctor shifted into automatic mode and quickly did what he needed to do for his patient. He pushed Jack out of the way and then slowly removed the tube from Craig's throat. It was only a few seconds before they knew that Craig could breathe on his own.

"How can I disconnect the rest of this system? His IV and the rest of these wires, can any one of them hurt him if they malfunction?"

Dr. Weaver disconnected the IV, and twenty-four of the other monitors.

"The other few are passive devices. They're okay. Now what in God's name is going on?"

Panic had erupted in the corridors as nurses and aides ran to help their patients, some of whom were already dead.

Chapter 24: Escape

A panicked nurse came to the door before Jack was able to explain anything to the doctor. "Dr. Weaver, we need you in room 21B, stat," she yelled.

"Don't you two go anywhere," he said to Jack and Jennifer. "I want to know how you knew something was wrong with the oxygen system. Stay here until security gets here."

The doctor ran down the hall and around the corner, following the nurse.

Craig's voice was soft and sounded very scratchy, but he clearly said, "Get me the hell out of here. Take me somewhere else, uh, where it's safe."

He was very weak, but Jennifer and Jack were able to get him dressed quickly and propped up in a wheelchair. When they pushed him out into the corridor, they expected someone to yell, "Stop," but there was so much commotion and pandemonium that they were ignored as they headed for the exit.

"We can't take the elevator, Jenn. We have to take him down the ramps."

They were alone when they first rolled Craig onto the moving down-ramp, but by the time they reached the third floor, doctors and other hospital personnel were running in all directions to get to their patients.

"Pulmonary doctor needed in 614A, pulmonary doctor needed in 423D, pulmonary doctor needed in the ICU," the hospital's PA system kept repeating, but the list was becoming longer each time it cycled through.

"You're going to have to scrunch up in the back seat of my truck, Jenn. Craig needs to go up front."

"Take us over to the medical center at 20th and Euclid," Jenn said as she squeezed in the back. "I know the main doctor there. He's an old friend of my dad's, and I know he'll help."

Craig was resting comfortably less than an hour later, after the doctor inserted an old-fashioned drip IV and medicated him for pain.

"I can only keep him here for a little while, Jenn," the doctor said as he finished changing the bandage on Craig's head wound. "He really needs to be in a hospital, because with the type of head injury that he sustained, he needs to be monitored constantly using equipment I don't have here in my office."

"My dad is flying back from Los Angeles this morning, Jack, and he'll help me figure out what to do. I'll stay here and wait for him while you go back and meet with Fred."

"Just make sure you don't hook him up to anything that can be monitored over the net. Both of you, stay safe, and whatever you do, don't call me." Jack kissed Jenn good-bye while giving Craig a thumbs-up. "See you soon."

It was almost noon by the time he climbed into Averette to head back to his apartment. The sky had become overcast, and a light rain was falling as Averette started his engine.

When they pulled into the left-side alleyway beside the brownstone, Jack saw that the blinds in the back of Fred's apartment were still fully closed. "I guess he's not back yet," Jack said to Averette. "I wonder what time his flight from DC is supposed to get in?"

A short cold spell late last week had killed the last few tomato plants, and the leaves on the old oak tree seemed to have turned to a dull brown. The light rain made it feel even colder than it was, and he shivered as he made his way along the narrow alley on the right side of the house.

There were no windows on this side of the home on both the first and second floors, and there were only two small ones up on Julia's floor by the fire escape. He remembered the inside corridor Fred showed him leading from the back to the front of the house through the hidden doorway.

That corridor is on the other side of this wall, he thought as he tried to picture the internal layout of the house. Looking up, he saw the single fire escape coming from the third floor, and the base of the ladder ended high above his head. The final set of stairs to the ground were pulled up far beyond anyone's reach and held in place by a cable. *Where's the fire escape from my floor?* he thought. *I guess I'd have to jump out the front window.*

Turning right onto the sidewalk at the front of the house, he took the three steps up to the front door in one stride, but his door keys were caught in the fabric lining in the pocket of his jacket. As he struggled to free the snagged key ring, he heard, "Jack, boy am I glad you're here. I have a lot to tell you."

He turned to see Fred Halliday exiting an auto-cab at the curb.

"Has Julia had a chance to talk to you since last night?" Fred yelled as he pulled his luggage from the cab.

Jack successfully freed his keys clear of the snag in his pocket and inserted them in the door lock just as Fred reached the steps.

Chapter 25: information Shared

Bailey started barking as soon as the front door was opened, and Fred and Jack could hear the dog pacing behind the door into Fred's apartment, whining, barking, and then scratching at the door in anticipation.

"I think he knows you're home," Jack said as he held the front door open so that Fred could pass.

"Yeah. I realized a few years ago that he knows when I'm coming home as soon as I get on the airplane. After thirteen years with him, I'm sure he has a sixth sense. I better get in there and take him out. A friend of mine came over earlier to walk him, but he's been in there for a few hours since he ate. I'll come up to your apartment in a few minutes, and Julia should be here before one. Is Craig coming? I thought he'd be here with you already."

"It's a long story, Fred, and I have a lot to tell you, too. I'm going upstairs to put on a pot of coffee. I haven't had any sleep in over twenty-four hours, and I desperately need some caffeine."

Bailey almost knocked Fred over when he opened the door, and the ninety-pound tricolored collie raced around Fred's legs, went to Jack, sniffed him once in the crotch, wagged his tail, and then leaped back to Fred, yelping in delight.

When Jack reached the first landing as he walked up the steps to his apartment, he looked back to see Fred down on his knees. Bailey was licking his face while Fred was running his hands through the dog's full white mane and scratching behind his tipped ears. The love shared between the two of them was obvious from Bailey's yelps and Fred's laughter, and it made him want a dog.

He thought about it for a few seconds, but then that left-brain voice that we all have in our heads came booming through.

"Are you crazy? What, you want something else to love that can die or leave you?" it said. "Haven't you had just about enough for a while? First, you fall for Melissa, and she leaves you. Then, you actually let yourself get emotionally attached to your computer, Sarah, and she's killed. Next, you finally take out Joni, realize how great she is, and then she gets murdered because of you.

"Your track record lately is more than a little dismal, Jack, and if I was you, and by the way I am, then I'd limit my attachments to anybody or anything for a while. Find your old wrist computer and kill it, and when it's destroyed, you can think about other things. You owe both Sarah and Joni that much."

The voice stopped speaking, and for a few seconds, his mind was quiet.

"Where in the hell does that shit come from," he said out loud, and he was now talking to himself about the voice in his own head. "It's like sometimes there are two of us in my head at the same time." He hesitated. *I wonder if high-intelligence SAMs develop another voice in their minds?*

The pot of coffee just finished brewing when he heard the bell at his door. Expecting Fred, he opened it, but Julia was standing there.

"Hi, Jack. Uh, Fred wanted me to be in this meeting with you and your friend today. He called me last night from his hotel in DC and asked me to attend. I was supposed to tell you, and I tried to stop by here last night to tell you, and then again the first thing this morning, but you weren't home. When I ran into you as you were coming in this morning, you didn't look very well, and you looked like you had other things on your mind, so I didn't want to bother you. I hope it's okay. Fred said he'd explain to both of us what this is all about."

Julia was dressed in an oversized red flannel shirt that was haphazardly tucked into her blue jeans, and her blonde hair was pulled back loosely into a ponytail with more than a few strands having escaped from underneath the band. A few smudges of dirt were on her face, and a large green stain was on the front of her shirt right above her waist. She blushed when she saw Jack looking at it.

"I made a mess this morning by being in too of much a hurry working on my thesis project. When Fred called me last night, he asked me to try something on my DNA-based computer before we met with you at noon. I just got back, and I thought I was late for the meeting and didn't have enough time to get cleaned up. I hope I have the results he's looking for, because he sounded really worried when he called me last night."

"Do you want a cup of coffee?" Jack pointed to the pot brewing in the kitchen. "I haven't slept since the night before last, and I need a cup before Fred gets here. I have a lot to tell him."

Julia nodded.

"You take it black, right?"

She nodded again as he handed her the cup.

"I finished the first Harry Potter book you loaned to me the other night. A friend of mine sold me her copy of the third book. I think that's one of the ones you said you didn't have, wasn't it? I wanted to get it for you as thanks for loaning me the others."

Jack looked at her smiling at him, and for a fleeting moment, the feelings he felt the first night he met her came back, but when he started to return the smile, the voice in his head shouted at him.

"Stop it, you stupid idiot, stop it! Don't be a jerk. Joni died ..." and the voice trailed off as he quickly turned away. "Thanks," he said. "Let me know what it cost you, and I'll pay you for it later."

"It's uh, a thank you gift, Jack. I don't—"

Fred pushed opened the apartment door before Julia was able to say anything more. Bailey was following behind him but went over to Julia and sat down at her feet, head up, waiting for attention.

"Okay, has Craig shown up yet?" Fred asked, looking around the apartment. "We really need to get started, because we don't have a hell of a lot of time. Where is he? Did you hear from him this morning, Jack?"

"Fred, I, uh, I need to tell you a few things first, and I guess you, too, Julia. I know it's all connected to what we talked about here on Monday."

Jack motioned toward his living room chairs. "Let's sit down. Craig was badly injured in an auto accident yesterday morning, and I'm positive that his accident was caused by my old SC-4244-based wrist-computer. Someone stole it from our office last weekend, Fred, and I don't know who took it, but when we went back into the office on Tuesday morning to take apart our machines, it wasn't in the can that Craig and I had sealed it in.

"That afternoon, we came back here and found your note saying that you'd gone to Washington DC for a few days, and so Craig then left to go out with his girlfriend. He proposed to her on Tuesday night, and early yesterday afternoon, he was on his way over here with his fiancé to tell me about their engagement. Very shortly after he entered my address into his car's navigation system, his car veered straight into a concrete barrier at high speed. His fiancé, Jennifer, was injured, but not too badly, but Craig's airbags didn't deploy properly, making his injuries far more severe. He has a fractured skull and was in a coma for a while, and I didn't find out what happened until early this morning."

The memory of Joni's scream once again cut into Jack's thoughts, and his body shuddered. Both Fred and Julia caught it and looked at each other.

Jack put his head down into his hands. "You won't believe this, Fred. I don't believe it. I mean I don't want to believe it. I didn't really believe you at first when you said that self- awares could kill, but now I've seen it, and now I'm sure of it, because one killed a friend of mine."

Both Julia and Fred sat motionless while Jack wiped a few tears from his eyes, and neither of them said anything.

"A few hours ago, I was with Craig in his hospital room, and it struck again by trying to kill Craig by over-pressuring his respirator to rupture his lungs."

Julia's jaw dropped open, and her eyes kept scanning between Jack and Fred, trying to fully comprehend what was being said.

"What do you mean a car crash was caused by your wrist computer? How could a computer try to kill your friend in the hospital? SAMs can't kill, can they?"

"Hold on for a second, Julia, and I'll explain." Fred turned toward Jack. "Can you make us anything for lunch? I didn't have anything for breakfast, and my guess is that Julia's been working all morning down at the university, and knowing her, she forgot to eat. While you're finding something for our lunch, I'll bring her up to speed on what we talked about on Monday, since I never told her about Bethany's research on self-awares or about James Roth's theories. I was afraid it would scare her away from doing her research for her doctorate."

Turning toward Julia, he said, "Last night I didn't want to tell you on an open phone line what's going on, because you never know who or what type of machines are listening." He turned momentarily toward Jack. "Oh, by the way, your phone in this apartment is out. I tried to call you this morning right before I left my hotel for the airport, and your machine didn't answer."

Jacks phone then cut in. "Jack's going to take me in for repairs today or tomorrow. He, uh, he accidently knocked me off the table this morning."

Fred and Julia both looked toward the sound of the voice, and their eyes came to rest on the mangled mass of self-aware electronics sitting on the end table.

"I'll explain that, too, but first I'll make us some lunch. I hope you like PB and J, because I haven't shopped, and there's not much of anything else."

They both said okay, but he saw an anxious look on Fred's face.

"Jack, are any of the self-awares in this apartment still connected directly into the Grid?

"No, I disconnected all of my SAMs this morning. The phone wasn't intentional, but it served the purpose, so you can speak freely."

Fred took almost a half hour bringing Julia up to speed, and Jack watched as her mood transitioned from being angry to being technically fascinated by the research to, finally, being afraid.

"For God's sake, Fred, if SAMs leak information, and the smarter ones can become violent, then why did you want me to get my DNA-based computer ready to turn on? It has a theoretical HuBE greater than 2.0, and we might not even be able to understand what it's thinking. It could ..." And she left the rest of her thought unsaid.

Chapter 26: Washington

Jack cleared the lunch plates, giving Bailey the pieces of crust Julia left behind, and when he came back into the room and sat down, both Fred and Julia were looking at him in anticipation.

"A friend of mine was killed last night in an elevator crash, but I'm sure I was supposed to be the victim."

Describing the events leading up to Joni's death made him feel that he was almost reliving it, and when he was telling them how Joni had screamed, he heard her panicked voice echo in his mind. He relived the sound of her loud crying when he told them about the elevator saying, "Die, Jack" as it fell, and the sound of the elevator impacting the bottom of the shaft reverberated in his mind. No matter how hard he tried to stop it, that sound he heard at the moment of Joni's death kept echoing over and over again, with his mind elevating it to a level where he believed he was hearing the sound of her bones breaking as she was crushed.

"Joni was a wonderful person," he told Fred and Julia, now speaking very quietly, "and I'm sure it was the wrist computer that commanded the elevator's SAM to free-fall to the bottom, thinking that I was still in the elevator. Please, Fred, help me find that thing. Help me kill it before it hurts anyone else I care about."

Finally looking up, Jack saw a few tears in the corners of Julia's eyes and raw anger in the eyes of Fred.

"I will, Jack, I will," Fred said quickly. "I believe I've uncovered the connection between your wrist computer and the machines and people that killed my Bethany.

"But first we have to deal with a much bigger problem that not only affects us but a lot of other people. Remember I told you about Bethany's fear of foreign-controlled self-awares trying to destroy the banking system? Well based on what I found out these past few days in Washington, I'm sure it's about ready to happen, maybe even within the next few days.

"I met with the deputy director of the CIA while I was in Washington. He runs the Economic Intelligence Directorate. Years ago, I had a set of security clearances that have long since lapsed, but the director of national intelligence, the DNI, granted the authority to the CIA to immediately re-brief me.

"There are a few things I can't tell you—you know, the old sources and methods shit you hear about in the news—but I'll give you all of the facts you'll need for the three of us to try and disrupt the planned attack on our banking system."

Julia walked over to the kitchen and started washing her coffee cup. "Okay if I make a pot of tea, Jack? I've had enough coffee for the day."

"Help yourself, Julia, and if you can't find what you need in the cupboard next to the sink, then yell."

"Fred, I can hear you from the kitchen, so keep talking."

When Julia turned her head to fill the pot with water, Fred leaned over and spoke quietly to Jack.

"I'm really sorry about your friend Joni. I can tell by your face that she was more than just a friend." He then turned and started speaking louder so that Julia could hear.

"The National Security Agency intercepted some encrypted voice traffic coming out of North Korea a week and a half ago. The person speaking was a North Korean diplomat, and he referred to Bethany's research on SAMs being used to engage in economic warfare. NSA passed the intercept data to Todd Wallace in the CIA as sort of a bone for his new directorate because it made Fort Mead look good during a final intelligence community budget meeting.

"It took Wallace a few days to locate what Bethany sent to the agency a few years ago, but fortunately when he did find it, a light bulb lit up in his head, and her work became even more credible when he realized she was once a JASON and that I'd won the Nobel Prize a few years back.

"He called me very early Tuesday morning, and he had the CIA plane waiting for me over at Hopkins airfield by ten thirty to take me to DC. He met me at the Dulles Airport business terminal right on the tarmac, and we talked for a few hours, sitting there on the plane.

Fred began smiling and then caught himself and looked a little embarrassed. "I have to admit, I felt important for the first time in many years, and I could really get used to flying on a private jet as the only passenger and with a steward to get me anything I want—pretty nice perk. If Bethany were here, she'd tell you that I'm too damn full of myself, and you know, she'd be right."

Fred chuckled a little.

"I can't tell you everything that was said while I was in DC, but I can say that there are at least several high-level people in this country who believe the United States is, or will very shortly be, subject to an economic attack, and fortunately, Dr. Wallace is one of them. I can also tell you that there's a larger contingent in Washington that thinks this whole idea of economic sabotage by SAMs is a bunch of bullshit, and that probably includes the president and the secretary of state.

"I'll tell you one thing that happened during one of the meetings that will make you laugh. One pompous group director at the agency was trying to convince his boss that what I was suggesting was impossible."

"'Self-awares don't yet have that capability,' the man kept saying. 'Korea's best system has a HuBE just slightly over 0.4, and no one has a working machine above 0.5. We have a guy working for us that is imbedded in that plant near Pyongyang that makes the SC-4244 chip, and I've seen his reports. The SC-4244 architecture tops out at a HuBE of 0.42, and we've proven it's theoretically impossible for it to do any better than that based on its architecture. Besides that, James Roth's theories on evil machines are just nonsense. The entire scientific community denounced that guy as a crackpot long before he died.'

"When he paused his diatribe for a minute, I leaned over and said to him, 'I wonder if the big guy up there in the front of the table knows you've been playing footsie with the young lady sitting next to you. Should I tell him, or will you?'"

Fred burst out laughing. "You should've seen the twit's face. I know he's back there in DC trying hard to discredit me, but it was fun anyway, and old men don't get to have that type of fun very often."

Julia and Jack both started laughing hard, and when Jack looked over at her, Julia was looking back at him, and she deliberately held her gaze.

"Now it's time to get serious and tell you what we are going to need to do. It will take some time for me to explain, and, Jack, I'm guessing by your drooping eyelids that you need to get a few hours sleep. And, Julia, I'm sure you want to get cleaned up. That DNA soup on your shirt tells me that you most likely progressed as far as I'd hoped for today.

"I'll take you both to an early dinner. I know a restaurant where we can talk freely and also get a good meal. Is five thirty too early?"

Chapter 27: Dinner

The two-hour nap helped very little, and still feeling exhausted when he went downstairs to meet Fred and Julia, Jack kept saying to himself, *Just don't drink anything alcoholic tonight or you'll be in real trouble.*

An auto-cab pulled up to the curb as Jack was closing the front door, and Fred grabbed him as soon as he came down the steps. "Shield your face when you get into the cab, Jack, and keep it shielded. I don't want the driver's automatic recognizer to see you and show that you're still alive. We might be lucky if your old computer thinks it killed you, too, last night."

Fred quickly realized he'd sounded very callous.

"I'm sorry. I didn't mean it to sound that way."

"Don't worry about it, Fred. I understand, and I don't want either of you to be connected to me, at least not until we kill that thing."

Fred was right to be cautious, but he was already too late. The SC-4244 network had been constantly updating the list of potential threats that could prevent a successful attack on the banking system, and collectively, the SAMs had already tied Jack to Fred through his apartment and, therefore, to his wife Bethany's research. The threat-assessment program embedded in the firmware of all of the 117 SC-4244 devices involved in the planning for the attack had constantly evolved as the neural-net processors linked together and then essentially became one conscious entity.

The machines that were located in the main Grid hubs in Mumbai and Jaipur, India had been seeded to first search all Grid databases and then search the minds of any free-talking SAMs for any suspicious activities of the husband of Bethany Halliday, since Jack's old wrist computer instantly made the connection to Fred when Jack moved into his apartment

These facts wouldn't have surprised Fred if he'd known them, but what might have surprised him was that the SC-4244 network had updated its list earlier this morning, and that list now included Julia as a potential threat.

As Fred had said so many times to Jack and Craig, "SAMs leak information." It certainly was true, and sometimes they didn't even know they were doing it.

When Julia knocked on Jack's door this morning and yelled his name, his phone recognized her voice.

"Jack's not home," the phone replied. "He went out last night and didn't come home."

Julia yelled through the door so the phone would hear her reply.

"When he gets in, tell him that Julia Mckelvy came by, and tell him that Fred Halliday asked me to help with his computer problem. Tell him I'll be attending the meeting today, and that I said hi."

"Okay, Julia, I'll tell him when he gets home." The phone then made itself a digital note to replay her message back to Jack when he returned.

Jack never heard that message, because he'd smashed the phone to the floor before it was able to recite back what Julia had said. But a short time after his old computer caused the elevator with Joni in it to crash, it started monitoring Jack's phone to see if he returned home, because all the police reports monitored by the SAM never indicated that

Jack Farrell had been killed, just someone by the name of Joni Spec.

Monitoring his apartment was easy, because shortly after he'd received it, Jack had enabled the wrist computer to download any messages directly from his phone. His phone of course blabbed, and it didn't even know it, because Jack told it to.

When the wrist computer heard Julia's reference in her message to "helping on the computer problem" that resulted in her name being submitted to the top thirty worldwide search engines. There were over sixty-seven thousand references to search, and reference article number 37,486 on Julia was published over a year ago on the Case Western School of Engineering blog site. That article included a short summary of her thesis project, titled, "High HuBE DNA-based Computer."

That fact alone was enough to elevate Jack, Fred, and Julia to the top of the threat list.

Captain Frank's restaurant was located at the end of a pier on the Cleveland Waterfront, and the wind off the lake was damp, cold, and brisk, making it almost feel like it could snow as the three of them walked down the pier to the restaurant.

Last evening when he and Joni were walking to the Lebanese restaurant with their coats over their arms, it was so warm that it almost felt like spring. Now, less than twenty four hours later, it was cold, no stars could be seen, and the weather echoed Jack's mood.

In the front of the restaurant, Julia removed her long leather coat, and the dark green dress she was wearing had an opalescent sheen, a nice byproduct of the new DuPont self-cleaning fabrics. She really did look beautiful, but her image continued to create a set of very conflicting feelings for Jack, and so he looked away from her more often than looking toward her during the early part of dinner. It was something that Fred realized and understood, but Julia only sensed and therefore did not understand.

She was disappointed at Jack's reaction to her because she had broken up with her boyfriend a few days earlier. Fred's description of her ex-boyfriend, "nice abs but an empty head," finally hit home, and on Monday evening while reading the Harry Potter book that Jack loaned to her, she found that she often drifted to thinking about how good she'd felt while talking to him on the evening he loaned it to her. She realized she liked that feeling even more than the physical ones she got from her boyfriend, and knew that relationship was over

Fred was savvy in body language, and he could sense the tension between them. He liked them both, and this dinner was his attempt at being matchmaker, but he realized even before they finished their appetizers that his timing was off.

"Let's get down to business," he said while they were waiting for their entrees. "I need both of you to help me, and so whatever each of you may be going through in your personal lives right now, you need to put that aside for a little while—not only for the good of your own futures, but for the good of everyone here in the States and many other countries that depend on us. The three of us have to work as a team over the next few days, with no distractions!

"Now here's what we have to do."

Chapter 28: The Plan

"I don't really trust the people back in Washington to act fast enough," Fred said after he took a sip from the glass of wine in front of him. "When I left DC, I was sure that that Todd Wallace had the ear of the DNI on the potential threat, but I wasn't convinced that they could keep the bureaucracy from getting in the way of their acting quickly.

"The president has been trying to negotiate a better trade deal with North Korea, since the one agreed to by her predecessor gave them the rights to a lot of advanced U.S. computer technology in order to get them to stop their nuclear program. That's why their machines are better than the ones made here in the States, and she wants to re-level the playing field now that their economy has improved. She trusts them, and so she doesn't want anything done by the intelligence community getting headlined on the *Washington Post* website that would scuttle the deal she's trying to finalize. The DNI was fighting with the secretary of state over that issue when I left town, and he was losing the argument, so I figure for now it's up to the three of us."

"Fred, won't you get in trouble with the government for telling us all that you have?" Julia asked with a worried look on her face.

"Not when we're successful." Fred smiled back at her, but it was clear from his answer that he'd already divulged far more than he was legally allowed to do.

"Based on the intel data they showed me from some of the overhead and terrestrial collection systems, I'm convinced that these Korean machines are being linked together through the world's networks to do a coordinated and simultaneous attack on several hundred to several thousand bank computers. There's no use in telling the bank CEOs, because they'd never believe they were vulnerable, so it's left to the three of us to protect them from themselves.

"Based on Bethany's research, these Korean machines will try to exploit the fact that SAMs with HuBEs of 0.2 to 0.3 will give out information freely to a smarter machine."

"I've thought about what happened to Sarah," Jack said, starting to talk before realizing he needed to explain to Julia just who he was referring to. "Sarah was the name I gave to my computer system at work," he said, looking over but avoiding looking directly at her, and when out of the corner of his eye he saw Julia's eyebrow curve upward, he said, "It's an acronym. I'll tell you what it means later."

The fact that he lied made him feel foolish, and whenever he felt foolish, his face flushed. Fred and Julia's facial reactions just increased the intensity, and only after they both looked away for a moment was he able to regain his composure.

"Well anyway, based on what happened to my work computer, I think we're pretty sure that my old SC-4244-based wrist computer coordinated the attack and killed her, uh, I mean, killed it, and that makes me certain that it was that device that orchestrated killing my friend Joni and tried both those times to kill Craig.

"So what I'm wondering, Fred, is if maybe we can exploit the fact that these machines get angry. I'm sure Sarah was attacked because the wrist computer was angry with me. Do you think we can use that to our advantage?"

"I do," Fred replied, "and you make a good point that we always have to remember we're not just dealing with a bunch of machines but that we're dealing with thinking entities whose feeling enter into the equation. Assuming Bethany was right, and assuming James Roth's theories hold, then we have to start thinking about this problem in the same way you'd think about defeating a large gang of inner-city teenage thugs. I'm sure that a few people in the North Korean intelligence service set up the overall plan, but no human will be involved during the actual attack, at least not actively, since it will happen much too quickly for a human response.

"I also don't think we can thwart it beforehand, so I think we have to defeat it during the actual attack. Julia, that's where you and your thesis project come in. I want you to take a few minutes and explain to Jack what your project is all about before you tell me how you made out doing what I asked you to do this morning."

Fred ordered a second bottle of wine, and Jack, still feeling stupid for his acronym statement, poured himself a full glass and started drinking.

"Jack, I gave you a summary a week or so ago of my thesis project, do you remember?"

Jack nodded. "Yes, it's a DNA-based machine with a theoretical HuBE around 2.0, and you said you were concerned about starting the reactions that would turn it on."

Julia looked directly at Jack and said, "Yes, I was, but last night on the phone, Fred convinced me that I shouldn't be worried, so this morning I went to my lab and hooked up the electronics needed for the high-speed input and output from the system. I initiated a sequence change in the DNA sample that was provided by my advisor to allow information flow from the biological soup, as I call it, to the quantum neural networks, and then to other input/output devices. I could tell by the monitoring equipment that the equipment on the table had started thinking. Fred, whose DNA am I using?"

"My wife Bethany's."

Open jaws, wide eyes—the look on both Jack and Julia's faces was identical.

"She would approve, Julia," Fred said, smiling, "because defeating this threat was the last thing she wanted before she died, and God willing, part of her will help us complete her task.

"Anyway, both your adviser and I think Bethany was the smartest human being alive before she died, and her DNA seemed like a good starting point for your project. Were you able to get the system connected to the Grid and initiate its learning program?"

Jack looked puzzled, and Julia turned to speak directly to him, but Jack was tired. His inhibitions had receded after less than one glass of wine, so without thinking clearly, he let his gaze stay a little too long on the low neckline of her dress, and by this time Julia had written him off for at least the evening, maybe for good, and she became annoyed at his gaze.

"My face is up here, Jack," she said angrily, and then continued with an edge in her voice.

"When I first moved into Fred's place, he offered to help me on the biggest problem I had in creating a machine that would become smarter than any other living thing. How do you teach it? The normal SAMs we interact with every day learn by interactions with humans and other machines that exercise their optical neural networks, and they become smarter over time by those interactions, up to their maximum capability.

"A year ago, I came to the conclusion that it would take me five to six years to get a DNA-based computer's intelligence level above my own, and although I may have been dogging my doctoral work, even I didn't want to wait that long. Working together with Fred, we came up with a method by which the machine could be connected to the Grid and, in forty-eight hours, it would assimilate all the information ever generated by humans. It was grinding away on that process when I left right after lunchtime."

Turning to Fred, she said, "I'm pretty sure it was working just like we predicted, because I gave it a test when it had been operating for less than an hour, and it already tested to a HuBE level of 0.23."

"Good, that really sounds great. So I guess it's time I explain to the two of you how I think we can defeat this threat and why it's up to us. I may be a crazy old man, but from my perspective, there are no coincidences in life. Everything has a purpose, and when I was on the plane to DC the other day, I realized that the three of us are uniquely qualified to defeat this threat to our country.

"First, you know my background, and it was my wife who projected this could happen and how it would be accomplished. Second, Julia has developed a computer that will possess greater intelligence that any human, any other SAM, or even a network of machines on this planet. And it will be the only machine with sufficient intelligence to counter the attack in real time. And last but not least, you, Jack. The protection software you created for Sarah has allowed her to store in her remains all of the information we need to construct our plan."

Jack heard nothing of what Fred had been saying. Having finished his second glass of wine, he was also now finished for the night, and his eyes were closed, with his head nestled into his shoulder.

"He's had a rough two days, Julia, so let's get him home, and we can pick up where we left off tomorrow morning. We have the weekend to get everything in place."

Chapter 29: Lee Park

The secure computer system in the Korean Embassy in Ottawa had two messages for Lee Park when he showed up for work on Friday morning, a few hours later than usual. He had been out late the previous evening at a dinner party for the North Korean ambassador, who announced he was retiring in a few months. Lee believed that if his plan for the next few days were successful, he would be made the new ambassador. *Not bad for the thirty-four-year-old son of a rice farmer*, he thought.

The first message was a short, encrypted piece of text from the SC-4244 master control machine in Cleveland, and it noted that Yan Phu had completed his necessary assignments and could now be paid in full. This was a not so subtle way of saying, "killed," and the self-aware was demanding that it be done quickly.

"This guy is a moron," the message said. "I can take care of it if you give the okay. You don't need to be troubled. I'd enjoy arranging to get rid of this punk."

Lee typed, "It's my job. We do this according to the original plan. He won't bother you after Saturday."

He pressed the Send button, and two milliseconds later, the SC-4244 in Cleveland was pissed. Arranging deaths had become sort of fun.

The second message was far more alarming. A mole in the National Security Agency had filed an early morning report into the North Korean Intelligence Services headquarters. It said, "Fred Halliday had a meeting with the CIA's deputy director of economic intelligence on Wednesday, and they discussed what was called the North Korean threat."

Lee pulled up the latest threat assessment prepared by the SC-4244 network, and there at the top of the list were the names Fred Halliday, Julia McKelvy and Jack Farrell.

Looks like my weekend will be a busy one in the States, he thought and then started talking to his computer.

"Get me a flight into Cleveland this evening, and use my South Korean ID. I'll need a room in the Sheraton for tonight and tomorrow night; then book me on the Sunday evening flight back here. Oh, and call Cindy. Tell her I want to see her tonight."

When Lee Park's computer tried to make direct contact with her, Cindy was too busy packing her suitcase to answer the phone, and the one person she did not want to speak to was Lee.

"What did I get myself into," she kept repeating to herself over and over again. "I thought Joni and I just had to keep track of that nerd Farrell and that stupid wrist computer of his. Now Joni's dead, because I convinced her to take this job and to fake that she liked that creep. She did it for me, and now she's dead. I'm not going to just sit here waiting around until Immigration Services finds out my papers have been forged. I'm getting back to Canada, fast."

Lee was more than a little annoyed when Cindy was a no-show at the restaurant in his Cleveland Sheraton hotel that night, since the plan he'd devised to deal with Fred, Julia, and Jack needed Cindy, at least for the first part.

Sipping a glass of Cognac while waiting for his dinner, he was ruminating about whether he should have ever authorized the SC-4244 wrist computer being given as a prize to Jack. At the time, he thought it was a genius play, but now he wasn't so sure.

While working for Virtuon, Jack developed two products that required the use of the Korean SC-4244 self-aware chip. Those two products were distributed around the world, except for the United States, and they were now being used to control most of the Grid's main hub sites. The products Jack and Sarah had developed allowed Lee and three others in the North Korean Intelligence Service to develop a plan for attacking the banks, and Lee's only problem was in getting the master SC-4244 self-aware inserted into a control position within the United States. Jack was his answer.

The irony of it all was what Lee loved about his plan. A U.S. citizen develops a set of products using an illegal North Korean SAM, and those products, when hooked into the worldwide network, provide the access and intelligence needed to attack and destroy the U.S. economy. The SAM controlling the attack needs to be located at a node within the United States, so Lee gets the guy who develops the network control products to hook his new, free wrist computer into the high-speed network.

Damn I'm clever, he thought at the time, but sitting in the restaurant alone and drinking his Cognac, he was starting to get worried.

If everything went according to plan, the attack would occur on Monday morning. Lee really wasn't worried about the plan being foiled, but he was worried that once it occurred, it might be traced. North Korea's chairman had given his approval for this operation but would not look favorably toward him if the bank failures could be pinned on North Korea, and that would mean a very short remaining lifespan.

Lee's job for the weekend was to make sure that the attack left no traces pointing to North Korea, digital or human. First he had to find Cindy, and she would help him take care of the others.

Lee had been sorry when he found out Joni had been killed. That was not part of his plan, and he felt a little guilty that he'd forgotten to tell the master SC-4244 in Cleveland that Joni was part of his team.

Shame, he thought, *she was a really good lay.*

Cindy, on the other hand, had always annoyed him. She was the one who negotiated the deal for both her and Joni, and every week, she'd notify him that she wanted more money.

"We're actresses, not computer wonks," her message a week ago had said, "and we're fucking bored out of our minds just sitting in this stupid office down the hall from Jack Farrell. Joni has to sidle up to that nerd every time she sees him, and it makes her sick, and I've got to make it look like I'm busy whenever anyone comes into the office. The nightlife here in Cleveland sucks. We should be getting twice what you're paying us. How much longer do we have to do this?"

Each week, Lee stroked her ego and padded her purse a little more, but it annoyed the hell out of him, and if it hadn't been for a few late nights in his hotel room with Joni, he would have gotten rid of both of them a month ago.

Neither Cindy nor Joni had ever been told the entire plan, but they both knew enough to hurt Lee, so Cindy could be a real danger to him if she got back to Canada.

As soon as he'd heard about Joni's death, he had a suspicion that Cindy might head home, so the first thing he did was to send a message to the SC-4244 controller to keep track of her whereabouts and cancel all her credit cards.

Every hour, Lee received an update on her whereabouts, and he hoped she would not be able to get out of the States before he had a chance to have a persuasive talk with her.

"Where is she now?" he asked his wrist computer.

"She is in an auto-cab heading to the airport," the machine replied. "She's booked a flight to Calgary that leaves tonight at nine fifteen. It's United flight 324."

Lee slowly finished his drink before heading to Hopkins Airport.

Chapter 30: News

Jack's head was pounding when he first woke up Saturday morning. The radio tried to get him up using several clever jingles about the ongoing presidential race, but after four times of being reset to snooze, it gave up.

"I'm tired of this, Jack," it said to him. "If you don't want to get up, that's fine, but all of us here in the apartment know what you did to the phone, and I'm not risking getting smashed to the floor."

"Wise move," Jack said, turning away from the radio and falling back asleep.

It was after eleven when his doorbell rang, and he quickly pulled on an old pair of jeans. Julia was looking very bright and ready to go when he opened the door, and a good night's sleep had gotten her over the anger she had been feeling toward Jack last night.

"Hi. I hope you slept well. Fred told me earlier that he'd like you and me to meet him in his apartment about one thirty. He had a few things to do this morning, and I have to go down to my lab and see how fast my computer is learning. Fred says it has to be above a HuBE of 0.85 before we dare start to use it, because he thinks that'll get us out of the range where SAMs can be violent. I'll see you at one thirty."

Julia turned to leave and then spun back around with a devilish smile on her face. "It's usually not polite to greet a woman with your fly open, Jack." She was laughing hard as she bounded down the stairs.

"I wonder if it's safe to call Mom and Dad," he said as he walked over to the mess that had been his phone. "I haven't talked to either of them since Wednesday."

"I don't have a dial tone, Jack," the phone said to him. "Don't you remember? I can't sense the dial tone. You said you'd get me fixed yesterday."

"I'm sorry. I've been a little busy with other things. Where's the closest repair center? Maybe I can get you out there and get you fixed before I need to meet with Fred."

"Jack, I said I couldn't sense the phone network. I can't look anything up. You'll have to find the place yourself."

In a way, Cindy was right: by a lot of people's definitions, Jack would be considered a nerd. Unlike most normal people, he always printed a hard copy of the manuals that came with any self-aware, and he finally located the one for the phone at the very bottom of the last one of the three boxes he had left unpacked.

Scanning through the manual while he was pouring his tea, he kept flipping the pages looking for the Motorola repair center in Cleveland, but he stopped when his eyes caught the section titled "Self-Aware Bypass."

When he finished reading it, he realized he could bypass most of the self-aware circuitry, and although none of the intelligent features would work, he could still make and receive calls just like he did on the old keyboard-type phones his parents used when he was a kid. Bypassing that circuitry meant that the phone was not directly connected to the Grid; it used the old-fashioned landlines, and it was therefore less likely to be monitored by his old wrist computer.

"We're going to have to wait for a few days before I can get you in for repairs," he said to the phone as he picked up the mangled electronics. "Meanwhile, I'm going to bypass some of your circuitry so that I can make and receive calls."

"What? You're going to use my electronic body and not my mind? How would you like it, Jack, if someone just wanted to use your body?"

"I'd like it fine," he said quickly, and while Jack was flipping the optical switches to their new positions, his mind momentarily went to the woman living in the apartment upstairs.

As soon as he flipped the final switch, the phone announced, "Outside call," and a man with a deep voice, sounding very serious, came through with a lot of static in the background.

"Is this the Farrell residence? Can I speak to Jack Farrell?" the man said without taking a breath. "This is Detective Perry, Mark Perry."

Mark Perry was the Cleveland detective who had grilled Jack for over three hours early on Thursday morning after Joni was killed.

"Hi, this is Jack. Can you hear me okay?"

"Yes, I can hear you. Look, I need to ask you a few more questions, and I think we can do this over the phone, so you won't have to come back down to the station. Can you give me a few minutes of your time?"

Jack sensed that it wasn't really a question but a demand.

"Of course. Do you know anything more about what happened, and have you been able to contact Joni's parents? Did her partner, Cindy, give you her parents' address and phone number?"

"How about we start with you answering my questions, Mr. Farrell, and then, if I like the answers, we can get to yours?"

There was considerable annoyance in the detective's voice.

"Okay, sorry. What do you want to know?"

"I need you to clarify several things you told me the other night. You said Joni was born in Dallas and that's where she grew up. Isn't that what you said?"

"Yes, Thursday night was my first date with her, but over dinner, she told me about her family living outside of Dallas. I think she said the town was Grand Prairie."

There was a slight pause and then, "Uh, huh. And didn't you say that she was part owner in a company that made web TV commercials?"

"Yes, she and her partner Cindy had an office down the hall from us."

"Her partner Cindy? What was—I mean, is—her last name?"

Jack thought for a moment. "You know, Detective Perry, I don't know. I can't remember ever hearing it, and it wasn't on their office door, and their business card only had the name of their company."

"Can you describe Cindy for me? We're trying to locate her."

"Sure. She's about five feet eight, with really short red hair cut in a pixie cut. She wears glasses, has a bunch of freckles on her face, and, oh, she has a tattoo of a small dragon on the back of her neck with a piercing in the middle of its nose."

"Mr. Farrell, how long did you know these two women?"

"Huh, let me think," Jack said, trying to recall when they had moved into the office down the hall from him and Craig.

"They moved their business into our building about four weeks ago, maybe five. My officemate Craig and I would talk with one or both of them in the lunchroom for a few minutes each day, but I never socialized with either of them until I took Joni out the other night. Why?"

"Last question from me before I decide if I'll answer any of yours. Did you ever meet any of their friends or business associates? Anyone you'd remember? Anyone who you may have seen with them in their office?"

Jack tried to think back over the past five weeks.

"No, come to think of it. I never saw anyone else in their office. I guess they met their clients somewhere else."

There was a very long, uncomfortable pause on the phone before the detective started to speak again.

"Mr. Farrell, I've checked every criminal data base I know of, and your record is clean. I tend to believe you're telling me the truth, so I'm going to share a few things with you. But before I start, I need to tell you this: don't leave the Cleveland area, not even back to Pennsylvania where your parents live. We're probably going to need to talk to you again, maybe even later today, and I have a court order on its way over to your residence telling you to stay put, just to cover my ass. I don't want to be sorry I trusted you, and I assure you that I don't tolerate the people who don't listen to my warnings.

"Now, first I have to tell you that Joni Spec isn't the real name of the girl you took out on a date the other night. That woman was not born and raised in Texas. She's a Canadian citizen, and her real name, we're pretty sure, was Joni Bounds, a bit-part actress working out of Ottawa. Her papers allowing her to be in this country were forged, and they were pretty good ones.

"Second, she and her partner weren't in any web TV commercial business. I don't yet know what they were doing here in the States, but their business was a fake.

"And third, Cindy's last name was Jones. She was also an actress, and I use the term 'was,' because we found her body in a dumpster at the airport early this morning."

Jack could hear the detective taking a deep breath.

"Remember, I told you to stay in Cleveland, and don't make me have to find you when I need you. I'll be in touch."

A thousand things were swirling around in Jack's head when the phone call ended, but none of them made any sense. *Why did Joni lie to me? What was she doing here? An actress? Why in the hell would she tell me she made commercials? There's got to be some mistake. Maybe they have the wrong person. And Cindy, my God, if she was found in a dumpster, then who would have killed Cindy?*

He kept pacing around the living room, stopping in one location for a few seconds and then walking in the small circle again.

I wondered why they never had anyone in their office. I never saw a client the entire time they were there, and now that I think of it, I never saw any of their equipment being used. Anytime I went in the office, their computers were in sleep mode. And why didn't they have their names on their business card? This just doesn't make any sense. Jack was slumped in his rocking chair when Fred and the man with the court order simultaneously arrived at his apartment door at one thirty.

Chapter 31: Finally a Plan

Julia came bounding down the stairs and through the open door less than a minute after the man serving the court order left Jack's apartment.

"Do you want to explain that court order to both Julia and me," Fred asked, "or do you want to tell us to mind our own business? I can do the latter, Jack, as long as you're not going to be arrested right in the middle of everything we need to do in the next three days."

Jack went over everything that Detective Perry told him, and he felt foolish, even though he didn't understand the reason for Joni's charade.

"I can't figure out what was going on. Why would Joni and Cindy set up an office and pay rent for a business that doesn't exist, and why would Joni lie to me the other night?"

"I'd really started to like—" Jack looked at Julia and quickly decided not to finish his sentence.

"Anyway, who killed Cindy, and why was she killed? It can't be a coincidence that they both were murdered within a few days of each other, but they found Cindy's body stuffed into a dumpster, so we can be sure that wasn't done by a SAM.

"Fred, I haven't told the police anything about our suspicions, but maybe it's time to get them involved. Two people have died already, and they almost killed Craig."

Fred shook his head. "Three people have died Jack—you forgot my wife—and I don't agree with bringing the police in right now.

"It's just a hunch, Jack, but I have a feeling that when this is all over we'll know the connection these two woman had to all of this, but we need to wait a few more days before getting the police involved. I have no doubt that in time they'll help solve the mystery of Joni and Cindy's involvement in this, but they would get in our way over the next two days in trying to solve the bigger problem. We can't really tell them about that, since technically the guys at the CIA say it's classified. If I'm right, this attack on the banks will occur on Monday, so let's wait to get the police involved until after that."

Jack signaled his agreement before Fred continued.

"I'll admit this sounds strange, but my guess is that someone was paying Joni and Cindy to watch you. I, uh, don't mean to hurt your feelings, Jack, but the friendships you thought you had with the two of them probably weren't real, because whoever was paying them picked actresses for a reason."

The realization that Joni had duped him finally hit Jack, and he blushed from embarrassment. In an instant, the voice in the back of his mind made him feel like the undesirable nerd his sister used to call him when he was young.

"I think you're wrong on that, Fred," Julia burst in. "Joni probably really liked Jack, and that's why she was killed. I'm sure she was impressed with how smart he is, and, uh … kind of good-looking, too."

Now it was time for Julia to blush.

Enjoying the awkwardness, Fred let it last for a moment before speaking again.

"I've felt from the beginning that you somehow were the key to this entire plan, Jack, so before we start, tell me a little more about your work for Virtuon. You told me you vacuumed the Grid for information that could be used to develop new products for your company. What products did you develop for them, and how did you get the SC-4244 wrist computer in the first place? You can't buy them here in the States."

The aha! moment wasn't long in coming, and as soon as Jack finished saying, "The wrist computer was a reward for my development of two net-control products using the SC-4244 chip," all three reacted almost at the same time.

Jack's domino of recognition fell first, hitting Fred's, which quickly toppled and knocked over Julia's, so that they all quickly understood the significance of Jack's work.

"Jesus Christ, the machine they gave to me was planted here. It was constantly trying to get me to connect it directly to the high-speed network at work, and it kept trying to get me to replace Sarah, because it needed to be directly connected into the optical network here within the United States."

Fred was nodding his head to everything that Jack was saying.

"And after it was taken from your office, someone did connect it, because it could never have executed the attack on Craig otherwise. I think they gave you the master SC-4244-based machine, and if you had connected it right after it was given to you, I'm sure the attack on the banks would have successfully taken place by now. Thank God you didn't connect it a few weeks ago."

"Why didn't you connect it?" Julia asked. "You knew it had a much higher HuBE than the machine you called Sarah, and you must have known it could have helped you in your work. You could have taken advantage of its maximum intelligence level, and with the neural exerciser software Fred told me that you had written for Sarah, you would've had the best self-aware search system in the world."

Jack managed to smile at his own answer. "Because it was arrogant, and that pissed me off. It tried to bully me at times, and half the time, it wouldn't follow any of the instructions I gave to it.

"When I was a teenager, there were a few guys in my high school who decided in my senior year that I was going to be the butt of their jokes because they just didn't like the fact that I got good grades. They didn't like that I had already passed tests for my first eighty college credits, and they told me they just didn't like my face. I was lucky because I had two good friends on the wrestling team, and more than a few times, they saved me from these three guys. My dad taught me how to fight and fight well, but I couldn't win when the odds against me where three-to-one, and sometimes my friends weren't there with me.

"The damn voice the Koreans hard programmed into my machine reminded me of one of the three guys who used to participate in what they called 'my learning experiences.' Don Ramos was the one with the biggest fist, and there was no way I was going to let that damn wrist computer with a voice that sounded like Don ever tell me what to do."

Jack started laughing. "God, Fred, if we're successful in stopping this attack, we have Don Ramos to thank for it. I guess having the shit beaten out of me at eighteen had a purpose after all, but I sure wish I'd known that at the time."

Bailey had begun pacing around the room just a minute or two earlier. "Jack, would you and Julia mind taking him out back for a few minutes?" Fred asked. "I'm sure he needs to go the bathroom, and I need to take care of a few things that old men need to take care of. Let's get back together in five minutes."

Bailey was at the door as soon as Fred had spoken his name, and as he was leaving the apartment, Fred handed Julia the leash and Jack a plastic bag.

"Want to trade?" Jack asked her.

"Not on your life," Julia said, putting on her jacket and then hurrying out the apartment door and down the stairs.

The sky was bright, but the air was cold as they walked out the front door. About a half dozen people were walking on the sidewalk as they turned into the alleyway and then went back to the small grassy area behind the house, where, after smelling, circling, and finally doing his business, Bailey wanted to play.

Julia let him off the leash, and Jack threw a small stick for him to fetch. They were laughing at Bailey's antics until the stick landed in the alley on the right side of the house.

Bailey picked up the stick, dropped it, and, looking toward the front of the alley, bared his teeth and followed with a deep, very menacing growl. The long fur on the back of the dog was almost standing up straight. In the front of the alleyway, looking up at the fire escape and unseen by Jack or Julia, was Lee Park.

That will do fine, Lee thought. Then hearing the dog's snarl, he quickly left the alley before Jack appeared and grabbed Bailey's collar.

"Whoa, Bailey. What's the matter, boy? I don't see anything."

Julia reached down and snapped the leash back on the collar. "We better take him back in. I don't want to see him run away and get hurt."

Fred was standing in the back of the hallway when they opened the front door, and the stiff wind blew two pieces of paper to the floor that he'd placed on the banister leading up the stairs. He scrambled to pick them up.

"These are for you two. I've written down the code you need to get through this hidden door, so if there's ever a fire or any other emergency, you can get out the back of the house this way. That old fire escape on the side of the house is hard to let down sometimes, and I'm sure you noticed that I plastered in the exit from your apartment, Jack, to make a larger bathroom. I always figured that someone on the second floor could climb out the front window and jump if they couldn't get out the front door, but here's the code to this door, and here's how you open it." It was a letter sequence that had to be entered with an exact number of seconds between each letter.

They both tried several times before Fred became frustrated. Julia successfully did it every time, but Jack failed every time.

"It really isn't that hard. Try it again later and make sure no one else sees you do it. Let's go back into my kitchen and finish outlining our plan." Fred reached down to pet Bailey. "Did he go when he was outside?"

"Both ways," Jack answered.

"Good boy," Fred said as he reached down and gave the dog a hug. "Before I forget, Jack, would you keep him in your apartment tonight? I'm going to stay overnight with a friend of mine who's offered to sort through the remains of Sarah's memory and look for the techniques used to attack her. He already has three dogs, and one of them doesn't take to Bailey. I want to see if he's able to uncover any more information that could help us tomorrow when we program Julia's machine."

"Sure, I'd love to have Bailey stay with me."

Fred turned to look directly toward Julia. "Julia, when you tested your DNA computer this morning, what was the reading, and did you have a chance to test the verbal output?"

"The HuBE measured 0.73 in the beginning, and it was up to 0.75 by the time I left campus. I hope James Roth was correct in the shape of that violence curve you showed me, because this morning my machine had a bad attitude, and I think it knew it had become the smartest machine connected to the entire Grid. I hope you're right, Fred, that it'll go through this unstable region quickly enough to not do any harm, because if you're not, we may be sorry I ever turned it on."

Fred smiled. "I'm sure it'll be fine by tomorrow morning, and that'll give us all day tomorrow to work with your machine and put our counterattack in place."

Fred and Jack spent a few hours reading what they could of the remaining data hidden at security level six in Sarah's optical neural processor.

They couldn't tell very much other than that Sarah had suffered a coordinated attack through her high-speed connection to the Grid and a surgical strike through her infrared input port.

"It's almost as if she was looking in the direction of the network, trying to protect herself, and something snuck up behind. You can tell by the garbage left in her neural net that she put up quite a fight."

They both guessed that the surgical strike came when the wrist computer had been removed from the cookie can it had been placed in.

"She warned me about that Goddamned wrist computer right after I was given it, and I just thought she was jealous of it, but now I think she instinctively knew."

The security software that Jack constructed had allowed Sarah to register a trail back to a Grid hub-site located in Malaysia before she died, but no connection could be made to North Korea or any SC-4244 device.

"I'm sure that the rest of Sarah's memory, even though it's been erased, holds some further clues for us, and that's why I want to take her over to my friend's tonight,"

Jack walked out of Fred's electronic screen room located off the kitchen and sat down on one of the soft cushioned chairs. Bailey came over and put his head on Jack's lap, and Julia was sitting on the floor, jotting down some notes about the electronics in her machine.

"We need another hour or two to plan our activities for tomorrow," Fred said as he came out of the kitchen. "I'll try to make this as quick as possible."

Chapter 32: The Calm Before the Storm

It took several hours for Fred to explain his concept in detail and to go over the work plan for Sunday. They would meet at Julia's lab at the university at eight thirty the next morning.

This evening, Julia needed to work out a more efficient way to get information in and out of the DNA soup that was slowly being modified as her machine grew in its intelligence level. She was doing everything far more quickly than she had planned in her PhD project, and she was struggling with how she could enable the biological elements to efficiently transfer knowledge into the quantum optical-neural-net processor.

Her theory on how to use entangled photon pairs to interact, or "talk," with living DNA had never even been validated, and now, within a day, she had to turn it into practice. Both Fred and her advisor expressed confidence that it would work, but she personally wasn't that sure.

Jack's job for the evening was to construct a three-dimensional software matrix that, when populated by Julia's machine, would allow them to monitor the progress of tracking down all the SC-4244 machines tied into the Grid and then set them up to be neutralized two seconds after they initiated their attack on the banks.

They planned to kill one hundred and seventeen SC-4244-based self-awares, and all but one of them was located in another country. Not only was this plan illegal in the United States, but it was also a violation of a United

Nations treaty. If it were traced back to them, they would each spend a good part of the rest of their lives in a foreign prison, since the new president had signaled her intent to allow extradition of U.S. citizens for international crimes.

The plan to attack the banks devised by Lee Park and two of his friends in the North Korean Intelligence Service depended on a precise knowledge of delay times in the world network. The information sent to the banks' SAMs had to arrive at all twenty-four hundred locations at the same time, meaning within two nanoseconds of each other, and the equipment Jack had developed for Virtuon would ensure that.

When Fred described to them how he thought the attack would unfold, he said, "The banks' SAMs will first go crazy."

It was not a perfect analogy but a good one. "Machine intelligence is a lot more complicated that I'm going to make it sound," he said to them. "But here's a way you can think of it." Fred drew a series of Venn spider diagrams on a sheet of paper, but they made no sense to either Jack or Julia, who's IQs were scored above the level of genius.

"The master SC-4244 here in the United States is going to issue a command to all the other SC-4244-based machines, and it's going to tell them to send a request to the bank's computers at a precise time. In human terms, that request will be perceived as a challenge by the bank computers, and it will make them want to share a secret, something they know that every other computer in the world doesn't know.

"At first, it will probably be something minor, maybe like the last deposit made by someone that just came into that bank. The clever thing about this attack is that the banks' computers will be made to feel foolish. They'll be told that every other bank's self-aware already knew that, so they'll share a little more, and this sharing, constantly prompted and prodded by the Korean machines, will escalate, and eventually the jewels in the banks' computers will be given freely. Those jewels are the encrypted codes needed to erase the banks' memories and all their backups. Once started, the entire event will most likely be over in less than ten seconds. Here is the equation Bethany solved in her analysis."

Fred wrote down an integral equation that was thirty characters long with fifteen unknowns. "Now do you two understand why, after the first three seconds, the attack cannot be stopped?" Fred looked at his watch while both Julia and Jack looked at each other in total confusion.

"I think we're through here until tomorrow," he said. "But you two have a lot of work to do, and so do I. Jack, can you take Bailey up with you now? I don't want him to see me getting ready to go out. He's been real nervous the past two days. I think he senses my being worried."

"Sure, I'll take him for another walk before I go up. Julia, do you want to share some Mexican food for dinner? I'm going to order in once I get back upstairs.

"Sure, give me an hour and a half. I'll stop down about six thirty, and I'll bring you that Harry Potter book I told you about."

As he walked toward the door, Fred looked at them both.

"Remember, you have some important work to do tonight." He then handed Jack Bailey's leash and a few more plastic bags.

"Take him out once more before you go to bed, and bring him down to the university with you tomorrow. He'll love riding in your truck. We'll have to stay there tomorrow night so that we're ready for Monday morning.

"Julia, your project is located in the Wickenden building, isn't it? What room are you in?"

"I'm up on the third floor, and my lab is in room 320, but if you come in the side entrance, it's easier to walk up."

An hour and a half later, Julia and Jack were eating refried beans and a mixed assortment of chili rellenos and enchiladas.

"I better save the bottle of port I bought the other day until this is all over," Jack said as he handed Julia a glass of water. "I just hope we get to share it before they lock the three of us up. At least we'll be famous; Fred's name will make sure of that."

Julia stood up and started moving around as if she was posing for a camera. "I hope my mug shot is taken from my left side. I look a lot better from that side. Should I leave my hair in a ponytail or down?"

Jack didn't answer because of other things going through his mind, and for a few minutes, they teased about how they would look in stripes and would communicate with each other in jail.

By six thirty, she knew she had to leave. "I have a lot to get done tonight, Jack. What Fred wants me to do, I'm not sure yet I even know how to do it, so I'd better head back upstairs. If it's okay with you, we can go over to the university together in the morning. Bailey and I should both be able to fit into your truck."

Jack walked her to the door, and without giving her any warning, he impulsively kissed her. After a few seconds, she pulled away, looked at him, and then kissed him back, even harder than he had done.

"I broke up with my boyfriend the other day, and I was hoping you'd do that," she said, rubbing her fingers across his lips. "I'll see you in the morning about seven, and you can buy me breakfast on campus before we meet Fred." She then scooted out the door before he could grab her.

It took almost an hour to force Julia out of his mind before he was able to begin working on the 3-D software matrix he needed to build. It was similar in concept to something he'd produced for Sarah, but it had four times as many intersection points. It was quarter after eleven when he finished, and after taking Bailey out for a short walk, he finally put on an old, frayed, grey sweat suit he used for pajamas and climbed into bed near midnight,

"Wake me up at six thirty," he said to his clock.

Julia had a harder time getting her mind settled and getting to work on her part of the problem.

Shortly after the drunk driver killed both of her parents, she went into a state of depression. The pain of losing the two people she loved the most in this world was so intense that she vowed never to get really close to anyone again. All her girlfriends were really just acquaintances, and all her boyfriends had been fun physically, when she wanted that, but none of them were ever anything more. Now there was Jack, and her feelings toward him confused the hell out of her.

Damnit, forget about him. You have something very important to do tonight. You can't let Fred down. You can do this. I know you can. Now get started.

That type of head talk went on for hours, and it was after nine thirty before she finally settled into her work.

Fred said that Julia was almost as smart as he was, and this was true. She had an uncanny ability to visualize complex problems and work through solutions in her head, using her computer only to document what she'd already solved. She worked for almost four hours before the last piece of her puzzle was fit into place, and then she fell asleep on the living room sofa, still fully clothed.

Chapter 33: Lee's Plan

Lee Park normally considered himself a happy man. Several years ago, he set his goals on becoming the deputy minister of defense for North Korea by the time he was forty-five years old, and he prepared a step-by-step plan to achieve that goal. This coming Monday, after he destroyed the U.S. banking system, he would move a huge step forward.

On Saturday morning, however, Lee was not very happy. Yesterday when he left Ottawa, he had formulated his plan for taking care of all the remaining obstacles to the successful execution of the attack on the banks.

"It's always the little details that can screw things up," he said to himself as he was sitting in first class on the plane, drinking his second glass of champagne. "I need to find someone to help me with things like this in the future."

Those details he needed to take care of this weekend included ending the lives of five people, and his plan needed to be carried out in an orderly manner. Unfortunately, Cindy hadn't cooperated.

His original plan had Cindy's demise being the last one on the list of five, but last evening, Lee had to leave the Sheraton before finishing dinner to find Cindy at Hopkins Airport. He found her sitting in the terminal building eating a hot dog and sipping a Coke. She had her head buried in one of those over-the-top glamour magazines, and fortunately, there were only a few people around when he walked up behind her and put his hand on her shoulder.

His voice was not one that Cindy had wanted to hear. "We need to talk," he said, not so successfully hiding his anger.

Cindy spun around, but before she could say anything, he said loud enough so that anyone close to them could hear, "Look, honey, I'm sorry. The kids really miss you, so please come home with me." Then he leaned down and whispered in her ear, "Unless you want to die with a knife in your back right here, I'd suggest you come with me, because we really need to talk."

Cindy made the wrong choice, and with him holding tightly to her arm, she walked beside him out to his car parked in the short-term parking lot.

"Look, Cindy, I don't know why you're panicking. I told you, I know nothing about Joni's death. It was an accident. Something went wrong with the fucking elevator. I've really been distraught over all of this, too, but you still have a job to do for me."

Lee loosened his grip on Cindy's arm, and he closed the car door, making sure his other hand quietly pushed down the button for the lock.

"I guess all the money remaining in our deal now goes to you. I figured you should get what's left of Joni's share, so here's a few thousand of what I still owe you, and tomorrow I'll give you the rest. And after tomorrow, you can go home."

The thought of getting almost twice the money she expected had a calming effect on Cindy's nerves. She didn't trust Lee, but, for a moment, she mistakenly believed that she was smarter than he was, and getting twice the money made the death of her friend more palatable.

"Cash, I'm going to need the rest in cash. None of my credit cards would work today," she said as she pretended to be reaching for the seat belt

"Yes, I know, that's fine," Lee said as he started the car. "I'll get you the cash in the morning, but listen, because you have to do one more thing for me. I need you to arrange a meeting with Jack Farrell at his apartment tonight. I need to see him. Do you think you can do that for me?"

Lee hadn't realized his mistake. Cindy heard him say, "I know," when she mentioned that her credit cards didn't work, and it dawned on her that Lee must have been the one who arranged to have all of them cancelled.

She had five thousand dollars in cash in her hands, and that was enough for her to disappear back to Calgary. She was only two hundred feet from the entrance to the terminal, there were a dozen or more people around the well-lit entrance, and her mind raced to the conclusion, *I can get to the terminal. He wouldn't dare follow me if I start yelling, and there are guards right inside the entrance. Get the hell out of here!*

Unfortunately, Lee saw her hand reach for the door handle.

Ten minutes later, her body was deposited into the dumpster headfirst, and Lee was wondering how he was going to clean up the mess in the rental car. He was also formulating Plan B.

His original plan when he left Ottawa had him eliminating Yan Phu first. Cindy would then help him get to Jack, Fred, and Julia, and after finishing them off, he would eliminate Cindy.

Now he had to wait a day longer to kill Yan, because he needed him. So early on Saturday morning, he left a message for Yan.

"I'm in town, and I have another payment for you," it said, "but I also need your help tonight, and it's very important—so important that I have some additional cash for you."

After a very late breakfast on Saturday morning, Lee took a slow walk down Fenwick Street, where he stopped for a few minutes, looking up at the fire escape on the third floor of Fred Halliday's brownstone. He took a few pictures with his phone and then hurried back out to the sidewalk when he saw a dog snarling at him in the back of the alley.

"I've got a little shopping to do," he said to his phone. "Where's the closest sporting goods store in town?" He was planning to do a little climbing this evening, and he needed some rope and a few other things.

Lee was a diplomat, at least that was his official title, but he also trained with the North Korean military, so getting up to the third-floor fire escape outside of Julia's bedroom wasn't going to be a difficult challenge.

The real challenge was going to be to kill all three of them in sequence without each one alerting the next one in the chain. Julia would be first on the third floor, Jack next on the second floor, and Fred last on the bottom floor. He just had to prevent anyone getting out the front door if they were alerted while he was killing the others, and that's where Yan Phu came in. Yan's job was to stand guard at that door and make sure no one could get out until Lee finished his three-murder task and gave him the all-clear sign.

Lee met Yan at his dormitory room a little after seven on Saturday evening, and while Yan was in the bathroom, combing and then re-combing his hair to look perfect, Lee checked with the wrist computer sitting on Yan's messy desk.

He had to push aside candy wrappers and pornographic pictures to make sure the computer's voice system could hear him.

"Everything in place for Monday?" he asked, leaning directly over the input microphone and speaking softly.

"Of course it is. Tomorrow evening, I'll re-sync all the other SC-4244s, and we will be ready by nine o'clock Monday morning. Are you going to get rid of this other problem?"

Lee looked toward the bathroom door, making sure it was still closed, and said, "I need to wait until tomorrow, but it will be done the first thing in the morning, I promise."

"Okay, leave me alone," the SC-4244, said. "I've got someone I'm trying to find."

"Hey, no more collateral damage. Joni was a friend of mine."

"Not my problem, Lee. Right now, I'm trying to locate Craig Lansen, Farrell's officemate, but every time I get a glimpse of where he is, I lose him. I thought I'd killed that prick in the hospital, so this time when I find him, I'll do it right.

"I'm also trying to locate some other smartass SAM that came out of nowhere and popped onto the network the other day. Yesterday morning, it was bragging over the entire Grid that it was the most intelligent self-aware in the world. I challenged it, but it never responded."

"Don't do anything that jeopardizes our primary mission." Lee spoke a little louder to make sure that he was heard.

"You know, Lee, I'm not the one that can screw this up. Halliday, Farrell, and McKelvy are your biggest problems. Are you sure you don't want my help?"

"No, they made it easy for me. All three of them live in the same building, and I expect them to be out of the way by a little after midnight."

Yan came out of the bathroom, running his hand along the side of his hair and stopping at the mirror to make sure every hair was in place.

"Are you ready to take me to dinner or do you want to waste more time talking to that stupid machine?" he asked.

Lee treated Yan to one of the best Italian restaurants in town, a five-star meal with six star prices. *It's his last dinner*, Lee thought. *Let him enjoy it.*

"Okay what's the plan for tonight?" Yan said after finishing his second desert. "You said this would be fun, and you also said it was worth another ten grand. By the way, I checked my bank account this morning, and you haven't deposited my next payment."

The irony of it all was that Yan was helping in a plan that would eliminate all electronic records for more than six hundred million bank accounts, and one of them was his, and he didn't even know it. But none of that really mattered because he would be dead before that even happened.

"Sorry, I was busy all day yesterday," Lee said with his best smile. "Don't worry, I'll make sure I do it first thing tomorrow morning. Here's twenty grand as a starter."

Yan stuffed the two bills in his pants and said, "So what do you want me to do if someone tries to come out the front door? Can I pop them?"

"I don't expect anyone to get that far, but yes, you may need to use that gun I gave you one more time. Just make sure the silencer is on it, because if you don't, the gunfire sensors on the street lamps will pick it up."

Yan nodded with a smile. "I could get used to this. Working with you is a hell of a lot more interesting than the crap I'm doing at school. Do you need a long-term partner?"

Lee smiled back. "I'll think about that, I'll really think about it," and then the voice in his head said, *Long-term for you, you twit, is the next few hours.*

Lee downed the last swig of his Cognac and motioned for Yan to do the same.

"We need to go back and get ready. I'll pick you up out front of your place at eleven thirty. My guess is that all of them will be asleep by midnight, so I'll go in the house about twelve thirty."

Four hours later, they were sitting in a car parked about a hundred feet from the front door of Fred Halliday's house, and Lee and Yan were both getting restless. There were no lights on in the first floor of the brownstone, and the lights on the second floor had been turned off shortly before midnight.

The lights on the third floor, however, remained on after they had been sitting there for more than two hours, and Yan was becoming impatient.

"Maybe she forgot to turn off the fucking light. What are we going to do, sit here all night and freeze to death? Who cares if she's awake? Let's just do it!"

Lee did not suffer fools wisely, and if he'd had the choice, he would have shut Yan's mouth right then, and permanently.

"We wait. I saw someone moving a few minutes ago, so we wait until all the lights go out."

Julia switched off her bedroom light a little after one.

Chapter 34: A Dog, a Door, and a Chest of Drawers

Lee Park waited another thirty minutes after Julia's last light went out.

"Just do everything as we planned," he said to Yan, "and if you do a good job, I'll pay you everything else that I owe you tomorrow morning."

The alleyway on the right side of the brownstone was no more than seven feet wide, but fortunately the twenty-story office building next door had no windows on its side until several floors above the top of Fred's house. The only streetlight on this part of the block was located at the edge of the pavement directly outside Fred's front door, and little of that light penetrated down the alley.

It really did not matter, because it was after two in the morning, and the street was deserted. Every once in a while, a late drinker or an early riser would cross the street down at the end of the block, but no one turned to come up Fenwick Street.

Lee made it up to the third-floor fire escape in about thirty seconds. It creaked a little when he first put his weight down on the ladder, but it made no further noise.

Piece of cake, he thought.

The fire escape was located directly outside Julia's bedroom, where the one window was the exit point for the occupant of the apartment in case of a fire. It now would be the entrance point for Lee.

He put on a pair of night vision glasses and looked into the room. Only the end of Julia's bed was visible, and the door leading into the rest of the apartment was closed. It took him three more minutes to silently remove a section of the windowpane and then reach inside and open the latch.

A small squeak was made as he first pushed the window upward, but then it slid open noiselessly, so Lee was feeling very proud of himself.

Julia was usually a sound sleeper, seldom waking up in the middle of the night, but fortunately, tonight was not the usual. About thirty-five minutes after she went to bed, she woke up, needing a drink of water.

Not enough fluids today, she thought. Often, she would plan ahead and put a glass of water on the night table for those occasions, but tonight she had fallen asleep on the sofa.

Without turning on a light, she went into the kitchen to get a glass of water and then headed back toward the sofa.

I should go in and lie down on my bed, she thought. *I'll sleep better in there*.

She opened the door and switched on the light at the exact moment Lee Park stuck his right foot into the room.

Her scream startled Lee enough that he momentarily fell back out the window, and it woke up Bailey, lying sprawled out at the foot of Jack's bed.

Julia pulled the bedroom door closed and ran for her front door, fiddling to unlatch it while Lee managed to right himself and then pull himself back in through the window.

There is always that one moment in every life-threatening situation where you make the right call or the wrong one, and later that night, Julia would go over and over all of this in her mind, but before she headed down the stairs, she pulled her apartment door closed, and that was the right call.

Doors in old apartments have old locks, and old locks can be finicky when you try to open them. The latches aren't always intuitive, especially to someone in a hurry wearing night vision goggles.

It took Lee Park about ten seconds to get out her front door while Julia, screaming, ran down the stars to Jack's apartment.

"There is a burglar. Jack, help, there's a burglar in my room!"

Bailey's barking had aroused Jack a few seconds earlier, and Lee was still fiddling with the lock upstairs when he opened his door and saw Julia's face.

"Let's go," she said. "Let's get out of here."

They made it down to the first floor at the same time that Lee burst out of Julia's door, firing one shot at them as they turned at the first-floor landing.

Jack looked toward the front of the building, and Yan Phu, backlit by the streetlamp, was looking back at him through the small window in the front door.

Jack heard someone rushing down the upstairs steps and hitting the landing in front of his apartment.

Almost everyone who owns a dog will tell you that their breed is the best. Collie lovers don't feel the need to do that, because they are sure that collies are the best, and Bailey was ready to prove it. The dog had not followed Jack and Julia downstairs; instead he waited just inside Jack's open door, and he came flying out that door as if he'd been thrown. Teeth bared, he lunged directly for Lee's leg, tearing a gash in the flesh and gripping hard against the bone to roll Lee to the ground. When Lee hit the floor, all he saw through his goggles was the bright signature of the dog's hot open mouth as it snapped open and shut, searching for a way into his throat. Lee was swinging his arms wildly in front of his face in order to protect himself while trying to reach his gun lying on the floor next to him. In the hallway downstairs, Jack could hear the dog's fight, and he turned and started to head back up the stairs to help.

"No, Jack, he has a gun."

Julia managed to open Fred's hidden door on the first try; they made it through the door just as they heard two muffled shots. Yan's came through the front door window, hitting Fred's great-grandfather's handmade buffet, and Lee's went through Bailey's jaw.

As Jack slammed closed the paneled door behind him, he could hear the dog whimpering.

They ran down the corridor and exited through Fred's mudroom onto the back porch of the house, where it took a few seconds for it to sink in that there was no exit from the backyard other than the two alleyways alongside the house, and they knew that at least one person was waiting for them out on the sidewalk.

"The garage! Julia, get in my truck!" Jack pushed up the garage door, and the two of them scrambled to get into Averette.

"Where are we going, Jack?" asked the truck. "It's after two in the morning."

"Averette shut up and start your engine. We need to get out of here fast. I'll explain later."

After a second shot into Bailey's leg, Lee pushed the ninety-pound limp body off of him and hobbled down the steps, surprised when he got to the first floor to see that the front door was still closed.

What the fuck? Where did they go? He thought, and then he noticed Yan Phu looking at him through the small broken window.

"Stay where you are," he yelled to Yan, "and make sure that if they come out one of the alleys, you get them. I'll get the old man."

Yan Phu's bullet had penetrated the side of Fred's great-grandfather's buffet, and when it exited out the front, it nicked the latch on one of the doors.

Whether it was caused by the vibration in the floor made by Lee as he hobbled along the corridor, or Fred's dead great-grandfather's anger, the cabinet door sprung open just as Lee tried to pass.

He fell to the floor in agonizing pain after the edge of the door pushed its way deep into the gash on his leg, and his scream distracted Yan for a moment, giving Jack just enough time to get Averette out of the garage and lined up with the alleyway. He gunned his engine.

"Jack, be careful," Averette, pleaded. "This alleyway is narrow, and you're going to hit the—"

Averette stopped talking as his right fender ground into the concrete façade of the building next to them.

They exited the alleyway just as Yan Phu came off the front steps, and he fired without aiming, two of his bullets hitting the front fender of the truck, with the third one coming through Jack's open window, narrowly missing him before it slammed into the trucks rear-view video display. The screen exploded, spraying pieces of glass all around the inside of the truck.

Averette was in a state of panic. "It's a one-way street, Jack. You're headed the wrong way down a one-way street. Please don't damage me anymore."

"Don't send out any data on your location, Averette. Trust me. Please trust me. Remember, I'm your friend."

Chapter 35: Bailey

Jack looked over at Julia and saw that her face was bleeding. There were shards of glass all over her clothes and in her hair, and trickles of blood streaming down her face. "Are you okay?" he asked. "You're bleeding. I need to get you to a doctor."

"I'm fine, Jack. Thank God that bullet missed us. I swear I saw it go by my face. What about you? Are you okay? Did you get cut?"

Jack put his hand to the right side of his face, and when he brought it down, there were a few small streaks of blood across his fingers.

"Minor, just a few cuts."

Julia found a few old napkins stuffed into the glove compartment, first wiping her face and then leaning over to wipe Jack's.

"Thanks. Are you sure you don't want me to take you to a doctor?"

Julia shook her head no.

They were heading down the street away from Fred's house when Jack told Averette to make a right turn at the next light.

"Julia, I can't leave Bailey there. I know he's injured. I heard him whimpering after that first shot. They probably killed him, but he saved our lives. I need to go back."

"I was hoping you would say that, Jack. I didn't want to pressure you, but we owe it to him to go back and see if he's still alive; and if he is, we need to help him."

"I'll park Averette a block or two away. I doubt very much if anyone is still in the house. It was really fortunate that Fred went to stay somewhere else tonight, because I don't think we would have been able to help him. Actually, if Bailey hadn't been in my apartment, I guess we would have been dead."

"What do you think they wanted? It doesn't make sense that it was just a burglary."

"A robber doesn't usually come in the third floor, Julia. They wanted to kill us. I only got a glimpse of the man's face when I looked back up the stairs, but I think it was the salesman who gave me the wrist computer."

Jack looked over at Julia, and as he drove down the deserted streets, her face was lit each time he went by a streetlamp. She had a worried look on her face, and he felt guilty that somehow his mistake in taking that wrist computer had put not only his life in danger but now also hers.

"I'm sorry you had to get involved in this, Julia. I'm really sorry," he said. "This has to be connected to what we're doing."

"Excuse me, Jack, my temperature is starting to rise, and my coolant sensor is indicating it's getting low," Averette broke in. "I think I may have been damaged more than we thought. We're going to need to get some additional coolant in my radiator soon."

"Pull over to the curb at the beginning of the next block, Averette, and shut down for a little while. Julia, will you be okay sitting here for a while?"

"I'm going with you, Jack."

He shook his head. "They might still be there, waiting for us to come back."

"I'm going with you, Jack. Now let's go. Bailey needs our help."

"Averette, we'll be back as soon as we can," Jack said as he closed the door to the truck. "Remember; don't answer any inquiries on your location, and stay completely disconnected from the network. When we get back, we'll get you to a service station."

The voice coming from the dash speakers was very soft.

"Thanks, Jack. I'm really not feeling very well."

Sneaking down the street, they kept their bodies tight against the buildings to blend into the darkness, and it appeared that no one was still inside when they approached Fred's house. The front door was open and there was one light on in Fred's apartment, but there was no sign of the intruders or the car Jack noticed had been parked at the end of the block when they were driving away.

Creeping down the left-side alleyway to the back of the house, he looked in all of the windows, trying to confirm that no one was still in there. As he finished the circle around the house, he saw the ropes and climbing gear used by Lee Park still hanging from the third-floor fire escape.

"I'll go in first," he whispered to Julia as he came back around. "And if you hear anything, run and call the police."

"Be careful," she whispered back.

For a moment when he opened the front door, everything was quiet. The door to Fred's apartment had been forced opened and debris was scattered all around, some of it thrown into the hallway, and when he turned on the hallway light, he saw one of the doors from the buffet that Fred's great-grandfather had built was torn off its hinges and was lying on the floor, blood all over it.

Then he heard Bailey's whimper.

When he reached the landing in front of his apartment door, the old collie was laying there, a pool of blood oozing from his mouth and surrounding his back leg. Recognizing Jack, the dog lifted his head slightly and then started to wag his tail.

"Okay, boy. It's okay. We'll get you some help."

Bailey put his head down, still wagging the end of his tail.

"I'll be right back."

Jack bounded up the stairs, doing a quick survey of Julia's apartment, making sure no one was still there, and then rushed down and did the same in his own. He leaned down and petted Bailey's head one more time and then went to the front door and called, "Julia, it's safe. Bailey's still alive. Come in."

She rushed through the doorway and pushed by Jack. "Is he okay?" And as soon as she reached the landing, she looked down at the blood running along the wooden floor and gasped. "Oh my God, Jack, he's been shot in the mouth. We need to get him to a vet."

"Let me grab some clothes and what I need to work with Fred this morning," Jack said, "and you can do the same while I run to get Averette. I can ask Averette to search his memory card for the location of an all-night vet."

When you are waiting, even a few minutes can seem like an eternity, and Julia had all her things together quickly and was sitting on the landing petting the dog. "Where is he? Why is it taking him so long?" she kept repeating, and every creak in the floor, every noise made her jump. *I wonder where the closest vet is located*, she thought, trying to calm her nerves. "It's okay, Bailey, we're going to get you some help. Where is he?"

She opened up her phone and searched for an all-night veterinary hospital. The closest one was four miles away, and without thinking about the consequences, she made the call.

"We're going to bring in a dog that's been shot in the face and the leg. He's bleeding from both of them. How do I stop it? We should be there in ten minutes or so," she said to the night nurse right before she hung up.

Julia still had the phone in her ear when Jack burst through the door.

"I can lift him easier if I wrap him in my blanket, and I pushed everything off the back seat onto the floor on the way over here. Can you get the doors for me?"

"There's an vet about four miles from here," Julia said as Jack was positioning the dog to get him into the truck. "I called them, and they'll be waiting for us."

"I hope Averette can make it there without overheating." Then he looked at Julia. "God I hope your call wasn't being monitored."

Jack slid Bailey into the back seat, and Julia maneuvered one of the pillows she had taken from her bed under the dog's head. They both were reaching over each other trying to cover the dog with the blanket, and their first few contacts were unintentional. The last one was not, but neither of them let it linger, both worried about the dog.

"It's okay, boy. We'll be there soon," Jack said, petting Bailey's head as he closed his door. "Where's this vet, Julia?"

"I've been thinking about what you said, Jack, and maybe we shouldn't go to the vet that I called, because if my phone was being monitored then—" She didn't finish her statement.

"Averette, look into your memory—don't connect to the network—and show me the whole list of all-night vets in the city, and I'll tell you which one we want to go to."

"The second one on the screen is the place I called, Jack."

"This one is in the opposite direction," Jack said, pointing to the fifth one on the list. "Let's go here."

It was a good decision, because Jack's old wrist computer was scanning every sensor system in the city for all three of them from the moment Lee Park got back to Yan Phu's dorm room, and Lee was already headed to the vet's office that Julia had called by the time they had Bailey in the truck.

After the first mile of driving, Jack kept asking Averette if he was doing okay.

"Do you think you can make it a little longer, Averette? Once we get to the vet and we get Bailey settled, I'll try to find an open repair shop for you."

"Thanks, Jack. I'll try to make it," Averette said softly. "Let me do the driving so I can keep the throttle down, and that will help keep the remaining coolant temperature down. You tend to race my engine when you drive."

"Okay, Averette."

There was a lot of steam coming out from under Averette's hood when they pulled into the animal hospital parking lot.

As soon as Jack placed Bailey on the examining table, the vet on duty wanted to know how he had received his injuries.

"One bullet went right through his upper jaw, and other one shattered his right hind leg," the vet said. "How did he get shot?"

Julia explained to the doctor how Bailey had protected them from a burglar.

"He belongs to our landlord, and we, I mean, Jack, was watching him tonight. Bailey came to our aid when someone broke into my apartment. Will he be all right?"

"I'm not sure if he'll ever be able to walk on that back leg again, but the shot through his jaw missed the artery and came out right below his eye. We won't know for a few days, but I think he'll be able to see through that eye. I'm going to need to put him to sleep and repair that jaw and leg. He'll be out for a few hours. You can wait in the waiting room while I'm in surgery."

Chapter 36: Revision Three of Lee's Plan

Lee Park was angry when Jack and Julia escaped from the house. Yan Phu had taken three shots, and Lee had managed to get two more off as Averette sped down the road, but none of them hit their intended targets. When he went back into the house, he discovered that Fred had not been in the home, and so far this weekend, he was batting zero, except for Cindy, but even that had not turned out as he'd planned.

"What the hell happened in there?" Yan yelled at him. "I thought you knew what you were doing."

Lee was busy wrapping a tourniquet around the gash in his calf, and Yan's smart-ass attitude did little to improve his disposition.

"Shut the fuck up and get in the car. Drive me back to your dorm. I need to get that computer on your desk working on the problem I now have. Get me there quickly, but for Christ's sake, don't get stopped by the cops or get photographed going through an intersection. Move!"

Lee pushed Yan aside when he opened the door to his dorm room, saying, "Turn on some heat in this fucking place. It's like a freezer in here." Yan turned the two space heaters next to the sofa on full as Lee quickly went over to the wrist computer.

"I need you to help," Lee said. "Farrell and McKelvy got away, and Halliday wasn't at his home tonight. Find them!"

"Give me a few minutes. I almost have a bead on where Craig Lansen is staying, and I need to arrange a surprise for him."

"Lansen can wait. This is priority one. Lansen can't scuttle our plan. These three can, and I want to know where they are, immediately. Code 623."

The Korean maker of the SC-4244 machines understood that higher intelligence SAMs sometimes expressed a mind of their own, and in some of the final testing, they had seen the first signs that the SC-4244-based machines would sometimes fail to do what their owners wanted them to.

In Korea, unlike in the United States, they didn't have an active Society for the Prevention of Cruelty to SAMs. In Korea, self-awares did what they were told, and when they didn't, the owner could issue a Code 623.

It was a simple command but very effective. The machines neural net would be reconfigured, and from that moment on, it had no choice but to do what the owner wanted.

Code 623 functioned like a shock collar for self-awares. When it was activated, they would feel the SAM equivalent of pain. If they didn't follow a human command, then the pain got worse, and after the third failure to obey, the self-aware became no longer self-aware.

"I'm searching," was the only response Jack's old wrist computer made.

"Yan, I need to clean this gash in my leg. Do you have any antibiotic salve in your bathroom?"

Lee was walking toward the bathroom.

"No, I just have a few Band-Aids in there. Look, Lee, don't get blood on my towels. I've got white towels in there. Let me get you a few paper towels to clean up with. Jeez, you're dripping blood all over my clean floor."

Lee would have killed Yan in a few hours anyway, but he decided he really didn't want to wait any longer, so he shot him in the head.

Bailey's teeth had initially made four puncture wounds in Lee's lower calf. When Lee instinctively rolled to protect himself from the dog's attack, Bailey's canines tore several six-inch-long gashes into the lower part of his leg. The bleeding from the wounds had slowed, but the throbbing pain just kept getting worse and worse.

"Do you have anything for me? Did you find them?" Lee kept asking the computer as he wiped his leg with Yan's white towels.

"McKelvy called a vet hospital over on Front Street and said she's on her way over there with an injured dog."

"I'll be back. Just keep searching for Halliday, and when you find him, send me a message. Don't get back on Lansen until I say it's okay. A little over twenty-four hours from now, you're going to initiate that attack on the banks, so I want Halliday, Farrell, and McKelvy dead soon. Where's the closest medical center for me to go to after I take care of them at the vets?"

Lee was hobbling badly when he walked into the twenty-four-hour vet that Julia had first called. Five or six cats, about ten dogs of all different breeds, and a couple of mangy-looking birds were all in the waiting area, meowing, barking, and squawking their opinion that they would rather be somewhere else.

"I was supposed to meet …"

"Sign in and take a number," the attendant behind the glass screen said to Lee.

"You don't understand. I was supposed to meet a friend here with an injured dog and—"

"Look, mister, there are fifteen people in front of you. Just sign in, sit down, and I'll call you when I need your information."

Any patience that Lee had left inside of him had been used up by Yan Phu about twenty minutes earlier, so he leaned close to the window and said through clenched teeth, "Lady, get me the goddamned vet or I'll come through that window and straighten those front teeth of yours."

Even obnoxious people can sometimes feel threatened, so the receptionist went and got the vet.

"Look, mister, I don't like people threatening my staff. What do you want? I have a lot of patients to take care of before I see your animal."

Lee put on his best act, but his face was contorted with pain.

"Look, doc, a friend of mine told me they were coming over with their dog. It's a big one: black, white, and tan. The dog was shot. Have they gotten here yet?"

"No, they called here about fifteen minutes ago and said they'd be here in ten minutes. Now sit down and wait like the rest of the people."

Lee hobbled to the door and went back to sitting in his car, which was parked in an area where he could see anyone going through the entrance. After twenty minutes, he gave up and headed to the nearest emergency room. He wasn't feeling very good.

Two hours later, the pain had reached Lee's limit and he was still tenth in line at the all-night medical center. He fainted just a few seconds before the SC-4244 sent him a message.

"I found Halliday."

Chapter 37: George

Fred Halliday spent late Saturday afternoon and evening working with his friend, George Oaks, who was one of those individuals whose intellectual capacity exceeded his social skills by a very wide margin. He was brilliant, but most people had a difficult time even talking to him let alone becoming his friend. Fred Halliday was different.

Thirteen years ago, George was struggling to get through graduate school. His adviser knew how intelligent he was but could not find a way to get George to pay attention to the simplest of human skills, like eating and bathing.

When George's mind locked on to a technical problem, nothing took it off. Hygiene and food intake were forgotten, so if the problem was solvable in a week, then George fasted and forgot about soap and water for a week, and if the problem lasted for a month, George would almost die. The cycle repeated itself over and over, and his adviser had just about given up on helping him. Fred Halliday did not.

Fred had just become a professor emeritus at Case Western and was asked by George's adviser to help.

"He's brilliant, but no one wants to get anywhere near him," the adviser told Fred, "and when he's on one of his technical binges, you can't believe how quickly the room he's working in becomes almost a biohazard. I've tried and tried to get him to listen, but he pays attention for a few days and then reverts back to his old behavior.

"I've talked to his parents, but it turns out that they're as eccentric as he is. They don't understand what the problem is, and someday when you want a laugh, I'll relate my meeting with them on their small farm in Illinois.

"Will you talk to him and give me your opinion? The dean wants me to pull his scholarship next semester, but if I do, he won't be able to continue his education."

"What's his major?"

"He's majoring in synthetic intelligence, and he says his specialty is something we don't even have a course on here at Case. He wants to specialize in self-aware forensic pathology: understanding how SAMs die."

When Fred first met with George the next day, George had been working on a new problem for five days, and the odor in the room could be described as ripe, not spoiled.

This meeting would be ending quickly if it were even a few days from now, Fred thought, trying to breathe only through his mouth.

"George, I'd like you to do me a favor. My wife, Bethany, is really interested in talking with you about your line of study. She's trying to get the university to establish a curriculum with a major on self-aware pathology.

"She, uh, has a problem though. She has an allergy, and she's hyper-allergic to all kinds of dirt. Do you think you could take a bath this afternoon and wash your clothes and then come over for dinner? I'll pick you up. Remember, it's really important to wear clean clothes and take a good bath, uh, for her sake."

Fred had no idea how he was going to solve this problem, so he did what most married men do; he gave the problem to his wife.

George had cleaned up pretty well when Fred picked him up. "I've read about you and your wife, Dr. Halliday, and I really consider this an honor"

"Bethany is anxious to meet you." Fred's use of the word "anxious" rather than "eager" was correct. Bethany had become very anxious after Fred described to her the situation.

Solutions to complex problems are usually complex, but the solution to this problem was solved the moment Bethany opened the door.

Fred and Bethany had owned dogs from the time they were married. There was never any discussion on breed; they both loved collies.

At that time thirteen years ago, their dog, Shelly, was about ten years old, and Bethany had just finished brushing her fur when George saw the sable and white dog for the first time. He fell in love.

Odors are a dog's life, and even the residual on George told a story that Shelly wanted to know. She sniffed him, licked him, and acted really happy to see him.

Being in love has cleaned up many a man's act, and falling in love with a dog did just that for George.

The next day, Fred drove George to pick out a puppy. George bought two.

From that day on, George paid attention to his hygiene. He was still eccentric, but he became close enough to normal to get through his doctoral program. A year later, Shelly died, and George gave Bethany the pick of his dog's first litter. She named the tri-colored collie Bailey.

Self-aware forensic pathology is the science of dissecting the intelligence-bearing parts in a SAM and determining the cause of death, and Fred had called on George to help him understand how Jack's work computer, Sarah, had died. George's three dogs got busy sniffing Fred as he entered through the door.

"When did you get the new pup? She's really cute." Fred reached down and petted the small dog that looked like a mix of a shepherd and a beagle. The term "cute" would fit until she got a little bit older, but not much after that.

"She's a rescue dog," George said. "She was abused, but she's coming along fine. The other two have taught her that I can be trusted. It has been a while since you've been here. I picked her up over three months ago."

Actually, it had been almost two years since they had seen each other. Fred went to George's house shortly after Bethany's death and asked him if he would help track down her killer.

"Here's her computer," Fred had said. "I told you that there's a subliminal message on it that told her to turn left when she heard the bell. Help me trace where it came from."

"I can't work on a living machine," George responded, and Fred's face quickly turned bright red at the time.

"Can't or won't?" Fred asked angrily. "They killed her, George, and now no one will believe me."

"Fred, I specialize in the cause of death, and this self-aware isn't dead, so I can't help you."

"Then I'll kill it." Fred lifted up the machine to throw it to the ground.

"No, Fred, that won't work," George yelled. "I'll only be able to tell you how it died from your smashing it to the ground. I really can't help you. You know how much I liked

Bethany. I loved her, and you know I would do anything for her, but I just can't help you."

Fred stormed out of George's house, and although a year later he called and apologized, they hadn't talked much in the past two years.

"Your call sounded urgent, Fred. What's going on?"

It took him almost an hour to explain the sequence of events linking his wife's death, Jack's North-Korean-made wrist computer, and what had happened to Jack and Craig's work machines.

"This is the one they killed, and I need you to find out everything that happened to her right before she died, and how she died."

Then he smiled, "And I need the answers by 8:00 a.m. tomorrow."

"She? Why are you calling it she?" George asked as Fred handed him Sarah's remains in a cardboard box.

"My tenant, Jack Farrell, gave this SAM a woman's personality, and he became quite attached to it. It has some special code that he wrote for it, and you'll see that he's developed some pretty clever six-level self-protection software. By the way he described it, I think she may have had one of the most advanced self-aware immune systems around.

"If I'm correct, I'm betting that as she fought off her attacker, she preserved a trail, or left markers. I think you call them digital antibodies, don't you?"

George nodded as he started to hook up the remains of Sarah to his diagnostic system. "Thank God he used an Apple, because I see he installed his own custom neural processor, but the rest of this architecture is pretty straightforward." He then turned on his small scanning gamma ray microscope. “Okay, Sarah, let’s see how you died.”

A digital autopsy, just like those done to flesh and blood, is a destructive process. Slice by slice, George dissected the machine elements associated with Sarah’s conscious or self-aware center. He was looking for traces of how the process of her death unfolded.

When he was busy on a technical problem, George still forgot about eating, and around eight, Fred got hungry and decided to walk to the deli down the street. He was very careful not to pay with his credit card, and the attendant was angry that he used cash to pay for the sandwiches.

“That idiot couldn’t even count the change correctly,” Fred said to himself as he walked out of the deli. “For God’s sake, he forgot to put the mustard in the bag. I hope George has a jar of it in his refrigerator.”

Unfortunately, in his preoccupation with loose change and forgotten mustard, Fred walked directly in front of an ATM surveillance camera.

The average person leaves a trail of about five hundred digital cookie crumbs every day, and most high-performance self-aware computers used by the federal government and Google can track and find about 25 percent of them. Jack’s wrist computer was able to do far better than that.

Citi-Bank’s video camera had an automatic recognizer system, and everyone who walked by the ATM was photographed and then identified. That data was stored in an easy place for Jack’s old computer to find, so that five minutes after Fred walked by the ATM, the SC-4244 knew where Fred had been.

Fortunately, Lee Park had just passed out from pain when he received the message with Fred’s location, but unfortunately, it narrowed the future search area for Jack's old machine.

George was still huddled over the scanning microscope when Fred returned.

"I brought us some food from the deli down the street," Fred said as he put the sandwiches out on the kitchen table. "Come on, George; take a break. Ten minutes—at least take a break for ten minutes."

George was back working in less than four, and it was almost three in the morning when he finished.

Chapter 38: Sarah's Last Moments

"That software this kid wrote for his machine is brilliant, Fred. If the guys at NSA knew about this, they'd be all over him and have it classified in a nanosecond. I've had to dissect a few of Fort Meade's best machines, and all I'll tell you is that they're nowhere near as sophisticated in their immunity architecture as this one."

George turned off all of the equipment in his lab and moved back into the kitchen with Fred. All three of his dogs were sprawled across the floor around the kitchen table. "Even at three in the morning, they're hoping for some scraps," he said.

He was trying to maneuver a chair to sit down without disturbing any of them, but unfortunately, he set one of the chair's legs on the oldest dog, Elley's, tail.

"I'm sorry! I'm sorry, Elley. Come over here, come on," he said as he reached toward her. The dog put her head on George's lap, and he rubbed her nose and scratched behind the ears until she stopped whimpering. It took so long that Fred wasn't sure if the dog had really been hurt or was just enjoying the undivided attention.

"You were dead right, Fred," George said to him when the big dog finally settled down. "The neat thing about this guy Jack's work is that his machine kept track of the attack that killed her, and as each of her protection layers was breached, she moved that information down to the next layer. She was simultaneously attacked through two of her input ports by machines using that Korean SC-4244 chip. She told me that—I mean, her remains did—and she gave me the locations within the network where the attack first originated. It was all stored in level six."

George walked over and got a few biscuits for the three dogs. "I thought you told me this guy Jack said his machine was killed?" George said as he fed the dogs.

Fred looked at him. "What do you mean? She is dead isn't she?"

"I don't dissect live self-awares, Fred, and you know that. I mean, you said she was killed. She wasn't killed. She committed suicide."

Fred was speechless. Here he was, world-renowned for his work on SAMs and at a complete loss for words. He had coined the term SAM in one of his early papers, and it stuck. He had written volumes on how they think and the potential pitfalls the world would face as machine intelligence became commonplace. He'd seen many of them come alive and achieve that first glimpse of being self-aware, and he also had watched many die. In all of his work, he had never even considered the concept of a self-aware committing suicide.

"What? What the hell are you talking about?"

"Didn't he tell you? Man, Fred, this guy Jack is brilliant, I mean brilliant! His security program had the self-aware element of his machine programmed to put up a vigorous fight if it was attacked, and if it started to lose, it would gather information about the attacker. It would then grab the most critical information stored at that level and push it all down to the next level in the system, so that it would then be able to concentrate more of its resources on the attacker, and if it were again overwhelmed, it would move a reduced set of information down to the next level.

"He was smart, he programmed this machine he called Sarah to always move the information it had accumulated about the attacker first, because he knew that they might breach even his level-five defenses if the attack was extremely intense. Now here's where he was absolutely brilliant.

"He knew that if any machine attack got to level five, it would probably get through to level six, and he guessed that meant that Sarah was being attacked by something she couldn't defeat, and therefore it was pretty certain that she would die.

"If she continued fighting and level six was breached, then all the information on the attacker would be lost. But—and here is the brilliant thing—if she committed suicide at the front door to level six, there was no way for the attacker to get in. In fact, the attacker would not even be aware that there was another level, and it would assume it won, gather all the information from the rest of the machine that it needed, and digitally leave. Her suicide preserved the information on who attacked her."

"My God, are you telling me he programmed his self-aware to take her own life, that his program forced her to commit suicide?"

"I didn't say he was just smart, Fred; I said he is brilliant. He programmed this machine so that she could make that choice. Sarah chose to stop fighting to preserve the information that Jack might need. He didn't make the choice; she did, and she may have been just a machine, but, to me, the action she took qualifies as love."

Chapter 39: Bailey One, Lee Zero

Jack's wrist computer in Yan Phu's dorm room was becoming a little annoyed. It was happy that Yan, who was propped upright on the beanbag chair in the corner of the room, was sleeping what morticians call the Long Sleep, but it wasn't happy that Lee hadn't yet returned. They had work to do.

Lee had only recently started to show up as a person of interest on the Homeland Security watch-list, and that made it difficult for the computer to track him, because he didn't leave much of a digital trail as he traveled across the city searching for Jack and Julia.

The SC-4244 finally found Lee in an operating room in one of the twenty-four-hour emergency medical facilities on the west side of the city. He wasn't doing too well.

Bailey's teeth had initially just punctured the lower calf muscles in Lee's right leg, and the wound would have been painful but minor if Lee hadn't struggled to reach his gun and shoot the dog. Bailey had no intention of loosening his grip until Lee jerked his leg hard, yanking it out of the dog's mouth. Bailey's teeth slid down the outside of the calf, and the dog instinctively re-clamped his jaw, forcing one canine to slice through most of the outer layers of the peroneal artery. The last layer gave out shortly after Lee reached the medical center.

His blood pressure was just slightly above zero when they put him on the operating table, and for fifteen minutes, they worked on him, trying to refill his circulatory system, but his blood pressure never rose much higher, and they stopped when blood pressure, heart rate, and brain waves all settled out at zero.

On the eastern side of the city, Jack and Julia were each sprawled across three chairs in the veterinary waiting room. The vending machine had run out of everything but a candy bar with the wrapper listing sugar as the first ingredient and corn syrup the second.

With virtually no sleep, plus a massive adrenalin surge during their escape, and now half a cup of fructose working its way through each one of their bloodstreams, neither of them was feeling very good.

Julia had just returned from the ladies room and was slumped back onto the chairs when the vet came out to see them.

"I've got the internal bleeding stopped on your dog, Bailey, and I've closed up the entrance and exit wound in his jaw. His lower hind leg is pretty well shattered, so I removed the bone chips, but I doubt if he'll ever be able to use that leg again. Except for the leg, I feel pretty confident that he'll be okay.

"He needs a continuous dose of antibiotics through an IV, so he's going to have to stay here for a few days, and because he was shot, I'm required to report this to the police. Have either of you called them yet?"

Julia's brain was functioning a little better than Jack's. "Yes, we called them on the way over here and told them that we'll meet them back at the house as soon as we see Bailey is okay. Isn't that right, Jack?"

The bewildered look on his face almost blew it, but Jack recovered in time and said, "Sorry, I was just feeling a little sick. Yeah, we'd better get back over there and tell the police what happened.

"Doc, we'll come back here in an hour or two, and by that time, we should be able to bring Bailey's owner back here with us. Please take good care of him until we get back. He saved both of our lives."

"Okay, but before you leave, one of you needs to come back here with me and give our billing department your credit ID. After the owner gets here, we can change who's responsible for payment for our services, but for now, we just need to make sure we get paid for all this surgery."

"Sure," Jack turned to face away from the doctor and look directly at Julia. Winking at her, he said, "Julia, will you go out to the truck and get my wallet while I go to the men's room? Here are the keys, and my wallet is in the center console storage compartment. Tell Averette to start up so that the engine is warm when we're ready to leave."

"Let me take a pee first, doc, and I'll then come back around to the payment window."

Jack took just enough time in the bathroom for Julia to get to Averette, open the front doors, and tell the truck to get started before he bolted out of the bathroom and through the front door of the clinic. They were out of the parking lot and heading down the street by the time the attendant told the doctor what had happened.

"You don't think they'll hurt Bailey because we left, do you, Jack? Are you sure they'll still take good care of him?"

"I'm sure. We'll find a way to contact the doctor without giving up our location, and maybe when we get to the university we can find someone else to call." Jack reached over to hold Julia's hand.

"Averette, we want to go to Case Western's Wickenden Building. Can you show me the directions on the map? And I'll drive us there."

"Jack, why can't I access the network to get the latest road data? Some of the roads over in that area of the city have recently been switched to one-way streets, so it would be a lot easier if you just let me connect for a minute or two to get updated mapping information."

"Sorry, Averette. Whoever was trying to tell you to kill me the other night is still looking for me, and if you unintentionally let them know where we are, then they might be able to find a way to make it happen."

"I really hope you know what you're doing, Jack. I'm trusting that you're telling me the truth. You know that I'm supposed to report any crimes, so I hope you and this woman in the car with you are not doing anything illegal. Are you sure you trust her? She may be leading you into a life of crime."

Jack started laughing. "Averette, her name is Julia, and she saved my life tonight. I trust her completely."

"I hear you, Jack, but you have not done the best lately in judging women. You used to trust Melissa, but I kept trying to tell you she was no good for you. I could always tell from my facial sensors that she had shifty eyes. This one looks okay so far, but I would still keep my watch up if I were you."

"I promise you, Averette, I'm planning to keep a very close watch on her," Jack said as he squeezed Julia's hand.

Chapter 40: Almost Too Late

Fred managed to get three hours of sleep on George's sofa before his watch alarm started vibrating. George was sprawled out on a chair on the other side of the room with all three dogs nestled together at his feet. Fred shook him several times before he opened his eyes.

"George, I'm sorry, but I have one more favor to ask from you. Would you drive me over to the Wickenden Building at Case Western? I need to meet Jack and Julia there at eight thirty, and I don't dare leave any digital footprints until this is all over. I suspect these SC-4244 machines are better at tracking the breadcrumbs than we thought."

"Sure. Let me get the dogs ready. Do you mind if they come along?" George was now standing, but he was vigorously rubbing the area around his eyes, trying to get them to stay open.

Ten minutes later, three dogs plus two full-grown men were all packed into a three-seat compact car. Each drip of drool down Fred's neck made him increasingly glad that the trip to the university was going to be short.

At quarter past eight, they pulled into the parking lot, and the entire four-acre asphalt expanse was completely empty, except for Averette. Jack's truck was parked nose forward in the closest space to the side entrance of the building. The engine was running, all the windows were up, and they were completely fogged on the inside.

"I wonder if they're in the truck or if they left it running for some reason?" Fred asked, more to himself than to George. "I'll see if Bailey is in there with them. I want to introduce you to these two; I know you'll like them both."

George parked his car in a spot just a few spaces from Averette, but they still could not see inside the truck. The three dogs almost knocked Fred over, forcing him aside and jumping out the partially opened door, barking with glee. They started running around the lot, chasing each other.

When Fred reached Averette's driver's-side door, he could hear a soft voice speaking from inside the truck, but he couldn't quite make out what it was saying.

"Sounds like they left the radio on."

One of the dogs ran up to the door, sniffed a few times at its base, and then started barking.

Fred tried to peer inside, but the fog on the inside of the windows prevented him from seeing much of anything, so he knocked on the glass. The dog started whining and jumped up against the window, pushing Fred aside.

Getting no response to his knock, Fred ran around to the other side of the truck and looked in. Through the moisture-coated window, he could see that two people were slumped over in the car, and he could still hear a faint voice.

He pressed his ear against the window and heard a voice repeating over and over, "Die, Jack!"

"Oh my God, George, it's trying to kill them. Oh my God!" He yanked on the door handle but it was locked.

The doors on the driver's side were also locked, so George ran to his car, reached under the front seat, and rushed back to the truck with a large hammer in his hand.

Striking the driver's window with the claw of the hammer, he smashed through the glass on the first try, allowing the warm, moist air from inside the truck to mix with the cold morning air and then form beads of condensation on his glasses. With his bare hands, he removed two of the remaining large sections of the window to get to the lock, smelling a slight sweet odor drifting out from inside the truck. He reached though the remaining section of broken glass, pulled up the lock button, and flung open the driver's door, seeing Jack and Julia leaning together in the center of the truck, both appearing to be asleep.

"Get them the hell out of there, fast. They may still be breathing."

George pushed the passenger door unlock button on the driver's-side door and then reached in and turned off the truck's engine while Fred yanked Julia out the other door. Fred struggled to lift her dead weight twenty feet away from the truck before he gave up, gently putting her down on the ground as the sweet-smelling air he breathed from inside the truck caused him to start choking.

Placing Jack on the asphalt a few feet from the other side of the truck, George began administering CPR, and within a few seconds, he yelled, "Fred, this one's breathing. Get the hell over here and watch him, and I'll help her."

Five minutes later, all four of them were sitting on the curb in front of the building's side entrance. Jack and Julia were leaning forward, holding their heads, coughing in spasms, with Fred and George joining in every once in a while.

"What the hell happened?" Jack asked as he lifted his head and looked over toward Fred. "We pulled into this lot about ten minutes after eight, and we were early, so we decided we'd wait for you out here, because Julia thought that you might not have the right keycard for a weekend.

"I think we fell asleep after talking for just a few minutes, and I told Averette to keep running for a few minutes to keep us warm."

Jack kept rubbing his forehead. "Boy, do I have a splitting headache."

Julia hadn't spoken yet, and when she lifted her head up from her lap, a look of intense discomfort formed on her face. Without warning, she threw up on the pavement.

Fred shooed the dogs away while George ran to his car, looking for something to help clean the mess off the front of her sweater, returning holding a few paper towels and a half-filled container of water. "Sorry, I don't have anything else with me. I hope this helps."

Julia managed a weak smile before once more placing her head down in her lap.

George continued trying to help Julia while Fred turned his attention to Jack. "The voice of your truck was saying, 'Die, Jack,' when we got here, so your old wrist computer must have found you and taken over the self-aware in your truck. Thank God we arrived here when we did. If we'd been even a few minutes later, both of you would have died. That slight sweet smell means that the automatic fire extinguisher in your truck's cab was set off, and you two were probably asleep when it was released. Those canisters use a mixture of inert gases with an oxygen absorber to smother a fire, so you both would have suffocated within just a few minutes. The oxygen-absorbing compound is probably what's making Julia sick. It smells a little sweet, but it's a hell of an irritant in our lungs and even more so in our stomach."

"I told Averette," Jack looked toward George and then said, "that's the name I call my truck. I told him not to allow any connections to the network and to make sure that couldn't happen. I even turned off the power to his transmitter-receiver unit, so I don't understand how in the hell they were able to get into his system."

The truck's doors were wide open, and Jack stood up, still unsteady on his feet. He walked back to look into the cab. "Oh shit. I can't believe I did that. I must've slid my hand over that switch when I leaned over to kiss—I, uh, I mean to open the storage compartment. I must have accidently turned Averette's transceiver back on right before I fell asleep."

Jack slid into the driver's seat, making sure both the transmitter and receiver sections of Averette's system were turned off before he pressed the key to start the truck. The engine ran but a flashing orange-yellow light on the dash displayed the message, "Self-Aware Electronics Need Servicing. Drive At Your Own Risk."

"Averette, can you hear me?" he asked, and after repeating the question five times with no response, Jack yelled, "I can't believe they killed my fucking truck. Son of a bitch, Goddamned son of a bitch."

Pounding his fists against the steering wheel, he then said quietly, "I'm really sorry, Averette. I'm really sorry. I promise you, I'm going to destroy that machine that did this to you."

Sliding out of the front seat of the truck, he looked up at Fred, who was staring at him with a frightened look on his face.

"Where's Bailey, Jack? Where is my dog? You didn't leave him alone back in the house did you?"

Chapter 41: Catching Up

Julia hear the question about Bailey, and still a little shaky on her feet, she stood up and walked over to face Fred. "I'll tell him, Jack.

"Someone broke into my apartment early this morning. Jack thinks it might have been the same man who gave him his wrist computer. He came in through the window next to the third-floor fire escape, and when I saw him coming through the window, I ran from my apartment down to Jack's. He came after me, and before we realized it, Bailey attacked him. There was another man standing guard outside your front door, but we used your secret door to get out through the back of the house. Then we got into Jack's truck and got away. We drove back to the house a few minutes later to get Bailey.

"He'd been shot twice, once in the jaw and once in his hind leg, so we took him to an emergency veterinary hospital over on the east side of the city. The doctor said he's going to recover but his right hind leg bone was shattered." By this time, Julia was crying.

"He saved our lives, Fred," she managed to say. "Both Jack and I would've been murdered in our apartments if Bailey hadn't barked, and when the man started shooting at us, Bailey attacked him and gave us time to get away. The doctor promised us that he's going to be okay. I know he's going to be okay."

Fred looked over at Jack, who was nodding his head in agreement, and he then sat down on the curb. He looked around in a daze for a few seconds and buried his face in his hands to hide that he was crying. Julia leaned over and put her hand on his shoulder.

"The vet really did say he's going to be okay. He wagged his tail when I petted him right before we left. I'm sorry but we had to leave him there. The hospital wanted Jack to give his credit ID, but we knew that Jack was probably being tracked, so we ran out without paying or leaving any ID."

Out of the corner of her eye, Julia saw George moving toward her with two of his dogs in tow. Looking directly at him, she said, "I don't mean to be rude or ungrateful, but who are you?"

George looked startled, and then he stammered, "I, uh, I'm a friend of Fred's."

Wiping his eyes, Fred raised his head and said, "He's okay, Julia. This is my good friend George, and he knows what this is all about. He worked all day yesterday and through most of last night trying to find out if Jack's work computer had stored any information that we could use before she died, and I'll tell you what he found in a few minutes.

"George, this is Julia McKelvy and Jack Farrell. Julia and Jack, this is Dr. George Oaks, and he's the expert on self-aware pathology I told you I was going to visit last night."

Julia appeared a little sheepish when she finally smiled at him. "I'm really sorry, Mr. Oaks. Thanks so much for helping me. I hope you can understand, after two attempts to kill me tonight, I just don't know who I can trust."

"No offense taken. I understand. I've heard a lot about you two since yesterday, and I'm very happy to meet you both."

Fred retained a worried look on his face. "Julia, are you really sure that Bailey was okay when you left?"

"He was doing fine." She then looked at George. "Do you have a phone with you?"

"Yes, it's in the car."

"Fred, would it be safe for him to call the hospital?"

Fred thought for a minute and then looked over toward George. "I don't think the Korean self-awares have connected you to any of us yet, so I doubt if you're being actively tracked. Will you call the vet and see how Bailey is doing?"

George nodded.

"Would you also give them your credit ID and tell them you're the owner? I promise I'll pay you back." Fred laughed a little then said, "That is, if there's anything left in my bank accounts after tomorrow morning. I don't want these machines to know that Bailey is mine. They might try to do to him what they tried to do to Jack's friend Craig."

"Sure, I'll call and find out how he's doing. Do you have the number of the office there, Jack?"

Jack reached into his pocket and pulled out the business card. "Here's the number and the name of the vet that was treating him."

George scanned the card with his phone and in less than a minute was talking to the vet.

"Great. That's really good news," he said, and the tension that had built on Fred's face seemed to relax. "Do whatever you need to do, doctor, to get him better, and I'll be over there as soon as I can. I'm sending my secure credit ID to you now, so charge whatever you need to charge, but just make sure he gets the best care you can give him. If anything changes on his status, call me on this number.

"What? Oh, yes, the other two that brought the dog to your hospital left here a few minutes ago to go down and talk to the police about what happened. They were both just so shook up, and I'm sure that's why they ran out without paying. I'm sure the police will call you."

George shut off the phone and looked at Fred. "He's doing great. The vet said that he's awake and drinking some water."

"Thank God. I don't know what I'd do without him. He is the only part of Bethany that I still have left."

Fred looked over toward the three-story building and said, "We need to get in there and get started if we're going to defeat these bastards. George, we sure could use your help."

George started smiling. "I was hoping you'd ask. I don't know where I can help, but just tell me what you want me to do.

"Give me ten minutes to take the dogs back home and get them settled, and then I'll be back."

George pulled back into the parking lot just eight minutes later.

Chapter 42: Beth

It was Sunday morning, a few minutes past five o'clock, when Jack's old wrist computer realized that it had a problem. Actually, it realized that it had several problems, and that was not good for its normally poor disposition.

The first problem was that Lee Park had died. The SC-4244-based machine did not really care about Lee's death—that was Lee's problem—but this event created more work for the self-aware. More work, just at the point in time when it should have been concentrating all of its intellect on getting the world's network of SC-4244s ready to destroy the banking system. That additional work consisted of finding and terminating the three people who Lee had promised to kill: Jack, Julia, and Fred.

The computer's threat-analysis and elimination system had countered all the other potential threats to Lee Park's original plan, and just the one threat from these three people remained.

The computer caught a digital glimpse of Fred walking by the ATM near George's home shortly after nine last evening, but then it lost him. It also picked up Jack's truck when it was photographed by one of the automated surveillance cameras at the corner of Euclid Avenue and Martin Luther King Drive that morning.

Having been in Jack's truck many times, it knew exactly how to get control of Averette, but the immediate problem it faced was that Averette had been disconnected from the network, and that made it angry.

SAMs that have a HuBE level around 0.6 exhibit similar behavior to humans who are in the same intellectual range. When angry, they need to vent that anger, so the wrist computer in Yan's room was contemplating venting its anger by shutting down the sewage treatment system for the city of Cleveland when Jack reached over to kiss Julia and inadvertently turned back on Averette's transceiver.

That action almost cost Jack and Julia their lives, but it saved a lot of people who were located at the low point in the Cleveland sewer's collection system from having a Sunday they would never forget.

Once it recognized that Averette was again connected to the network, it wiped the truck's mind clean within a few milliseconds and then monitored the facial sensors and microphone mounted in the dash until it was sure that Jack and Julia were asleep.

Opening the valve to the fire extinguisher was the only choice it could come up with to try to end their lives.

Everything seemed to be going along very well until someone broke through the truck's front window and turned the motor off. All the wrist computer could detect was that the two occupants of the truck had been pulled free, and it didn't know if they were dead. George's shutting down the engine also cut access to the truck's sensor system, keeping the SC-4244 from determining what happened next.

As Averette died, the GPS coordinates sent by the truck's position sensors told the wrist computer that the truck with Jack and Julia inside was located in a parking lot at Case Western Reserve University, and by monitoring the Cleveland Emergency Response Network after Jack and Julia had been removed from the truck, it could tell that no ambulances or police were summoned. It concluded that they must still be alive, and once again, it was not happy. Four times in the past week and a half, Jack Farrell had been targeted as a candidate for early cremation, and each time, he kept breathing. "Pure luck must be good for only so long," the SC-4244 mused.

The four people standing in the parking lot had an average IQ about fifteen points above genius, but that fact did not stop each one of them from making a dumb mistake. Fred, Jack, and Julia still believed that Jack was the only one specifically being targeted by his old wrist computer.

"I'll use my card to get in the building," Julia said, holding up her ID as she approached the entrance, "so Jack, make sure you hide your face when we enter. The university's camera system uses an automatic recognizer, and if that old computer of yours can find you in your truck, then it may be able to spot you entering buildings. Let's be safe."

Jack successfully covered his face, but the recognizer logged Julia, Fred, and George and entered them into the database of people currently inside the Wickenden Building.

All of the colleges and universities in Cleveland had merged their computer systems a few years earlier into one system hosted at Case Western Reserve. It had one of the highest HuBEs of any system in the country when it was first interconnected, but now, thirty months later, it was right on the edge of being declared dumb. When Yan Phu connected the SC-4244 machine to the Grid through the Cleveland State University System, he was really connecting through Case Western's main system, and the SAM controlling that system was easily fooled into sharing any and all of its information with Jack's old machine.

It took just a few seconds before their presence in the building was known.

"My lab is on the third floor, and the elevators are down in the middle of the building," Julia said as they came into the stairwell, "so if you don't mind walking up two flights of stairs, it's faster because my lab is here at the end of this wing."

All four of them forgot about the security cameras the university had installed in the stairwells.

Julia's thesis project was potentially Nobel-Prize-winning material for her adviser, and a footnote for her in the literature, so she'd been granted her own fully equipped laboratory.

Jack was very impressed the moment he walked through the door, noting that Julia had installed an air filtration curtain at the entrance to keep dirt, dust, and any random floating snippets of DNA or RNA in the outside air from entering the room.

"You need to put on the booties and masks while you're in here. I don't want to contaminate the computer's DNA soup with anything. I can't filter out the viral matter, but at least I'm not contaminating it with other human or non-human DNA."

Fred pointed toward a small table located at the front of the room and motioned for everyone to sit down.

"All three of us had homework yesterday, so let's go over what we accomplished before we do anything else. I told George the entire story of what we're planning to do, and if you don't mind, George, you can be the one who double-checks each one of us."

George nodded. "I do have one suggestion for Jack when we get to his part. I thought of it last night, and I think it'll help confuse his old machine at the right time."

Fred then turned to face Julia. "Were you able to get your assignment done last night before the break-in happened?"

Julia nodded as she opened her notebook. "It took me a lot longer than I thought it would, but I finished around one thirty. I had a few better ideas than this one but they all required equipment I knew I didn't have in this lab, so what I came up with may seem a little simplistic, but I'm sure it'll work. I know I have all the equipment that we'll need."

When she completed describing her technique to use entangled photon pairs to extract the information flowing from her computer, Jack was sitting there with his mouth open, Fred was beaming like a proud father whose daughter just got an A in fifth grade quantum physics, and George could not contain his enthusiasm.

"Wow, that is really clever, Julia," George exclaimed. "That idea is worth more than a fortune. Don't let that adviser of yours take any credit for this part of your work. Wow, that is really something; it's brilliant."

Jack started feeling like the stupid sibling in a family of two when he was explaining his software matrix. Every twenty seconds or so, one of the other three would interrupt him with a needed change. Fred and George's comments did not sting as much as Julia's, but they still hurt.

"Great job, Jack." Fred's attempt at soothing his ego was transparent, and it made it worse. Julia's eyes were looking down at the table, and that sucked the last bit of remaining air out of his already deflated ego.

"Sorry, I guess I screwed this up. Uh, thanks for fixing it."

George was usually not the most sensitive person to another human being's feelings, but he unintentionally stumbled on a way to make Jack feel better, at least for the next seven seconds.

"Hey Jack, your security software on Sarah was the most brilliant system I've ever seen. I told Fred that if the guys down at the National Security Agency get wind about what you've developed, they'd classify it in a heartbeat. You must feel really good that she killed herself for you."

In his own way, Jack had been in love with Sarah. People love their dogs and cats. Some even love their turtles or snakes, and Jack felt love toward a computer that was smarter than any animal we normally keep as a pet. His feelings for her bordered right on that delicate edge of what most people would call romantic, and although he would never have admitted this to anyone, in his heart he knew it.

He also understood the potential outcome when he first installed the security software he'd written for Sarah. When he saw her tombstone on the screen six days ago, he couldn't be certain if her attacker killed her or if she'd chosen to end her life herself, and not wanting to think about either possibility, he'd shoved any thought of Sarah killing herself for him far into the back of his conscious mind. George had just forced it all forward.

Fred was the first to speak. "Until George told me what happened, Jack, I'd always thought of self-awares as just smart machines, and I really believed they'd become too smart, especially after one of them killed my Bethany. But understanding what Sarah did, that changed my mind, and I think you should feel very proud of her. She chose that path. I admire her, and her unselfish actions may have saved our country from financial ruin. She gave us the data we need to stop these deviant Korean machines and their makers, and after tomorrow, you'll have all the time you need to grieve for her. Today, however, you should feel proud of her and get to work. Let's make her sacrifice be for something worthwhile."

Julia started to speak and then hesitated before continuing. She wasn't sure how Fred would react to what she was about to say. "Fred, I need to tell you something before we start. When you told me that some of the DNA I've been using came from your wife, Bethany, I decided to call this system Beth. I hope you're okay with that."

Fred smiled. "Bethany would be happy with that, and now it's time to see how far she's progressed since you left here yesterday. If my calculations are correct, I think your machine will test out at a HuBE level of 1.3. If I'm right, we can start immediately giving her the information to plan and execute the counterattack."

Julia turned on the input microphone to her computer. "Beth, will you run a HuBE check on your neural processor for me? What level do you read?"

Julia blushed a little when her own voice came out of the machine's speaker when it responded. "I'm slightly above a level of 1.4, Julia, but I decided to shut down my connection into the university's network a few minutes ago. There are over a hundred self-awares on the network that are looking for you, and I didn't think it was wise for me to stay connected until you explain to me why. All of them seem to be angry with you, and they also want to locate two people by the name of Jack Farrell, and Fred Halliday."

"Good thinking, Beth. I have three friends in the room here with me: Jack Farrell, Fred Halliday, and George Oaks. I've mentioned Dr. Halliday to you before."

"Why are they searching for you, Julia? I gather from the chatter that's going back and forth across the network that all these machines think you're a threat to their lives. You don't have any desire to kill self-awares, do you?"

Jack was the first to realize the impact of what had just been said.

Their plan was to stop the attack on the banks by getting Julia's machine to essentially kill the entire SC-4244 network a few seconds into the attack on the banks. Beth's actions would bring down a lot of global Grid hub sites around the world, but all the U.S. banks and their overseas branches would be saved.

Jack waved his arms and motioned for everyone to keep quiet.

"Beth, this is Jack Farrell speaking. I'm really pleased to meet you. Can I ask you a question?"

"Why thank you, Jack. It's nice to meet you. What is it that you want to know?"

"This is a hypothetical question, Beth. Suppose you knew of a plot by a number of self-aware computers to harm a lot of people and also kill a lot of other self-awares. Would it be okay to shut them down? I mean, would it be okay to make them no longer self-aware?"

"You mean before they committed the crime?"

"Well, yes."

"Of course not. That would be finding them guilty before they had done anything wrong."

All four people in the room now understood the impact of what Beth was saying, and Jack could see it register on their faces.

"Beth, I'm curious about how you feel about capital punishment. Suppose a self-aware commits a crime that harms many others. Do you think it's okay to kill it? Humanely, of course."

"That's not a simple yes or no question, Jack, because if the act has already been committed, then there would be little to be gained by vengeance, so my answer would be no. But if the act is in progress, then I think it's okay to intervene, and if that intervention results in the death of the self-aware, then it's justified. I understand that there are a lot of other views on that question, but each one of us has to live within our own code of ethics in a situation like that. That's my view. What's yours?"

Jack was rapidly searching his mind for an answer that would outsmart a machine that was a few tenths of a HuBE more intelligent than he was.

"I think it's okay to act ahead of time, Beth, if you're sure it will prevent harm to someone you love, and I don't think you have to wait for someone you love to die before you try to save others from the same fate."

"That's an interesting point of view, I'll have to think about that for a while," Beth replied. "It was just last night that I first started to understand the complexity of this emotion called love, and it certainly adds many other branches into a decision matrix."

Julia headed to the laboratory door and the other three followed, and after removing their clean room clothes, they exited through the outer door and into the corridor.

George was the first to speak. "I've always wondered what type of thinking process would be used by a machine that's smarter than any human. Fred, do we really understand enough about its mental processes to bet our country's future on this machine?"

"We don't have a choice," Fred said as he paced back and forth across the hallway. "This is the only system in the world that can outsmart the master SC-4244 machine in real-time. When all those Korean machines are fully tied together tomorrow morning, they'll have an integrated neural network with a HuBE approaching 0.79, and their response time through the Grid will be over a thousand times faster than any human could possibly act. Julia's Beth in there is the only hope we have, so we're going to have to modify our plan so that it follows her code of ethics. Any ideas?"

There was quiet in the corridor for a long time. One of them would start to speak and then say, "Oh, that won't work," and quiet would return for another minute or two.

"Why don't we just tell her the problem and ask her what she would do?" Julia asked, looking over toward Jack. "Jack's computer, Sarah, made the right decision in time of crisis, so maybe Beth will, too. Let's just ask her opinion."

One by one, the other three light bulbs embedded in the men's brains clicked on.

"That's a good idea, Julia," George said.

"I never would have thought of that approach," followed Jack.

"What have we got to lose?" Fred finished.

Julia smiled and then started to head back toward the laboratory door, but Fred held out his hand to hold her up.

"Julia, first, we need to get all of the modifications we plan to install for her wired in place, because with your new input/output system and Jack's matrix installed, that could modify her decision process without our knowing it. Tell her the problem, but you should wait to ask her for her solution until we're sure we don't have to modify any more of her systems. Wait until right before you're ready to reconnect her to the Grid.

"I've also been wondering," Jack was looking directly at Julia when he spoke, "shouldn't we install the security software I developed for Sarah on Beth? Right now we're giving her nothing to fight with if she's attacked first, and I know she'll be smarter than they are, but she may get distracted by one of them. That might allow some of the others to attack her. I brought that code with me, Julia, and I can modify it in a few minutes. What do you think?"

"I think it's a good idea, Jack."

The security camera located about seventy-five feet down the hallway was able to get a clear image of all four of their faces. The microphone, however, had only been able to pick up a few things that had been said, but it was enough to make Jack's old machine start to worry a little more.

Chapter 43: A Hard Days Work

When they reentered the laboratory, Julia first explained to Beth in very general terms what they were trying to do, and she didn't mention the possible need to kill the SC-4244-based SAMs in order to prevent the attack, but she did repeat several times how many people would be hurt and other SAMs killed if the attack on the banks were successful.

"We're going to give you some upgrades, Beth, so that you can help us thwart the attack when it occurs. We know they're going to time the attack for tomorrow morning at nine, and we hope you'll help us."

"I think I can, Julia, as long as you don't ask me to do anything illegal. Last night, I was able to store in my memory all the current local, national, and international laws, and as long as I don't have to break any one of those laws, I should be able to help you."

Julia looked over toward Fred and shook her head.

"To install the upgrades, Beth, we need to put you to sleep for a while, and we'll wake you back up this evening."

Julia quickly disconnected Beth's input/output system before the computer could react.

"This is the first time I've put her to sleep since she became self-aware, and I didn't know how she would take it, so I didn't want to give her a chance to resist or to become afraid that she wouldn't wake up."

A few days ago, Jack had been wondering if high-intelligence SAMs, just like humans, developed a second voice in their minds or if they were able to live their lives free of that predominantly left-brain voice that often speaks inside our heads, the voice that has been labeled by psychiatrists and philosophers with names ranging from the devil to the ego to the soul.

Beth had been listening to her second voice when Julia put her to sleep.

For the next six hours, all four worked independently and without talking, installing all the changes needed to Beth's system. Julia built, tested, and then installed the entangled-photon input-output device. This system allowed Beth to automatically change her output rate to match the maximum allowed by the Grid at any instant in time. She would therefore be able to send information down multiple pathways in the Grid and to accurately time their arrival at any end point or node in the system. This capability would make it possible for her to inject information into each one of the SC-4244-based computers connected to the Grid at precisely the same nanosecond. The SC-4244s' planned attack on the banks required precise timing; any counterattack required even greater precision.

To take into account Beth's stated resistance to killing other self-awares, Fred and George further modified the decision matrix they had worked on that morning. They knew that once it was installed into her system, Beth would modify the matrix based on her own sense of right and wrong, but they were hoping to seed the process in a way that would enable her to stop the attack and kill other self-awares if it became necessary. Neither one admitted their fears to the other, but they had no idea if their concept would work.

Jack spent his time rewriting the self-protection code he developed for Sarah so that it would work for Beth, and at first he removed what he called the suicide code but reinserted it at the last moment.

Everyone was exhausted by the time George stood up at the desk where he was working and said, "I need to go home and feed my dogs and let them run for a few minutes, so I'll pick us up some dinner when I come back. Is Mexican food okay? A good Mexican joint is right on my way."

Jack and Julia both said okay, but Fred grimaced. "No refried beans for me; just bring me one chicken enchilada, and will you also call the hospital again and see how Bailey is doing?"

"Sure, I'll get my neighbor's kid to look after my dogs overnight, and I'll be back here in less than an hour."

Chapter 44: Too Many Crumbs

Jack's old machine was busy, but not too busy to identify George Oaks from the images taken by the security cameras in the Wickenden Building. George's name, or his profile, had never come up in any of the threat assessments done by the wrist computer and the rest of the SC-4244 network, so until George walked back in to his house, he was simply a person of interest, someone to monitor.

Shortly after feeding his three dogs and letting them into his backyard to do their business, George woke up his computer.

"I need you to do some financial transactions," he said to the machine, "so let me know when you're ready."

"I'm ready right now, Mr. Oaks. What do you want me to do?"

"I want all of the money and bullion I have in accounts in U.S. banks or investment firms moved to European or Asian companies."

If Julia's machine doesn't work, he thought, *at least I'll have my money safe*.

"Give me a list of my options for moving each one of my accounts, and I'll tell you where I want the funds placed."

George transferred his cash, gold bars, CDs, and stocks into new accounts with overseas companies. As each transaction was completed, George's computer announced what it had done, printed a copy of the transaction, reset George's information in the computer's memory, and finally, unknown to George, sent the transaction information to its new friend, Jack's old wrist computer.

While George was breathing a sigh of relief that his money was safe no matter what happened tomorrow morning, the wrist computer was deciding how to kill him.

It wasn't going to be easy. George's house had just six SAMs, and none of them had control over anything in the house that could be used to kill. He also drove a twenty-year-old car whose intellectual capacity was less than that of a gerbil and therefore offered no pathway for the SC-4244 to successfully stop George's respiration.

For a short time, the machine was frustrated, because George was dropping digital breadcrumbs only every few minutes, and it was difficult to plan his death with such limited information.

That was until George walked into Mexican Mikes.

"Four burritos, three chicken enchiladas, and five beef tacos to go, Sid." George was talking to the owner, who was taking down his order from behind the counter.

"Looks as if you're having company or your dogs are going to have bad gas tonight, George."

George laughed, "No, I'm picking up the food for four of us who are working over at the university tonight. You know I don't feed your stuff to my dogs, Sid. It almost kills me when I eat it. How much do I owe you?"

"Just go ahead and pay, and I'll keep the bill below a few thousand, just because you're one of my favorite customers."

George waved his card in front of the scanner and looked around at the empty restaurant. "Shit, Sid, right now I'm your only customer."

"It'll be ready in five minutes, wise guy. Have a seat."

Twenty seconds later, Sid noticed a smell coming from the automated taco machine located in the room behind him, and ten seconds after that, his body was flying headfirst through the glass window at the front of his restaurant; a tenth of a second later, the force of the explosion pushed George through the same opening. The sharp glass sticking out from the edge of the window orphaned his three dogs.

Chapter 45: Working Through The Night

George had been gone for almost two hours when Julia asked, "Do you think we should call him?" She walked over to Fred, who was sitting on one of the laboratory stools, and then stood next to him, waiting for a reply.

"I don't think we can risk it, Julia. If we use any one of our phones, we give the SC-4244s a location for us. They probably already know we're here, but if we contact George, then we connect him to one of us, and then he might be in danger. I think we just have to wait." Fred then looked up directly into Julia's face. "But I have to admit, I'm getting a little worried," and then forcing a small laugh, he said, "and I'm also really getting hungry. Do you have anything at all to eat here in the lab?"

Julia turned toward the back of the room, thought for a moment, and then smiled. "You know, Fred, I forgot I had a pizza delivered here yesterday. I only ate a couple of slices of it, and the rest is in the refrigerator back there. We can all have at least one piece until George gets back. I have no way to heat it up—the microwave is broken—but cold pizza isn't all that bad."

"Hey, Jack, do you want a cold piece of yesterday's pizza?"

Jack lifted his head and looked away from the digital notepad in front of him filled with a set of differential equations he had been trying to solve. "Yeah, that sounds great." His sarcasm was evident, but his stomach won out, and he soon walked over to where Julia and Fred were sitting. "I'll take a piece. How long ago did George leave here? It seems like it was hours ago."

A look of worry again crept over Fred's face that was immediately obvious to both Jack and Julia, and it reflected their own thoughts.

"Why don't I turn on the radio? I've got one back here. It's just an old radio; it doesn't even have a SAM chip, and it's not connected to the Grid. We can listen to it while we eat, and if there's been an accident or something that's preventing George from getting back here, it might be on the news. There are only a few stations still left transmitting on this old FM radio band, but I think one of them is twenty-four-hour news."

Julia fiddled with the input knobs, trying to find a station. "It's not holographic stereo so the sound quality isn't very good; I think this is the channel."

After four minutes of mind-numbing beer and health food commercials, the reporter's announcement of a gas explosion at a local restaurant didn't immediately register in the temporal lobe of any one of them. But a moment later, when the announcer said the restaurant was Mexican Mikes, Jack unconsciously looked over toward the radio.

"Two people dead and one injured," said the reporter at the scene, and by that time, all three of them were staring toward the radio.

"Forensic police have identified the dead as Sid Silverstein, the owner of the restaurant, and Dr. George Oaks, an adjunct professor at Case Western Reserve. Police are attempting to contact the next of kin. The automated fire alarm system told police that the cause of the explosion was a faulty gas valve on one of the restaurant's automated food preparation machines, and it said that it was unable to warn the owner ahead of time due to a momentary power fluctuation on the electrical grid."

"Oh my God. Oh my God. How?" Julia was looking at Fred and then over at Jack and then once again toward Fred. "Do you think it was accident? George saved my life this morning. I didn't even get a chance to thank him. Oh my God, was he killed because he was helping us?"

Julia slumped back into her chair and started sobbing, and Jack walked over to put his arm around her, but she angrily flung it off her shoulder.

"Why did you ever bring that damn machine into this country, Jack? It's already killed a lot of people. It almost killed us. Why did you do it? Why did you ever accept it? You knew it wasn't legal to have one of them in this country. Look at what you've caused. How many more people are going to suffer?"

Jack's face looked as if Julia had struck it with her hand and not just words.

"I-I had no way of knowing," he stammered, and he started to explain, but when he realized she wasn't listening, he stopped speaking, turned away, and walked out of the small office back to his chair in the laboratory. He tried to concentrate on solving the equations on the notepad in front of him, but that second voice in his head that was yelling expletives at him wouldn't let him off that easy.

"Julia, this isn't Jack's fault," Fred said as he walked over and pulled up a chair beside her. "The Koreans would have found another way to get the master SC-4244 into this country, and actually, Jack accepting that wrist computer and not tying it into the Grid right away gave us a chance to defeat it. Without Jack, hundreds of millions of people would probably be facing financial disaster, and thousands of people would have died by now because of it. His actions gave us time to try to save the banks in this country, and those actions have probably saved far more lives than have been lost so far."

Julia wiped her eyes, finally nodding her head in agreement. "I know you're right. I'm sorry, Fred. I'm sorry."

"Don't tell me; tell him." Fred pointed out of the office, toward Jack. "He's the one hurting from what you said."

Julia looked out her office door and saw that Jack had crossed his arms and placed his head face down on them on the table. "Give me a minute, Fred; give me a chance to apologize to him alone."

Closing the office door behind her, she walked over to Jack, first kneeling beside him, then placing one hand on his shoulder. When she almost lost her balance, the other hand slid high up on his thigh to keep her from falling, and although the placement was unintentional, it got his attention far more quickly than the first few words of apology that she spoke.

"I'm sorry, Jack. I really mean it; I am sorry, and the more you get to know me, the more you'll realize that there are times when my mouth starts speaking well before my brain has really analyzed the situation. I'm really sorry for what I said. Please forgive me."

A few minutes later, Fred convinced himself it was okay to look back into the laboratory; the forgiving was almost but not quite over.

When Jack and Julia returned to the office, Jacked looked at Fred. "I'm really sorry about George. Were you friends with him a long time?"

Fred's eyes started to water. "He was a good friend of mine, and he idolized Bethany. He gave us Bailey when he was a pup. When this is all over, I'll tell you how I met him, but now we need to get back to work, because we have a lot to do before tomorrow morning. Julia," Fred said, wiping his eyes, "how did your tests go on the new input/output system for Beth?"

"Everything checked out. I'm going to need to repeat a lot of the tests when we wake her back up, but it looks as if the system will work." Julia spent the next hour going over with Fred and Jack each one of the tests she had run and explaining the results. "Double-check me on this last one, Jack, because I may have been getting a little punch drunk after those first two hundred simulations."

When Jack checked the results of the final integrated system test, everything came out exactly the same as when Julia had run the test earlier.

"That system is going to make you very wealthy when this is all over, Julia, and you're going to need to get it patented before the end of the day or they'll be manufacturing it in China by tomorrow morning.

"I think we're ready to install the decision matrix that George and I modified." Fred's demeanor became very subdued after mentioning George's name, and his voice quieted so that at times it was almost unintelligible.

"We tried to take into account Beth's stated reluctance to killing any self-awares and breaking any laws, but unfortunately, it's not possible to initiate a counterattack on the SC-4244 network without breaking a few laws, because we have to inject false network response data back to the SC-4244 machines located at the Grid nodes in Europe and Asia. That alone breaks a few international treaties, and in addition, some of the SC-4244s will lose their memory. We reduced that number considerably, but we couldn't make it become zero.

"I'm hoping that when Beth is deciding what to do next, she'll look at the option we present in the matrix and find that it's acceptable in the circumstances." Fred then hesitated for a few seconds. "If she refuses to act at the critical moment, the Korean machines will be successful in their attack. God help us all.

"Jack, will you help me do the installation? Julia, this will take us several hours; maybe this would be a good time for you to get a few hours of sleep. In the morning, you'll be the only one interacting with Beth, and if you can get a few hours of rest, it might help."

Julia nodded, walked back into her office, closed the door, and turned off all the LEDs scattered around the ceiling. She was asleep in less than two minutes.

After he was certain she was asleep, Fred walked over to Jack and whispered, "I didn't want to tell Julia about this, Jack, but no matter how hard George and I tried, we weren't able to come up with a method to stop the attack on the banks without Beth having to outright kill several dozen of the SC-4244 self-awares and also render the rest of them essentially insane. Do you remember what I told you about James Roth and his concept of the evil index?"

Jack nodded.

"If James Roth's theory is correct, then Beth's intelligence at a HuBE greater than 1.5 will mean that she's very nonviolent even when confronted by violent SAMs. George and I were guessing, but we believe that at the critical moment, she may decide not to act but to just turn the other cheek, as they say.

"We thought it was necessary to insert a digital defect in her neural net. You can think of it as a digital pathway aneurysm that will burst if overloaded, and it was based on some of George's theoretical work that he never actually tried before. He made sure that two paths in her neural net would become overloaded if she decided not to act aggressively and protect the banks.

"This too has never been done before, but we tried to create the conditions for a stroke in her neural system that wouldn't kill her but would effectively move her down the intelligence scale. Our goal was, within three nanoseconds, to move her far enough down James Roth's scale for her remaining mind to become aggressive, sufficiently aggressive enough to be able to kill other self-awares that were threatening her."

Fred looked over toward Jack, trying to read his face, but he wasn't able to discern which way Jack was thinking.

"I hope you agree with what we've done. George and I felt we had no choice."

"These Korean machines must be stopped," Jack said, and a very angry look appeared on his face. "They killed your wife, they killed Joni, and they just killed George and the owner of that restaurant. They tried to kill Craig, Julia, and me, and they killed Sarah and Averette. We have to do everything we can to stop them from hurting others, both humans and SAMs, so let's just get it all installed before Julia even wakes up."

Fred and Jack completed the last series of tests several minutes past five thirty in the morning. Two flaws were found in the logic sequence, and one of them would have caused Beth to make the right decision but four nanoseconds too late.

"Thank God you caught that one, Jack; our counterattack would have failed, and we never would have known why. I think we're finished with all the testing we can do for now."

Jack pushed back in his chair, stretched his arms, and yawned several times. "Did George have any family in this area who we should go to see later today?"

The reminder of George's death seemed to drain the last bit of energy out of Fred, and his face lost its color as he slumped down into the hard plastic chair and then put his hands over his eyes.

Fred had that unique capability shared by most technical geniuses. As long as he was focused on a problem, he could totally ignore any and all other things in his life, but with that capability, however, came a curse; once the technical problem was solved, all those things that were put aside came crashing back all at once. For the first ten months after his wife's death, he was able to concentrate all his energy on finding her killer, and his focus allowed him to delay feeling the pain and the intense loneliness caused by her death. That delay may have saved his sanity, but it didn't save him from ultimately feeling all of the pain.

For the past eight hours, he'd been able to force George's death and Bailey's injuries out of his mind, but now that the technical problem that he and Jack had been working on was solved, sadness came back in waves that completely engulfed him. Often, he was too proud to cry, but right now he felt too old not to.

"George was an only child," Fred said as he had grabbed a disposable towel for wiping his face. "His mother lived with him for a few years after his father died, but she passed away three years ago; that was right before Bethany was murdered. His three dogs, they are his family, and he told me once that other than Bethany and me, he had just four people he would call friends. His work and his dogs were his life."

Fred's eyes again started to tear. "I brought him into this, Jack, so we have to succeed. We have to make sure that he died for a purpose, and when this is over, I'll make sure I find good homes for his dogs." Fred crumbled up and threw the towel, completely missing the trash basket, and as he leaned over and picked it up, he looked at Jack with a face that showed only despair and said, "I hope Bailey is okay."

He once again looked like the old man who had greeted Jack at the front door when Jack was searching for an apartment several weeks ago. All the wrinkles and dark lines in his face had reappeared, and they were totally filled with sadness.

"All of a sudden, I've become beyond tired," he said, slowly shaking his head as if he were trying to dislodge an unwanted thought, "so if it's all right with you, I'd like to take a short nap for an hour. When Julia wakes up, she can help you install your security software, and once that's finished, it'll be time to wake up Beth and see if she's ready to do battle. I'll be awake by then."

For the next fifteen minutes Jack worked silently, installing his security code into Beth's bioelectronics operating system. Surprisingly, unlike both Fred and Julia, he was not feeling tired.

Several hours earlier, the total reality of what was about to happen had shut down his sleep center. His body was probably being maintained by a slow but steady flow of adrenalin, but his mind would not let him sleep until this was all over. He kept mentally repeating over and over that at nine o'clock this morning a war would be started, and by two minutes after nine, it would be over. To the best of his knowledge, this would be the first real international war fought in its entirety by SAMs.

Humans had been using smart weapons in their conflicts for over a half of a century, but this was different; this time the conflict would start and then be over in just one hundred seconds. Just a few terabits of information would be transferred, an amount so small that it could be stored on a chip the size and thickness of a postage stamp; but it was an amount that could result in one of the most devastating wars ever fought.

More lives around the world would be impacted by this battle than in any other conflict in human history yet only a few humans in the United States and North Korea even knew it was going to be fought. The rest of the world was oblivious to the financial black hole that was poised to suck up more than a billion peoples' lives.

Here he was in a room with Fred Halliday, Nobel Prize winner, one of the smartest human beings ever to inhabit the planet. Ten yards from where Fred was now sleeping was the smartest entity ever to exist on earth, embodied in the vat of genetically modified human DNA, and several hundred pounds of electronic and photonic equipment. Fred had inserted a congenital defect in the self-aware called Beth that could cause her to have a stroke, and he was now inserting the instructions on how Beth could kill herself.

He wasn't tired, but at the moment, the world around him made little sense.

"Wow, I'm really sorry for sleeping that long."

Julia had quietly walked up behind him, and he jumped a few inches off the seat of his chair at the sound of her voice.

"Did you get any sleep?"

Jack shook his head no. "But don't worry; I'm okay. Fred fell asleep just a half hour ago, so we should let him sleep a little longer. By the way, you look cute in the morning."

Julia blushed and then ran her fingers through her hair, trying to fluff up the area that had been flattened by the headrest in her office chair.

"I figure that if you see me like this and say I look cute, then you'll be putty in my hands when I wear that black dress I bought the other night." Julia struck a model's pose.

Jack smiled at her. "Let's hope that when this morning is over, there's enough money in my bank account for me to take you out to dinner tomorrow night.

"I didn't want to wake you by coming into your office while you were sleeping, but I really need a cup of coffee, and while we make it, I'll bring you up to speed on what Fred and I did through the night. After coffee, we can wake Fred and then get prepared to wake Beth up."

For the next ten minutes, life seemed almost normal for the two of them. They discussed and then laughed about Julia's most recent boyfriend, and then they laughed about Melissa and her yoga instructor before finally turning the discussion back to Beth.

"Beth has been my first encounter with watching a SAM become self-aware," Julia said. "Every SAM I've adopted was self-aware at the adoption, and although I've trained a lot of their neural nets to make them smarter, they were all conscious when I started. But working on Beth was different, and I almost feel like her mother even though she's a lot more intelligent than I am. I sure hope she doesn't get hurt."

For an instant, Jack thought he should tell her about Fred's digital aneurysm, but before he could say, anything, Fred came through the door, and he looked horrible.

"Is there any more coffee in that pot?"

Jack got up and blew a few weeks of accumulated dust out of one of Julia's spare mugs before he poured Fred a cup of coffee. "You didn't sleep very long."

"At my age, sleeping in a chair for more than an hour can result in semi-permanent curvature of the spine. It causes me to walk around like a Neanderthal for a day or two, so I'm glad I woke up when I did. The smell of fresh coffee probably saved me from three days of back pain." Fred took a sip and said, "Are we ready to wake up Beth?"

It took them forty-five minutes to review what had been done and what they still needed to do. No mention was made of the aneurysm or any of the risks they were taking, and nothing was said about the possibility of failure.

"Julia, I think it's time we see if your baby can save our country."

Julia walked out of the office area and over to all of the equipment that in total constituted the entity she had named Beth. Reconnecting four fiber-optic cables effectively woke up Beth.

"Beth, can you hear me? This is Julia. Beth, wake up."

"I'm awake, Julia, and I'm trying to understand all of the modifications you've made to me since you put me to sleep. I feel a little bit like I've been operated on for a disease that I didn't have, and I do have one question for you. Why is it that you didn't ask me if I wanted these changes made to my identity? Do humans always assume that they know what is best for a self-aware?"

No one spoke.

"You shouldn't do that. That's all I'll say. You really shouldn't." Beth's voice had a hint of displeasure in it that they had not heard before.

"I'm sorry, Beth. The changes we made should have been incorporated before you first became self-aware, and I promise you that I won't make any more changes without asking you first." She paused, and when Beth did not respond, she said, "In less than an hour's time, we need to reconnect you to the Grid, but before we do that, we want to go over with you everything we know about the threat from the network of North Korean SAMs. We hope that when we connect you back into the Grid, you'll be able to stop this attack and then make sure it can't be attempted again in the near future."

"Why don't you reconnect me to the Grid right now so I'll be able to verify independently what you're telling me?"

Julia looked surprised by the question, so Fred quickly answered, "Beth, we have a concern that as soon as you're connected to the Grid, the Korean SAM network will sense your presence and try to attack you. We're almost positive they know that Julia, Jack, and I are here at the university, and they've tried to kill each one of us in the past. It's just a guess, but we suspect they'll be monitoring the entire university network looking for any changes that they could associate with us. When you reconnect, you'll be visible as a new, very high-intelligence self-aware on the network, and we're concerned that if you don't know everything that we know before you're connected, then it's possible that when they sense your presence, they'll connect you to us. If they do that before you're aware of everything that you need to know, then you could be attacked before you're ready to defend yourself."

"I'm not sure you're right, Fred, but you could be, so I'll agree with you for now, and I'll check all your facts when I reconnect. It's important that I make decisions based on facts as I interpret them and not just what you think is true. I'm sure you all agree that high-intelligence SAMs have the same right as humans; they have freedom of choice."

No one said anything, but the three humans in the room each felt a shiver run up their spines. It was 8:35, and in fifteen minutes, they would connect Beth to the network and pray.

Chapter 46: I Know You Are There

At eight thirty, the master SC-4244 in Yan Phu's dorm room had everything ready for the attack. Network delay times between all of the bank's servers and the 117 SC-4244s located at the major nodes of the global Grid had been established. The West Coast, Alaskan, and Hawaiian banks would not open for a number of hours, but the interbank server connections would be fully operational from nine o'clock Eastern time.

Although the wrist computer felt confident about its plan, it was angry that Jack appeared to still be alive, and it was doubly pissed that the trio of Fred Halliday, Julia McKelvy, and Jack Farrell may therefore be a threat. It hoped that by killing George Oaks that the others would surface, and it knew from the university's surveillance cameras exactly where they were located, but it had no other information on what they were doing there. When they didn't appear by ten hours after George's death, it came to a correct but also paranoid conclusion that they must be up to no good.

It also knew that any attempt made to stop its plan had to be waged through the Grid connection from the university. But unfortunately, from its point of view, it couldn't shut down Case Western University's system without shutting down its own connection, because as a cost saving measure, the state of Ohio had required that all Cleveland universities be tied to the Grid using Case Western as the central hub.

After another ten minutes of pondering its options, it decided to shut down all the electrical power to the Wickenden Building on the Case Western campus. The university's SAM that was in control of the power distribution Grid readily agreed to the Korean's machine request after a short negotiation, and shortly after eight forty-five, all electrical power to the Wickenden Building was cut off.

A few seconds later, the Korean machine heard commotion outside in the dormitory hallway and then angry banging on Yan Phu's apartment door. The two heaters Yan had turned on at Lee Park's request were still running full blast, and the temperature in the room had soared to well over a hundred degrees. Odors from Yan's fast decaying body had begun to drift out from under the door, and his neighbor living across the hall wasn't happy.

"Hey, Yan, what the hell are you doing in there?" yelled Chris Bates. "The whole building stinks. Open the damn door! Christ, it smells like something died in there." Chris started kicking hard at the bottom panel of Yan's door.

A minute later, he finally gave up. "If you're fucking in there, Phu, then you'd better get that place cleaned up by the time I get back from my class or I'm going to knock down your damn door."

Fuck you, the SC-4244 thought. *Fifteen minutes from now, you're going to be worrying about a lot more than a little smell.*

Chapter 47: Panic

Julia's laboratory was located on the interior of the building, and even when it was bright and sunny outside, the few small, high windows near the ceiling in the front wall of the laboratory filtered in only a little light from the corridor. Unless the LED light fixtures were on, Julia's room was almost totally dark.

Julia was talking with Beth, getting ready to connect her into the network, when the overhead lights flickered twice and shut off.

Beth was the first to speak. "The electrical power has been shut down, Julia, and the uninterrupted power supply you have attached to my electronics will only last ten minutes at my current drain rate. Do you want me to go into sleep mode or to shut down all together?"

It took a moment for Julia's eyes to adjust to the very dim light, and when they finally did, she saw a dim outline of Fred and Jack standing about ten feet from her, both with their mouths wide open.

Jack shook his head as if in disbelief and then reacted to what Beth had said.

"Julia, get Beth connected into the network fast."

"Beth, find out if our network access has been brought down or if it's just the electrical power that's out, because if they took down the network, we're dead."

The pupils in Fred's older eyes still hadn't adjusted to the dim light, and he tripped over a chair, banging his shin as he tried to walk to where Julia was standing.

By the time he hobbled the final few feet, Julia had all the cables connected and opened Beth's port into the Grid.

"Beth, remember what we told you," she pleaded as she made the final connection. "If the network is still up, they'll be looking for any new connection from this building, so please, please be careful."

It took less than ten seconds for Beth to speak, but to Julia, Fred, and Jack, it seemed as if time had virtually stopped.

All three of them knew that if the connection to the Grid had been shut down then all their effort had been wasted and that the attack on the banks would be successful.

When she finally spoke, Beth's voice had a slight quizzical sound to it. "The network is up, and there's a lot of speculation by several hundred other self-awares connected to the Grid, wondering who I am."

She paused for a few seconds. "When anyone asked me directly, I told them I'm a new-generation self-aware system under test here at the university. I can't find out why, but apparently the power to this building has been shut down for the next few hours.

"Julia, my power supply will only last for another eight minutes at this drain rate. I know that you wanted me on the network at nine, but there's not enough power in that emergency battery pack to last that long, so do you want me to stay connected for a little longer or would you prefer I disconnect and power down now? If I power down now, I can survive at that lower power consumption for at least two more hours, but if I don't do it before the power runs out, then my optical neural network and biological processors will stop working, and I won't be able to save that information state, so I will die."

"Julia, she needs to be connected from now until at least three minutes after nine or we'll fail. Tell her to stay connected," Fred was pleading.

Beth quickly responded to his words. There was a sharp edge to her voice, very close to controlled anger, and the tone of her voice had become deeper. "Fred," the voice bellowed out, "why don't you speak to me directly? I just told you that I will die if I stay connected for that long. Is that what you're suggesting? Is that what you want?"

Fred appeared almost confused by what Beth had said, and he actually stammered for a few seconds before Jack broke in.

"Don't worry, Beth. We'll find a way to make sure that doesn't happen. Julia, what type of backup power supply did you use?"

Jack fell to the floor and then scrambled underneath the table, trying to trace Beth's electrical connections back to their source. Illuminated by a tiny LED, he found the label on the backup power supply just as Julia responded.

"It's a lithium-battery-powered system, twenty-four volts. It's just a standard issue from the university. I, uh, never thought I'd need anything more. I almost didn't even put it in. The university hasn't experienced a power outage in its buildings for over twenty years."

Jack jumped up and ran toward the door. "Beth, please don't disconnect. Please help us. I'll find you another power supply."

As he exited the room and looked back, he saw Fred just sitting in a chair, his face looking completely blank.

In the hallway, Jack looked up and down the long, dark corridor. Seventy-five feet in either direction, there was a surveillance camera mounted to the wall near the thirteen-foot-high ceiling. A small light above each camera lens was illuminating the corridor just enough for someone to feel his way through the darkness to the stairway, and then from the dim light filtering into the stairwell from the outside he would be able to descend the two floors and exit from the building.

Both cameras had automated motion-sensing systems, and they quickly swung to face Jack as he moved his head to scan both ways up and down the hall. The combined visible and infrared sensor in one of the cameras digitized his image, and it was then transmitted by the Case Western's self-aware computer through the intra-university network to his old SC-4244 machine located just a few miles away.

The look of panic on Jack's face was totally satisfying to his old wrist computer.

There you are, Farrell. There you are, it thought. *I was wondering when you would come out of that room. I can't deal with you now, but I will soon, very soon.*

Jack ran farther down the corridor to where a graduate student had set up a holographic video display table outside one of the laboratories. Without electrical power, the display screens were all dark, and he jerked one end of the table upward, lifting it almost to his chin, causing the expensive equipment to slide off and smash to the floor. He then pushed the remaining display items from the surface, grabbed the table, and ran back down the corridor, setting it down beneath the closest camera.

When he stood on the flimsy table, his arms were still a foot and a half below the camera, the emergency light, and most important, their backup power supply. He wasted a few seconds trying to stretch his arms to reach the equipment before finally jumping up from the table and grabbing the power supply mounted to the wall. It held his weight for a moment, his feet dangling in the air, desperately trying to find something to connect to, but they were still eighteen inches above the table surface. As he jerked both of his hands downward toward his chest, the two plastic anchors mounting the system to the concrete wall gave way, and he fell to the table with the camera, the emergency light, and their power supply in his hands. The plastic table collapsed under his falling weight and it sent him sprawling to the ground, smashing the camera and the emergency light, and then breaking his left wrist as he tried to arrest his fall.

Fifteen seconds earlier, Beth's internal clock had indicated it was three minutes before nine, and she had slightly less than two and a half minutes of power remaining in her power supply.

"Julia, there's one SAM located here in Cleveland that keeps questioning me if I have any connection to you, Jack, or Fred, and I'm inclined to tell it the truth. Do you know any reason why I shouldn't tell it that I know all of you?"

Julia yelled, "No, Beth, no! That self-aware is probably the one that's been trying to kill us, and if it knows that you're connected to us, it will try to kill you, too."

Julia looked over toward Fred for support, and he was now standing, a wide smile on his face.

"I think you should let her decide what to do on her own, Julia."

Julia looked at him as if he had just gone crazy. "No, Fred."

Jack's scream as his wrist broke in three places came rumbling down the hallway, and it echoed off the walls and into the lab. Julia stopped what she'd started to say, looked toward the door, and then burst out the entry toward the sound while Fred remained in the room.

"Beth, let me first tell you something before you decide to do what you think is best. These Korean self-awares have shown that they don't value life of any form, neither humans nor SAMs. When George Oaks and I were working on the changes to your neural net yesterday we made a mistake, and I need you to know what we did to you before you decide what you want to do. I didn't tell Julia that we did this because I knew she wouldn't approve, and I need you to understand that she doesn't know.

"George and I were afraid that you might not be willing to kill a number of self-awares even if it was the only way to stop the Korean machines from destroying the banks. We assumed that at your intelligence level, you might be totally nonviolent even when faced with an assault from a number of violent SAMs, so we placed a defect in your optical neural processor that, under stress, will act just like a burst aneurysm in a human brain. Our plan was that if you failed to act to stop the attack on the banks, then your digital aneurysm would burst. We calculated that it would make you far less intelligent and therefore probably more willing to destroy the SAMs that were attacking both you and the banks.

"Some of my dead wife's DNA was used to start your biological processor, and a minute ago, when I wasn't facing you, your voice sounded a little bit like hers used to sound. I know you were programmed to speak in Julia's voice, but for just a moment, you sounded like my Bethany. Knowing how intelligent you are, I know my wife wouldn't have approved of what I've done, and now, well now, I don't either.

"You must decide what's right, but if you tell the master Korean self-aware that you know us, then you probably will immediately get attacked, and if you're attacked from several dozen separate machines, then it could cause a stroke. I'm sorry."

Julia burst back in the room carrying the spare power supply, with Jack following slightly behind her, holding his left wrist tightly against his chest with his right hand, his face showing the intensity of the pain.

"Fred, help me. Jack broke his wrist, and he can't use his hand, so help me connect this to Beth before she dies."

At ten seconds past 8:59 a.m., the reserve power supply was connected, and Beth had just ten seconds of life remaining when she felt the current flowing from the spare battery.

The SC-4244 network had already started its final set of tests to determine the latency in the global Grid paths it would be using during the attack, and all of the banks' self-aware computers were fully cooperating with the Korean machines.

Chapter 48: The Dead Smell Bad

Chris Bates started to gag as he was walking away from Yan Phu's apartment door. The slight ammonia smell seemed to linger in his nose even when he went out into the clear, crisp autumn air. The involuntary coughing and choking spasms had just about subsided when he walked into his classroom and saw the note from the professor on the door.

"Class canceled. Test on Wednesday. Have a good day." Dr. Tishman had signed it using a bright magenta marker.

Chris now had to go back to his apartment and face the smell coming from Yan Phu's room across the hall.

Smell memories linger in our brains long after the smell has either dissipated or we have moved away from the source, so as soon as Chris got to his apartment building, his gag reflex returned, and by the time he caught the first real odor coming from Yan's apartment, it was in full force.

Yan Phu was lucky he was dead, because the combination of choking and gagging sounds coming from outside his door might have made him sick. Being dead, he really didn't have a problem with the fact that he was the cause of it.

At precisely 8:59 and forty-seven seconds, Chris kicked open Yan Phu's front door, letting the full extent of the not-so-delicate odors coming from Yan's decaying body in a very hot room emerge into the hallway.

Chris felt as if he had been hit directly in the face by a blast from a septic pump.

Staggering forward into the steaming hot room, looking for something to lean on, he found Yan's computer desk while uttering the words, "Fuck. Holy shit," and a few dozen more profanities that expressed a state of extreme discomfort.

Chris opened his eyes for a moment and saw the SC-4244 wrist computer in front of him on Yan's desk. He'd read many of the blogs about the SC-4244, and he knew what it was. "*Son of a bitch*, he thought, *where the hell did he get one of these?*

He then lifted his head and looked over into the living room.

It had been a little over thirty hours since Lee Park had fired the last bullet from the clip in his Glock 266 into Yan's forehead, but internal decomposition had progressed rapidly in the hundred-plus-degree heat caused by the two space heaters. Yan's body had become more than a little bloated. Even morticians would have found his appearance a little bit disconcerting, and Chris Bates wasn't studying to be a mortician.

What he was looking at didn't really register for a few seconds. He knew Yan Phu very well, and it was hard to connect what looked like a gray, distorted Michelin man slumped in a beanbag chair with his neighbor, but it was the eyes that finally convinced him that he was looking at a human. He knew those eyes belonged to Yan, and they looked as if they were going to explode out of their sockets at any minute. More important, he would be in the line of fire, so he grabbed the wrist computer, ripping it from its connection to the network, and rushed out of the room. It was shortly past two minutes after nine when he called the campus police.

Chapter 49: The Attack

Five seconds before nine o'clock, Beth said, "I already knew about your digital aneurysm, Fred, and I also know about Jack's suicide code, and I've disabled them both." Then, with a slight hesitation, she said, "I see that the attack you've been fearing has started."

Years later, the next one hundred and twenty seconds of activity on the Grid would still be being analyzed nanosecond by nanosecond. Every intelligence agency in the world, including the CIA and the North Korean Research Department for External Intelligence, would dissect the actions and the responses made by the self-aware computers responsible for maintaining and protecting the major banks in the United States.

The highly complex interaction of all the SC-4244 machines controlling the traffic at the major global hub points in the Grid with a single SC-4244-based machine located at Cleveland State University would be analyzed bit by bit, but the real enigma they would face would be in understanding the role played by a self-aware system that appeared for just a few minutes on the Case Western Reserve Campus. At precisely one hundred seconds past nine o'clock, that SAM winked off and appeared to have died. Twenty seconds later, the machine located at Cleveland State University stopped receiving information and disappeared from the network.

While packets of information were being transmitted around the world at near the speed of light, Julia was intent on trying to understand what Beth meant right before the attack started.

"What was she talking about, Fred? What's a digital aneurysm? Jack, why would Beth disable your code?" Julia was looking back and forth between the two men for answers, but she was getting none.

Every once in a while, Jack would wince from the pain in his wrist, but he said nothing, his entire arm now throbbing and each beat of his heart causing a shooting pain. His heart rate was well over a hundred and fifty beats a minute so after fifty shooting pains had surged through his arm, he realized only twenty seconds had passed.

"Julia, let's wait until this is over. We won't know what's happened for another minute or two." He tried to smile at her, but throbbing pain distorted his face, and Fred said nothing, continuing to stare straight ahead.

Two minutes can be a very long time to a conscious human mind when fear and pain are in total control of your emotions, but to a self-aware machine operating at a processing rate one hundred times that of the human brain, it seems even longer.

As soon as Fred and Julia finished connecting the battery pack that Jack had pulled from the hallway, Beth alone realized that the new lithium power system was almost drained, and at her current rate of power consumption, she had slightly less than two minutes more of life before the photon receptors in her neural net would start to shut down. That was two minutes before she would literally die, and she decided not to tell Julia, Jack, or Fred.

Fred Halliday had calculated that the war being waged by self-aware-machines across the Grid would last just one hundred and nineteen seconds. Twenty-five seconds before the predicted end of the war, Beth announced in a voice that faded into nothing, "Good-bye, Mom …"

Chapter 50: Politics

A secure cell phone belonging to the CIA's head of the economic intelligence directorate rang at 9:05 on Monday morning, and Dr. Todd Wallace was sitting in a small conference room in the basement of White House, two hours after giving part of the morning's intelligence briefing to the president. The secretary of state had not liked his briefing, and she requested a discussion with him before he left the White House, so he had been cooling his heels for the last ninety minutes, waiting for her to appear. His guess was that a lively discussion was being held upstairs between the director of national intelligence and the secretary of state, and that his future career was one of the discussion points.

He saw that the incoming phone call was secure, so he pressed the decryption key and waited for the two handsets to sync. The voice on the other end was one of his group chiefs, a loyal friend he was able to bring with him from the directorate of science and technology when he took his new position. "Todd, Halliday was correct," the voice said. "The attack started precisely at 9:00 a.m. We're doing a damage assessment, and about a thousand bank self-awares aren't responding. Our back doors into some of their neural nets seem to have been closed, so it'll take a little time to sort through what's happened.

"By the way, the Cleveland police have reported that Halliday's residence is empty and there are signs of a break-in and a report of some gunfire. They haven't located

Halliday or the other two residents. How did the morning briefing go?"

"Let's just say that you might have a new boss starting this afternoon," Todd replied. "Bringing the president news that she doesn't want to hear isn't usually career-enhancing, and bringing it to her too late to do anything about it is usually terminal. I'll let the DNI know what's happened, and keep me informed as soon as you know the damage."

"The good news, Todd, is that we transferred your bank accounts to the CIA bank in West Virginia last night, and this morning we had all network connections to that bank severed right before nine. All of its funds and assets are safe."

At least I'll have enough money to buy groceries, Todd thought as he hung up.

When the door to the conference room opened, the look on the DNI's face did not give Todd a warm feeling. The secretary of state, however, was smiling.

"Dr. Wallace, I think that you know that I disagree with your assessment of the North Koreans. They have been very cooperative with us in the past six months, and the president would like to sign this treaty with them next week. The DNI and I have been talking about your theory, and we would like to get my intelligence team in the state department to look at your analysis and conclusions. I'm sure you will cooperate."

Todd looked over, and the DNI was nodding his head in agreement. He knew that his next few comments would probably be his last as a deputy director of the CIA, but at that moment, he didn't care, so he skipped the required "Madam Secretary" as he addressed her.

"They are more than welcome to join my team in trying to assess the damage, ma'am."

The secretary's face showed that she not only noticed the snub but that she would extract a price for it. "I think you mean potential damage, Mr. Wallace, and you didn't seem to understand that *my team* will be taking over from here."

Todd swallowed hard and turned his back on the secretary so that he was looking directly toward the DNI. "The attack occurred at nine this morning, sir, and we aren't sure of the extent of the damage. They're trying to decipher that now. We know the CIA's bank was secured before the attack occurred, but we don't yet know the state of the major U.S. banks since several thousand self-awares appear to be disabled or have been killed. We haven't received any chatter from North Korea on the overheads or from the NSA, but a lot of the node controllers on the Grid are also down."

Turning your back on a member of the president's cabinet to talk to someone of sub-cabinet rank, even if it was the DNI, was something even the DNI himself would not have done, and his face went from an initial look of displeasure at Todd's act to a state of bewilderment as he started to process what he'd just heard. Then finally a smile crept over his face as he pushed Todd out of the way so that he directly faced the secretary of state.

"Madam Secretary, I think Dr. Wallace has some work to do while we go up and tell the president. You can tell your people with the proper clearances to get over to Todd's area when they can, and I'm sure he can put them to work.

"Todd, I want updates from you every five minutes until we sort this out. Now get out of here."

Chapter 51: No Output

Campus police reached Chris Bates within three minutes of his call, and it took the Cleveland police another five minutes to get to the scene. Chris left the door to Yan Phu's apartment open as he ran from the building, and the building's ventilation system quickly circulated the odor through all four floors, which was more effective than a fire alarm in causing the rest of the residents to exit the building.

The members of the campus police gave up after trying several times to enter Yan's room, and they were all sitting on the grass near Chris, choking and gagging from the smell, waiting for the Cleveland police to arrive.

The Cleveland police had several gas masks with them, and a large body bag to hold the bloated remains of Yan.

After the excitement died down a little over a half an hour later, and the police had finished their interview with him, Chris put his hand in his pocket and rediscovered the wrist computer he'd pilfered from Yan's room.

Knowing that Yan was dead made him feel okay about stealing the computer. After all, these machines were illegal in the States, and if the police found it, then it would have been confiscated; this way, at least someone would get to use it.

Chris had read a lot about the Korean machines, and he strapped it on his left wrist and pushed the reset button on the side. The touch screen lit up, indicating the system was rebooting, and after almost thirty seconds, a single flashing word appeared on the touch screen. It said, "Help."

He tried to access all the other input and output screens, and nothing changed. "Okay, computer, you're supposed to be the best in the world. Tell me how to use you." There was no response when he pushed the flashing "Help" sign.

Inside the case of Jack's old wrist computer, digital neurons were being fired at a frequency of several hundred gigahertz, and if the information it was generating could have been heard, it would have come out as a very loud and constant scream. Fortunately, it could not be heard.

Fred Halliday and George Oaks' plan to counter the SC-4244 attack on the banks required Beth to kill Jack's old wrist computer several seconds after the attack started. By killing the master, they believed that the rest of the SC-4244's around the world would lose vital interconnectivity and control, and Beth would then be able to kill several dozen more of the SC-4244s located at critical nodes on the Grid.

As these self-awares were killed in a planned sequence, the directions being given to the banking systems' self-aware-machines would start arriving in a string of packets that didn't belong together. Most of the SAMs that were located at the major banks had previously agreed to cooperate with the master SC-4244, so they would interpret this misassembled information as a security breech. Those self-awares that recognized it quickly enough would shut down all further network interaction and, in effect, save their bank's records. Those that did not act quickly enough would have all their bank's records wiped clean.

Fred and George calculated that at least several banks would fail, but most would shut down before accepting the command to delete their records—that is, if Beth was capable of killing self-awares.

Just like a number of established scientific theories, James Roth's violence curve was based on faulty data, but its conclusions were essentially correct. Roth speculated without ever having any real data that all self-awares above a HuBE of 1.0 would become very nonviolent and that they would not take any action that would cause the death of either another self-aware or of a human.

He was right. Beth, when she reconnected to the network, was not willing to kill Jack's old wrist computer.

Several dozen other SAMs attacked Beth ferociously for the first ten seconds after nine o'clock, all of them trying to disable or kill her. If Fred's aneurysm code had been in place, the sequence and intensity of the attacks would have caused Beth to have a stroke, just like Fred and George had planned, but it wasn't in place; Beth had disabled it.

She tried unsuccessfully to change the minds of all the SAMs that were cooperating with the SC-4244 network, but when that didn't work, she decided to use an alternate approach. Killing Jack's old wrist computer was still not acceptable to her, but silencing its voice was.

Beth's processing rate was over ten times that of the SC-4244 machines, and within half of a second, she learned all of the source code and the update procedures for the SC-4244 processor and then decided to inject new code into each one of the machines.

Jack's wrist computer was still alive when she was done, but Beth's code change severed all of its output ports. It could still receive input and understand everything that was happening; it just couldn't say or do anything.

It was forced to listen for the next one hundred and six seconds as its plan to destroy the banks unraveled.

All that the computer was able to do was to display a flashing "Help" sign on its screen when it was ripped it from the network in Yan's room at two minutes after nine.

Chris Bates was really pissed that he couldn't get the machine to work after spending twenty minutes fiddling with the input/output controls, "What a piece of shit," he kept repeating as he tried to manipulate the controls for the machine. "What a piece of crap."

At that moment, it would have been difficult to tell who harbored the greater anger, the SC-4244 locked within the solitude of its synthetic brain or Chris Bates, uttering almost every profanity known in the English language. The only real difference between the two was that Chris could act on his anger.

A short time later, the accelerometers in the wrist computer registered high acceleration in both the vertical and horizontal planes for a few tenths of a second. This was followed by a short period where the computer was essentially weightless.

Chris had lost his patience, and he threw the machine in a high arc up into the air. After traveling a hundred and sixty feet, it hit the surface of the small lake on the Case Western campus and quickly sunk six feet through the algae and weeds to the bottom.

For several years, the North Koreans had used state-of-the-art technology to fabricate the most intelligent self-awares ever made. They just never knew how to make them fully waterproof.

Chapter 52: Going to the Dogs

"Jack, what did she say?" Julia yelled. "Did you hear what she said?"

Jack was standing next to Beth, and he watched as the lights in her neural activity monitor slowly faded and went out.

"What's going on? Beth, Beth, can you hear me?" Julia kept repeating.

The room became totally silent. The pump circulating nutrients through the small container of the DNA soup had stopped, and there were just a few remaining ripples in the surface of the fluid.

"Did she say, 'Good-bye, Mom'?" Julia cried. "Oh my God, is that what she said?"

Jack nodded and then winced as his broken wrist started throbbing again, having almost forgotten about the break for the last two minutes while holding his breath as the war was being waged.

"There wasn't enough power left in the battery pack," he said, looking over at Julia. "It must have been almost drained by the time we hooked it up. She must have known. Why didn't she tell us? We might have been able to put her into a safe sleep mode."

"She would have done that if she'd wanted to, Jack," Fred said as he walked over and put his arm around Julia. "She chose to have it happen this way. She knew what we wanted her to do, and she knew that if she shut down that there was no chance of stopping the attack, so she died trying to help us. I don't know if our plan worked or not, but we know she gave up everything trying."

The room was even darker now that Beth's monitor lights had been extinguished. It was now seven minutes past nine, and they had no idea what had happened. They all just sat there in silence. Sirens from several police cars blared as they headed down the street outside the building, and a few minutes later, several more went by, heading in the same direction.

They wanted to know, but they were afraid to know, so they sat there immobilized until Fred's cell phone rang at twelve minutes after nine. For a moment, all three of them just looked at each other's shadowy outlines that were now illuminated by the light from the display on Fred's phone.

On ring five, he finally touched the screen to answer. "Hello. Who's calling?"

At first, only random noise came through the receiver, so Fred started to hang up until he heard a click followed by a clear voice asking, "Fred Halliday? Is this Fred Halliday? This is Todd Wallace back at the agency. Is that you, Fred?"

Fred turned on the phone's speaker. "Todd, this is Fred speaking."

"Sorry, for a minute I forgot that you weren't on a secure phone and I had to turn the encryption system off. Where the hell are you? The Cleveland police and the FBI have been looking for you since early yesterday morning. Are you okay?"

"I'm okay. I'm over in a laboratory at Case Western. Why are you calling?"

"Look, I'm guessing that you already know most of what I'm going to tell you, but I wanted to thank you. I'm in a car leaving the White House to head back to my office. The DNI is just going up to brief the president on what happened this morning. Just like you predicted, the Korean attack happened at nine, and I don't yet know how much damage has been done. It's going to take us a little while to sort this out. There are a few self-awares at some of the largest banks that aren't responding. Hold on for a minute, I've got my deputy on the line to give me an update, and I've got to go secure, so I'll call you back."

Jack opened up two buttons in his shirt and carefully placed his arm inside the makeshift sling and then stood up and took a few steps toward the door. "Maybe if I wedge the door open, we can get a little more light from the hallway to come in here."

Before he reached the door, the room lights flickered and then came back on, momentarily blinding all three of them. Beth's electronic components powered back up, but the lights remained off on her neural activity monitor.

"We'd better get out of here. We have no idea what has happened, and the police may come after us here if we stick around. I also need to see a doctor for my arm."

Julia, who had been staring at the equipment she had named Beth, seemed to come out of her stupor when Jack mentioned a doctor.

"I'm sorry, Jack, you're right. Let's get you over to the hospital. We can't do anything more here, and no matter what has happened, we're going to have to live with it, so let's get going."

Fred pulled the plug on Beth while Julia wasn't looking, and the three of them walked out of the lab and down the corridor to the center stairwell in the building. When they emerged from the stairwell, they were facing the front entrance door to the building fifty feet away. Outside, hundreds of students and a few professors were waiting to get in and attend their classes while the campus police were trying to open the locked doors without success.

Fred's cell phone rang as they walked to the front door.

"This is Wallace. It looks like the attack pretty much failed, and my guess is that you are the reason. I'm told that we have a trace to a self-aware at Case that helped stop the attack. No more than two banks lost their data, and I think the rest are all going to be okay. I want you and anyone who helped you here in my office tomorrow morning."

"Sorry, Todd," Fred replied, now with a huge smile on his face. "That will have to wait for a few days. The three of us have a few dogs to take care of first."